M000013282

Nov. 10, 2017

To Carolyn,

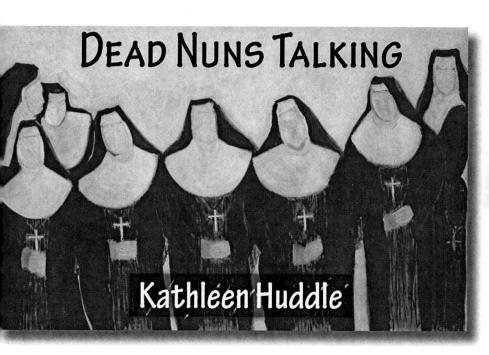

DEAD NUNS TALKING

Kathleen Huddle

Peace Out,
Kathleen

Wingspan Press

Copyright © 2017 by Kathleen J. Huddle

All rights reserved.

This book is a work of fiction. Names, characters, settings and
incidents are either the product of the author's imagination or used
fictitiously. Any resemblance to actual events, settings or persons,
living or dead, is entirely coincidental.

No part of this book may be reproduced or transmitted in any form
or by any means, electronic or mechanical, including photocopying,
recording or by any information storage and retrieval system, without written permission from the author, except for the inclusion of
brief quotations in reviews.

Published in the United States and the United Kingdom
by WingSpan Press, Livermore, CA

The WingSpan name, logo and colophon are the trademarks of
WingSpan Publishing.

ISBN 978-1-59594-599-0 (pbk.)
ISBN 978-1-59594-921-9 (ebk.)

First edition 2017

Cover design and artwork by Kathleen Huddle

Printed in the United States of America

www.wingspanpress.com

Library of Congress Control Number 2016959697

1 2 3 4 5 6 7 8 9 10

Dedicated to my world-class mother, Loretta Sperduti Mullen, who gave me the sweater off her back when she was cold and the food off her plate when she was hungry. Wise as a priestess, her pearls of wisdom have served me well, especially her most valuable advice: Stop picking at the thing on your face or it'll never heal, and never eat yellow snow.

ACKNOWLEDGMENTS

I would like to express my appreciation for my large Irish/ Italian family who surrounded me with love and laughter and to the sisters of IHM who gifted me with an excellent education.

Dead Nuns Talking

ONE

The dead nuns talked to me again. Maybe that was normal if you were Theresa Caputo, but I was a sixty-year-old artist and nun-o-phobic Catholic-school survivor who still had nightmares about my third-grade nun. Wasn't it traumatic enough to have been taught in Catholic grammar school by *live* nuns? Back then, I offered up as penance the unfailingly cruel and imaginative punishments of my third-grade teacher, Sister Attila the Nun, who was—*indisputably*—the meanest Sister in Nunsville. Her inflictions were legendary, say, when she ordered me to move my desk next to the radiator valve so that the steam would spray me.

"But, Sister, the steam is burning my arm. Please, may I move my desk?"

"You may *not!* During your lunch hour write: *I will not question Sister Attila's judgment*, 500 times."

Man oh man, once Sister Attila the Nun sentenced a defenseless student, not even exculpatory evidence and a papal pardon could save the poor wretch. If vengeance had been an Olympic sport, that veiled villain would have won a gold medal. If a kid found herself in the crosshairs of Sister Attila the Nun, she'd make a sincere Act of Contrition because she knew she was a goner.

Sister Attila the Nun had sentenced me to solitary

1

confinement in the cloakroom because—through no fault of my own—I'd contracted an advanced case of the giggles. You see, my mamma had used an Italian slang term, *coolie,* which I figured everyone used. *Coolie* refers to the general vicinity of the buttocks. So when Sister taught our history lesson about the Chinese coolies transporting people around China in rickshaws, I begged God to help me as I twitched with plugged-up giggles. She shouldn't have said *coolie* over and over. I couldn't save myself.

"Miss Credo!"

A jolt of electricity passed through my body, which made me quiver like a mass of *Jell-O.*

"Share with the class what you think is so funny!" she bellowed like an Army drill sergeant.

Yikes! How could I explain *coolie* to Sister Attila the Nun? I wasn't even sure if a nun had a *coolie.* I prayed like a convict on death row, Jesus, Mary, and Joseph *save* me and moved over in my seat to make room for my guardian angel.

Relegation to a dark cloakroom wasn't as bad as a knuckle cracking with a steel ruler. The imprisonment was probably designed to humiliate. But I was glad to get a break from that Holy Terror. I made a pillow out of my gray wool coat, opened my brown-paper lunch sack, and feasted on my peanut butter and green-mint jelly sandwich on soft Stroehmann's bread. When Mamma made my lunch, I loved to hold up the mint jelly jar to the light—it shimmered like a glass of emeralds. One time, Sister had locked Johnny Soprano in the cloakroom and he grew so hungry, he ate *everyone's* lunch.

At least I didn't get the steel ruler like the time Sister summoned Thomas Mullen to the front of the classroom and demanded he hold out his hand for a lashing. As Sister's heavy weapon came down for the kill, Thomas, a James Dean wannabe, swiped his hand away at the last moment and Sister Attila the Nun whacked her own hand!

2

Thomas and his brother, Tony, were fearless. The brothers Mullen were legend at our parochial school. Tony Mullen had talked the whole class into performing a group-practical joke on Sister Attila the Nun. *I know!* He'd said a teacher couldn't possibly punish the entire class and besides, she'd think it was funny. *Funny?* I'd never seen that heavy-breasted, mustached ruffian laugh or even crack a smile. If she'd tried to grin, Sister's face would have exploded and flown all over the classroom and we'd have had to duck-and-cover like we did during air-raid drills to avoid the nun shrapnel.

When Sister Attila wrote on the blackboard with her back to the class, Tony yelled, "Give me liberty or give me death!"

Sister was supposed to have said, "Who said that?"

The entire class was to have responded, "Patrick Henry."

Instead, Sister Attila the Nun turned around prematurely and lunged at Tony with her rosary beads flying and her veil swinging over her head like the Grim Reaper and boxed his ears.

Tony, the class clown, should have rolled with the punches, but he couldn't help himself and said, "Oh, no. She's giving me death!"

Then, that bully-in-nun's clothing squished Tony's face into the blackboard with her gold wedding-ring-of-Christ pressed into the back of his neck. You might chuckle now, but we were frozen with fear. Tony dubbed her a Sister of Show-No-Mercy.

One day in our classroom still lives in infamy. Sister Attila the Nun had turned her back to the class in order to demonstrate on the chalkboard the Palmer method of writing. As Sister's muscled arm swooped in large circles producing elegant cursive forms, my classmate, Freddy, had the poor judgment to flash Sister *the finger.* Flashed. The Finger. To. Sister Attila the Nun! Freddy was temporarily insane. Didn't Freddy know the nuns had eyes in the back of their heads? That their veils were sheer enough to see *everything?* Didn't Freddy learn anything from Tony Mullen?

With unparalleled ferocity, Sister Attila sprang like a coiled cobra on poor unsuspecting Freddy. The Sister of *Mercy*—the irony was not lost on me—grabbed Freddy's head and pounded it into her desk, which was dented from previous head-bashings. Then because Freddy "couldn't be trusted and Sister needed to keep her eyes on him," she flung open her bottom desk drawer and tried to stuff Freddy into it. She tried and tried. When Freddy, who was a big kid, couldn't fit into the drawer because it was a physical impossibility, she forced him to sit under her desk.

The entire class sat there watching with their mouths in the shapes of a perfect *O*. All of us looked like that man in Edvard Munch's painting, *The Silent Scream.*

Freddy sat under her desk for hours, bored out of his skull. He extracted his handkerchief from his back pocket and waved it, ever so slowly, as a flag of truce. Normal kids would laugh at that sight, but remember we were in the classroom of Sister Attila the Nun. We were scared mirthless.

Sister Attila the Nun must have had her black sensible shoes outfitted with tiny mirrors because she saw the handkerchief waving and kicked Freddy with her pointy nun shoes, *kid kickers,* we called them. Finally, Freddy had had enough and screamed obscenities at her. Screamed. *Obscenities.* At. Sister Attila the Nun! The collective gasp of the students sucked all of the oxygen out of the classroom.

Freddy was sentenced to a convent-basement lockdown. After that historic day when Fearless Freddy the Finger became an urban legend at The Scourging at the Pillar School, Freddy's mother pulled him out of Catholic school faster than a Hollywood divorce. Sister maintained that Freddy, who had a true phobia of rodents, was just cleaning out the convent basement and the old door must have been stuck. But we kids knew

Sister Attila the Nun had locked Freddy in the shadowy crypt among the cobwebs and rats.

On another momentous occasion, Sister Attila the Nun had laid waste to Ted the Thug, the class bully. After months of terrorizing his classmates and daily stealing Gregory the Geek's lunch money, Thug was busted when Gregory—who'd lost weight at an alarming rate—snitched on him.

Sister summoned Thug to the head of the classroom. The religious woman rolled up her bell-shaped sleeves, slowly and deliberately, taking great pleasure as she always did performing before her captive audience.

"This is for stealing Gregory's lunch money," she said as she drew her powerful arm back like a New York Yankee pitcher winding up to deliver a fastball. She slapped Thug's cheek so hard it produced a loud *thwack!* It sounded like a baseball hitting the bat for a homerun. It left Thug's face frozen in a profound profile. Then in a voice so artificially sweet it made my blood coagulate, that Bride of Christ said, "Now class, we do not want Theodore to go through life with a crooked face, do we?"

I just wanted Theodore to live. I sat straight-spined with my white-knuckled hands tightly folded and my right leg vibrating like a jackhammer under my gray and burgundy plaid uniform skirt.

"No, Sister," we replied automatically in one voice, like the reaction of trained laboratory rats.

She hauled off and whacked Thug's face in the *opposite* direction. *Thwack!* In a quiet voice, which was much scarier than yelling, Sister Attila the Nun said, "If you ever even *think* of stealing again, I *will* annihilate you."

I quietly retrieved my dictionary from my desk and looked up the word, *annihilate.* Horrified, I wondered if Mamma realized I was in the classroom of a dictator who threatened to wipe out little kids without a trace.

Dead Nuns Talking

Talking was considered a transgression by the nuns. During rehearsal for a procession in the church where we marched in two by two, like dumb animals on Noah's Ark, my classmate, Neil, was talking.

"Neil!" Sister screeched so loud it made the veins in her forehead stand out like worms. Her voice reverberated throughout the empty church, bouncing off the pews. I expected the stained-glass windows to shatter. Again, she screamed, *"NEIL!"*

All kids in that church dropped to their knees and knelt like saints under the cross.

So, you can understand why my history with nuns made me nervous, like swimming in a tank full of sharks. I suffer from a psychological disorder called nun-o-phobia, which is an overwhelming fear of nuns. I will do anything to avoid them. Some of my symptoms include, but are not limited to, severe shaking and full-body trembling, breaking out in a flop-sweat at the mere mention of a nun, facial tics, hyperventilation, profuse drooling, hallucinations, sudden onset of migraine headaches, apoplexy, hyperactive bowels, stuttering, fibromyalgia, incontinence, extreme dry mouth, hives, tachycardia, projectile vomiting, paralysis, tinnitus, seizures, plaque psoriasis, abnormal fear of being tortured by a nun, and premonitions of being murdered by a nun. These symptoms can manifest in a victim and are triggered by talking about nuns, looking at photos of nuns, sightings of killer whales, watching *Nunsense* the musical, visiting penguins at the zoo, watching the movie *Sister Act*, and viewing anything that is black and white.

It all started with the painting for St. Anthony's Hospital. Had I known what those dead nuns had planned for me, I never would've accepted that commission. No matter how badly I needed the money. Never.

TWO

"Get your hands up in the air," the throaty voice demanded. My octogenarian mother, Mamma Mia, and I raised our hands as we exchanged worried expressions. Sparks shot from Mamma Mia's black-olive eyes.

"Higher!" The raspy voice sounded like Darth Vader.

We reached for the sky as beads of sweat sprouted on our foreheads. Could my mother handle this kind of stress? I tried to figure out an escape plan.

"Don't think you can get away from me!"

My gaze ping-ponged around the room, searching for a back door.

Mamma's eyes flashed as she plucked her asthma inhaler from her pocket and held it with both hands like a pistol. "I have a gun and I know how to use it!" Then she swiped a linen handkerchief from its garage in her bosom and wiped her moist brow. "Judas Priest, I'm sweating blood."

The chubby, overly peppy exercise instructor dressed in a camouflage outfit barked orders in a gravely voice like a prison guard as she walked around the senior-citizen exercise class. Her nicotine breath assaulted the elderly residents as she made sure she kept them moving.

My mamma was exactly five feet and round in the middle, like Mother Earth. Her muscular legs, strong from years of pedaling her bicycle, were mapped with varicose veins in grape-like clusters. Although her legs looked as if they had road maps tattooed on them, they kept perfect time with Rod Stewart's "Do You Think I'm Sexy?" She had a classically beautiful face with few lines—a widow's peak, movie-star arched eyebrows, high cheekbones, and generous lips stained with ruby-red lipstick. She rubbed olive oil on her face to erase wrinkles and it worked, but she always smelled like a tossed salad. I was most impressed with Mamma's wicked sense of humor.

"Boy, this exercise isn't for sissies," Mamma Mia said. "Hey, am I the only one who noticed the Exercise Warden can stand to lose a few pounds?"

"Now, ladies, take you stretch bands, hold them high over your head, and pull hard, you need to feel the stretch in your upper arms!" the drill instructor shouted.

I surveyed the circle of white heads and noticed I was the only one still coloring my hair as I brushed a long, dark-chocolate lock from my face. Maybe Sergeant Sadistic would help me lose the twenty pounds that were super-glued to my doughy midsection.

The crooked lady opposite me stretched her over-sized rubber band and it got away from her and sailed straight toward me.

"Incoming!" I shouted and fell to the floor like a bad actor in a grade-B movie. My lanky body sprawled out as my face brushed against the cool beige linoleum tile. Sniffing pine disinfectant, I looked around, waiting for a few laughs. *Nothing.* At least Mamma Mia appreciated my humor—we made a game out of making each other laugh. Mamma always won.

"*Bene,* Artemisia," Mamma said, "that was a good one."

"Not as funny as your *gun.*"

"Ladies, bend over and touch your toes," the stony-hearted instructor commanded.

"Okay. Now she's getting on my nerves," Mamma said. "See that woman in yellow?" Mamma hitched her chin. "I wouldn't stand behind her if I were you. Cabbage alert."

A plump woman in front of me, dressed in a yellow sweat suit with multi-colored flowers embroidered over her sagging breasts, bent over and fiercely broke wind as if she sat on a giant whoopee cushion. It was a long, drawn-out fart—machine-gun toots trailed by a long whoosh. From my smiling lips a wayward giggle escaped, which quickly morphed into an uncontrollable laughing fit.

Man! I hadn't had a laughing convulsion like this since I was in third grade and Sister Attila the Nun locked me in the cloakroom...Okay, get a grip.

"She needs an ass muffler," Mamma said as she flared her nostrils and scrunched up her face as if she smelled rotten fish. She fanned her face with her flattened hand.

I closed my eyes and slowly shook my head.

"Artemisia, take me back to my room before that gasbag drops another atomic bomb," Mamma said a little too loudly.

Ah, vintage Mamma Mia. I never knew what was coming out of her mouth.

"Mamma Mia! Was that nice?"

"*What?* She almost asphyxiated you with her gas. Instead of flowers on her shirt, she should have a skull and cross-bones and a disclaimer: 'Stand behind me at your own risk.' Next time better wear a gas mask."

No hope remained of regaining my composure. I looped my arm through Mamma's as we slowly strolled down the long gleaming corridor of St. Anthony's skilled-nursing wing like Siamese twins.

St. Anthony's had become Mamma's universe. One time, I thought Mamma would like to visit my studio. She had a difficult time getting into my car and after I'd settled her into a comfortable chair in my studio, she had to use the bathroom.

When she realized that I didn't have a handicap-accessible toilet, she said she wouldn't be able to get up off the "commode" so we rushed back to her skilled nursing room.

"Mamma, the nuns sure keep this hospital clean."

"Clean as a whistle," she said. "It's always spic-and-span. Why, a doctor could perform surgery on the floor! When I was in training as a student nurse here back in 1934, we scrubbed the floors on our hands and knees with boar-bristle brushes."

In Mamma's room, the view from her large windows showcased the emerald dragon-backed hills with a glint of the serpentine curve of the Chemung river at their base.

Mamma sank into her blue-velvet recliner, which had molded itself to her short body. She released a loud sigh, like a tire losing air, as she blotted her face with her handkerchief. *"Aqua, per favore."*

I poured a glass of ice water from the sky-blue plastic pitcher and handed it to my mother. How remarkable Mamma was, especially in comparison to the rest of the residents, many of whom were bed ridden or mentally incapacitated. Mamma loved Latin, poetry, mythology, and art. Her lofty interests mixed with her earthy sense of humor made for lively conversations.

It fractured her heart to have sold the cute little bungalow my father had fixed up for his war bride. He built the wrap-around porch, which surrounded the house like a hug. Mamma recounted how they spent many happy hours on the porch. "Just me and my Giuseppe—watching the pine trees sway hypnotically in the breeze, holding hands, enjoying morning coffee, sipping Chianti on soft summer evenings."

Ever since my father died in a railroad accident when I was a toddler, it had been Mamma Mia and me against the world. If I fell, Mamma bruised and if Mamma were cut, I bled. Mamma said, "We were thick as thieves."

A few years ago Mamma had fallen at home and I couldn't

lift her, couldn't help her at all, except to call an ambulance. I feared she'd never walk again, but after three nerve blocks and loads of physical therapy, good ol' St. Tony's had worked a miracle. Now Mamma was able to walk a little for short periods with her four-pronged cane, but mostly her mode of transportation was her wheelchair.

I missed the cottage-like coziness of our home, but selling it was the only way to pay for Mamma's healthcare and secure a spot for her on St. Anthony's skilled-nursing floor. She was a private-pay resident until her money ran out. I thanked God for St. Anthony's, which had an outstanding reputation. Most of the employees of the hospital had worked there for years because St. Tony's was one big happy family. Mamma received excellent care and I visited her daily. Heck, I practically lived there.

"I have to get back to my studio. Left my paints out on my palette and I need to work on my canvas before they dry," I said.

"Have you sold any paintings this week, honey?" Mamma asked.

"Nope, but I took on two more students and I've written a grant for an interesting project. I get paid for teaching your Arts and Crafts program here. I'm fine, Mamma."

"Well, that should bring in a little money," Mamma said, trying not to look too worried about me as she rubbed my arm. "Before you leave, will you pluck the hair on my face? I have a five-o'clock shadow on my upper lip and I don't want the nurses to mistake me for Groucho Marx."

"Sure."

I carefully tweezed the wiry hair, taking care not to pinch Mamma. I saved the coarse chin hair for last. I had to tug hard on one stubborn hair, which I held up to show Mamma.

"Holy cannoli! Take a gander at that one, it had roots down to my toes." She inspected her visage in the magnifying mirror and smiled broadly. *"Bene! Grazie."* Mamma took my head in her hands and kissed both my cheeks.

I repeated the Italian kisses—*baci*, we called them—on Mamma's smooth face, which was soft as earlobes and smelled like fruity olive oil.

"You look beautiful! Hardly any wrinkles," I said.

"I have one big wrinkle," she said…"I'm sitting on it."

"Ciao, Bella," we said at the same time.

"Arté, honey, hand me my pocketbook."

I rooted around in the nightstand and found Mamma's black faux-leather purse and placed it on her lap. She checked inside the purse, and handed it back to me.

"These are for you!" she said grinning widely, like a child offering a fresh mud pie.

I peeked inside the purse. It was full of small packages of Lorna Doone cookies. "Did you steal these from the supply cupboard again?"

"Can I help it if the supply cupboard is next to my room?" Mamma said, shrugging.

"I can afford to buy my own cookies, Mamma," I said frowning.

"Listen, Arté, I wanted you to keep our house, but we *had* to sell it. I paid a fortune to live here before my money ran out. I *own* those damn Lorna Doones. Now, don't forget to bring back my pocketbook for the next exchange."

"Yes, Mamma Mia. But we're going straight to jail for cookie dealing."

* * *

As I exited the elevator in the lobby there was a commotion. I heard Sister Xavier, the administrator of St. Anthony's, amid the crowd. Her low-pitched vocals rang through the room. "Governor O'Shea, it's such a *pleasure* and a *complete honor* to welcome you to St. Anthony's! We're about to celebrate our centennial." Her deep tone had a fog horn quality. Her eyelashes batted wildly as if she had cinders in her eyes as she tilted her head at an odd angle. Was she having a seizure? She leaned in too close to him as she gave him a goofy smile revealing the red stain on her front tooth from her scarlet lipstick. A nun wearing lipstick! That was a new one for me.

The tall governor reacted to the nun's clumsy attempt at flirting with a wide grin, which crinkled the corners of his gray eyes. A bustling group of security guards, reporters, and TV cameramen surrounded the governor who was on a political campaign to gain votes for the upcoming election. He gave an impromptu speech droning on how great he was, how smart he was, and how he was going to create more jobs and make the state of New York vibrant again. " I know I'm going to win *bigly!* If you vote for me, I promise to approve hydro-fracking in Verdant Valley, which will bring in hundreds of jobs!"

Some of the crowd applauded and others gave the thumbdown signal.

Bigly! Is that a word in the dictionary?

"This campaign has taken on a life of its own. There has been a *huge* grass-roots swell," he preached, as he gestured wildly with his hands. "Why, it's a *movement!* A *movement* which the likes of New York state has never seen!"

A mysterious nun crowded next to me and quipped, "Tis a movement to be sure. A *bowel* movement."

That arrow slung from a nun made it doubly funny to me. Of course, the comment was lost on Governor O'Shea as he flashed his victory sign.

"I'd be happy to give you a tour, Governor!" Sister Xavier crowed.

"First off, I'd like to see the archive room." The politician flashed a phony smile, exposing his overly whitened teeth, which looked like Chiclets.

As the unlikely duo rounded the corner, I meandered through

the throng. The shrouded figure garbed in the old-fashioned, long nun's habit— a throw-back to my childhood— made me shiver with the heebie-jeebies. As she snaked through the crowd, she brushed against me and smelled like she'd strolled through a field of lavender. The nun glued her gaze on Governor O'Shea and she scowled at him as if he were Satan himself.

THREE

"*Goddamit!* What the *hell* do you mean St. Anthony's might close? My mother *lives* there!" My hand flew to my mouth trying to stuff the errant words back inside. Oops, now I'd done it—swore at a nun! I was going straight to hell with no hope of a stint in purgatory, where indulgences could have been saved up during my lifetime and redeemed like *S&H* green stamps to reduce my sentence. *Indulgences*...hadn't thought of that since I'd served time...um, I mean, attended Catholic-grade school. That concept got me in serious trouble with my eighth-grade nun, Mother Superior. She'd taught us about purgatory—the recycling bin for souls who hadn't been good enough to ascend directly into heaven or bad enough to plunge into hell. She said I could *rot* away in purgatory for one or two thousand years! My poor soul would exist in a state of severe suffering until it *expiated* my sins. She over pronounced *expiated* as if she were a diction coach—she over pronounced a lot of words, especially her favorite one, *expulsion.* But, the good news was that you could cash in your indulgences like poker chips (she didn't say poker chips—that was my term. I didn't think nuns were allowed to play poker... although, she had an excellent poker face). She explained that a lifetime of saying special prayers, attending Mass and receiving the sacraments would be most beneficial if you were to land in purgatory because of a redemptive-point system (RPS). There were two types of indulgences: partial and plenary. They had rigid rules attached to them, which were so complicated my brain couldn't comprehend. I carried a holy card, which had a prayer to the Immaculate Heart of Mary, and when recited was worth 500 days' indulgence. But if I said the *Jesus, Mary and Joseph* prayer, and the *Most Sacred Heart of Jesus* prayer, I'd garner a seven-year indulgence *each.*

Mother Superior also preached about eternity. According to her, eternity was like the individual grains of sand on all the beaches in the world and if a bird were to remove each grain of sand, which would take thousands of years, eternity would last longer than that!

I jerked my head. Wait a minute. *Three hundred days! Seven years? Thousands of years?* I scratched the back of my thirteen-year-old neck. Wasn't *time* an earthly concept? How could there be measured time in eternity? How could you suffer pain if you were dead? And whose brainchild was the indulgence insurance program? How did they come up with the days and years of remission for each prayer? Who kept track of all of it? Was there a wizened monk in a monastery bent over a dusty ledger scratching marks in a massive purgatory tome? I struggled to understand.

When I questioned Mother Superior about it, she balled her fists and turned the exact shade of an eggplant. She morphed into a screeching banshee. "How *dare* you question the teachings of the *Church!*" Her eyes narrowed into tiny slits. "Are you mocking me?" The crucifix resting on her bosom heaved up and down. Seething, the nun flung her arm like an arrow and pointed with her gnarled index finger to the door. "*Get. Out!* Pack up your books. You're suspended until further notice."

Jeez, I wondered how many extra days I'd spend in purgatory for pissing off a nun?

"Artemisia!" Sister Xavier said, returning me back to the

present, "Governor O'Shea confided in me that St. Anthony's is *fated* for closure. He held no hope for the future of this hospital." Her nostrils flared as she squared her broad shoulders. "Don't shoot the messenger."

* * *

I took the scenic route back to my studio. I loved my hometown. Verdant Valley, as lyrical as her name, was nestled in upstate New York. Surrounded by voluptuous breast-like hills, I felt safe and nurtured. I crossed over the black-iron bridge, its metal openwork casting lacy shadows on the macadam, to greet my river. The Chemung River sashayed through town like a blue satin ribbon. The name Chemung, which means *big horn*, was bestowed by the Senecas when they found vestiges of the wooly mastodons along the waterway. I smiled, imagining that scene with the Indians honoring the relics they'd unearthed. I felt renewed each time I saw the sunlight dancing on the water like diamond dust. In the winter my river transformed into a mirror with glassy reflections of the tree-lined banks edged with crocheted ice.

I passed my alma mater, set in the middle of town like a crown jewel. Romanesque buildings dotted the campus, each wearing lush ivy overcoats. Brightly painted Victorian homes stood stately as queens along the oak and gingko -tree-lined avenues. The green tremolo of the leaves, shimmering in the sunlight of late summer, would soon morph into the fall fireworks of scarlet, marigold, and tangerine. This caliber of beauty boosted my creative spirit, like taking aesthetic vitamins.

The urge to paint overtook me and I was not the one in control. I had no choice but to point my cruiser toward my studio.

I painted a few hours before it was time to meet my friend, Mary, for lunch. I didn't have a sister, but if I could choose one, it'd be Mary McKee, an artist in my age bracket who worked at St. Anthony's managing the business office. Although we were as different as fire and ice, we'd been sidekicks for twenty years. My petite friend was full of inexhaustible energy, excitable, and had a charming Boston accent. I loved it when she said *wicked pissa*—probably a Boston thing. Mary's husband, George, who also worked at St. Anthony's as head of Information Technology, towered several inches over her. They were a study in contrasts.

One time Mary called me and said, "Ethel, Lucy here. You gotta get over to my house right now and help me get this new picnic table out of my car before Ricky gets home."

"Lu-cy," I said, "you'll have some 'splainin' to do. Won't he notice a new table?"

"Nah, I'll just cover it up with an old cloth and put some junk on top."

Mary and I were starving artists...well, not really starving, but money was tight and our art supplies were expensive. Striking success in the art world was brutal, just like, say, making it in the publishing world or an actor finding recognition in Hollywood. We suffered for our craft. Mary constantly dreamed up harebrained schemes to win money—usually an outlandish contest or she signed us up to work wacky jobs for which we were not qualified.

We were always on the fringe of trouble, sometimes more like Thelma and Louise. Like the time Mary helped me sneak onto the skilled-nursing wing of St. Anthony's to make sure Mamma Mia was okay. Mamma had been sick during the flu season and the entire floor had been closed under quarantine. Mary hijacked a gurney, which was parked in the hallway. On a shelf underneath the stretcher were sheets, gowns, and a box of surgical masks. So Mary donned a gown and mask and I stretched out on the gurney as Mary covered me head to toe with the sheet. She even put a little tag on my big toe. She looked as though she were on her way to the morgue with a *stiff*, as Mamma would say.

Mary wheeled me into Mamma's room. I was afraid I might scare Mamma—what with me looking like a corpse and all.

Unfazed, Mamma Mia said, "Oh, hi, Artemisia," as if I pulled a cockamamie stunt like that every day.

"How are you, Mamma? Feeling better? Need anything?"

"Nah, everything's copacetic."

We exchanged Italian kisses and Mamma gave us a bunch of Lorna Doones.

Back at St. Anthony's, my stomach growled while waiting for the elevator. I overheard two nurses outfitted in Caribbean-blue scrubs talking about the possible closure of St. Anthony's. Then I rode the elevator with that nun I'd seen giving the 'stink eye' to Governor O'Shea. Tall and thin, her bushy eyebrows shaded her blue-denim eyes, which practically bored a hole through me. We were alone in the airless steel box and a strong scent of lavender filled the elevator car. An ominous shiver ran through me as I twitched like a wet dog shaking off water.

The hooded figure nodded. "'Tis a lovely day."

"Yes, Sister," I responded automatically.

I relived my Catholic-school prison sentence. "Class, line up in the back of the room for time tables. You may not take your seat until you recite with one hundred percent accuracy," Sister Attila had said. *Jesus, Mary, and Joseph save me!* Please, I *beg* of you, don't let me be the last one standing. I shook my sweaty hands and rubbed them on my plaid uniform skirt.

The elevator pinged, returning me to safety.

"Are you feeling well?" the old-fangled nun asked. "You're shaking!"

"Huh? I'm okay, Sister. Just…uh, too much coffee this morning."

"Did ye see Governor Scanlan O'Shea in the lobby?" she asked.

"Yes, Sister."

"In Gaelic, *Scanlan* means scandal. He wears his name well," she said.

Didn't quite know what to do with that information. I gave a short, choppy wave. "Have a nice day."

"Good day to you," she said, dipping her veiled head.

I strode off the elevator so fast, I nearly broke into a sprint.

I met Mary in the cafeteria and sank safely into a brown-leather booth, the seat of which had been hollowed out from years of wear. Mary called it 'an ass-groove.' Sniffing the institutional aromas of goulash and warm turkey gravy made me smile. We sat along the bank of windows and the sun warmed our backs like a heating pad as we discussed which pieces of art we'd submit to a juried competition. Mary, a stained-glass artist, used the glass in a nontraditional manner, depicting whimsical women.

"Think I'll submit the Pink Dancers," Mary said between sips of her peach smoothie.

"Yeah, wonderfully expressive. They'll be accepted for sure," I said, digging into my salad to stab a curly piece of spinach with my fork.

"You?"

"A diptych of Angels of Peace, most likely—if I can dig up the money for more twenty-three-karat gold leaf for the angel's wings."

"Why do we work in media that's so expensive?" Mary wailed. "My glass costs a small fortune too!" Mary emptied her smoothie and continued to slurp so hard I thought she might suck the bottom off the cup. "Okay. I'm going to *explode* and you'll have the unpleasant job of scrapping my guts off the wall if you don't tell me about your *date*," Mary said, holding onto the edge of the table.

"I am so mad at Mamma! She has to stop trying to hook me up with dates. This time it was with her nurse's brother. Didn't even ask," I said, slapping the table. "Told me when it was too late to back out. Mamma called me to the hospital because she was *so sick*. I rushed into her room and found this guy holding a pathetic bunch of wilted daisies."

"Was he cute?"

"*Cute?* Mare. You sound like a school girl passing notes in study hall."

"C'mon, tell me already."

"He could stand to drop fifty pounds. But he wasn't bad looking, not like Mamma's last guy—even Mamma admitted that guy 'had a face only a mother could love.'" I blew out a puff of air. "Remember Mamma's *fabulous* guy who said *fabulous* every second word? Who wanted to get into my pants?"

"Oh, *him*. He didn't look like that type. I thought he was gay."

"Mare. Literally. He wanted to *wear* my silk panties…and my red patent-leather stilettos."

"*Pissa!*" Mary said, slapping the table, unable to contain her big laugh.

"I am telling you. I'm *so* finished dating."

Mary bit her bottom lip as she fidgeted in her seat. "Arté… you can't live the rest of your life moping over your high-school sweetheart. Yes. It *was* tragic that Michael was killed in Viet Nam, but that was well over forty years ago! Sorry," Mary said quietly, "just keeping it real."

"Oh, Mary, I *know* that. I finally made my peace with losing Michael. The sad part is, I was supposed to have had beautiful Italian babies with Michael—we used to talk about that all the time…and now…my old eggs have turned to powder. How the hell did that happen?" Bitterness overtook me. I blurted out loudly, "We should have had sex before Michael left for his second tour of duty!"

"*Sush!* Keep your voice down," Mary said in a whisper looking around furtively as everyone stared in my direction.

"Maybe I would have had Michael's child...but no, the nuns absolutely brainwashed me about sex—talk about guilt trips! I was saving myself for my wedding night." A callous laugh erupted. "*My wedding night!* We had the Sons of Italy hall rented, had my gown...Mamma made dozens of Italian cookies ..."

"Sorry, Arté, didn't mean to make you sad."

"It's not like I haven't tried to find love again with a good man. I mean, yeah, I didn't date for a few years after Michael, but I knew he'd have wanted me to find someone special. Then I began an odyssey of dating a string of losers. I loved Marcus, but he was a flaming alcoholic—couldn't have babies with him. Finally, I fell hard in love with Jack who'd managed to hide the fact he was married. Can you believe I dated him almost two years? I was such a chump!...don't even get me started about *Richard!*"

"Don't beat yourself up," Mary said.

Slumping in my seat, I took a sip of water and a deep cleansing breath. "You just can't let your sorrows define your life. You can't control the situations, but you can control the way you process your pain—learned that from Mamma. My father died young, but Mamma didn't give up. So, after my failed relationships...*all of that*, I can honestly say my life is full and happy. I have Mamma Mia, kooky friends—like *you*—my work, my fuzzy buddy, Merlin."

Mary flipped her pomegranate-red bangs away from her amber eyes. "Nice acting."

Grasping the pepper shaker, I cracked a flimsy smile. "I'd like to thank the Academy ...my agent..."

"Your life sounds like a *crap fest*. Glad you're happy. So tell me about this last date—bet he wasn't that bad."

"Well, he was nice enough. Divorced with baggage. And

I don't want to say he was cheap, but Old Country Buffet wasn't my idea of a first-date restaurant. People there ate like convicts on death row, like it was their last meal. The way he ate corn reminded me of my miserable Ex, Dickk the Corn Machine, who always ate four pieces of corn. *Four!* When Dickk ate corn, it was like watching trees go through a wood-chipper. He made pig-slopping noises as his teeth *ripped* into the kernels, working his way back and forth on the cob—like it was an edible typewriter. The farm-animal noises made me sick. Had to hide in the bathroom until he'd finished chowing down. But, with *this* guy there was that teeth-picking thing too. He took a bunch of tooth picks and reamed his teeth, like it was an Olympic sport and he was in training."

"I get it. Prince Charming he wasn't."

"*Man!* I'm reading Mamma the riot act on her matchmaking. I don't understand why she's suddenly fixated on me having dates. How'd *she* like it if I hooked her up with Mr. Gomer who lives down the hall from her—you know the guy, the one with two strands of hair wrapped around his head, gums his food, spits when he talks, wears his pants up to his armpits?... Yeah, how'd she like *that?*" My voice rose as I pounded the table hard. Mary jumped. Then she giggled like Betty Rubble at my pure exasperation. "Whoa!" she said, checking her watch, "your fascinating love life is making me late for work—gotta go." She handed me a slip of paper. "Here's info for a great job, a print ad that pays 800 bucks! I figure that'll take care of your rent and utilities...maybe some gold leaf."

I frowned as I read the description. "Uh...Mary, it says here it's for Depend adult diapers."

"Oh, Arté," Mary said with a wave of dismissal, "*if* they were to use the photos—and they *won't*—it'd be in some obscure geriatric journal. Lighten up! You'll thank me later when you get a big fat check."

"I'll walk you to the elevator," I said as I handed Mary two packages of Lorna Doones from Mamma.

"Hope your mamma doesn't get busted for stealing cookies," Mary said.

* * *

In the elevator we stood next to a beautiful little girl on a gurney who whimpered. Her dark, damp curls stuck to her forehead. I had to hold my hands behind my back as I resisted the urge to brush them back.

"Hold the elevator!" a rich, deep male voice called out. A boyish-looking older man dressed in blue OR scrubs stepped in. His OR cap was stuffed in his pocket and he had a great head of thick curly hair—silver like Richard Gere's. His blue-topaz eyes, which matched his scrubs, were fringed with long lashes. He looked like a runner. "There's the little princess! I want to ride up to the OR with you."

"I want my mommy," she cried softly as her little body quivered. She rubbed her big brown-doe eyes with her fists.

The man in the scrubs said in the most charming Donald Duck-voice, "Your mommy will be waiting for you when you wake up from your nap. Would you like a funny balloon?" he asked as he blew up a surgical glove and knotted the bottom. It looked like a cow's udder.

The frightened child actually giggled at the silly voice and balloon.

Mary and I smiled.

"Just hold my hand," the Donald Duck voice said.

The elevator groaned to a stop and the doors slid open. The kind man held her tiny hand all the way down the long corridor as we heard the perfect imitation of Donald Duck mingled with the music of little-girl giggles.

"Mary, who is that man?"

"That, my dear friend, is Doctor Joseph Goodman, thoracic

and general surgeon. His wife died about five years ago—he's the busiest doctor on the staff. Surprised you hadn't seen him before."

"That was tender the way he comforted that adorable child."

"Hey! He'd be a good one for you, but better hurry. A slew of nurses are after him."

I did a double eye roll. "Jeez, you sound like Mamma."

"Just sayin'," Mary said, shrugging as she ambled down the hall.

"Peace out," I mumbled.

FOUR

As I painted blissfully in my studio, my cell phone inter-
rupted my work. Ugh! I wanted to hurl the phone into the
Chemung river.

Mamma had fallen. Fearing for my mother's life, I threw
my brushes in the sink, and sprinted to my car.

* * *

I spotted Mamma in the hallway of the X-ray department, a
unit of blood dripping into her bruised arm. I sucked in a sharp
intake of air. Mamma had a lump on her forehead the size of a
kumquat and a few stitches above her eye.

I rushed up to her and grasped her gnarled hand. "Mamma
Mia! Are you okay? Did you lose a lot of blood?" I gently ca-
ressed the papery-thin skin of her hand, stroking her distended
veins, which branched off like river tributaries.

"Artemisia...don't get your bowels in an uproar. I don't
think I need this blood. I bled a little—*piccolo*," Mamma said,
pinching her thumb and index finger together.

"Jeez, how the heck did you fall?"

"I dropped a magazine, reached over to pick it up, and my
momentum kept on going. Next thing I knew, I was on the floor.
Like that stupid commercial where the wimp-ass lady—pardon
my French—says, 'Help, I've fallen and I can't get up.' "

I bit the tip of my thumbnail as a zap of guilt surged through me. "Mamma, are you happy living here at St. Anthony's? Honest answer."

"Yes. I'm content and at peace. Thanks to Sister Xavier, I receive Holy Communion every day. I have no worries about bills, groceries, cooking, cleaning, laundry— why, it's the life of Riley!"

"After we sold the house, we had no room for all your furniture, dishes, and pretty things here. I always felt bad about that," I said patting her hand.

"Arté. Let me tell you something. I spent most of my life collecting *stuff.* And then I spent a good deal of my life getting rid of *stuff.* Had too much junk. I didn't own my possessions, rather, *my possessions owned me.* Now I feel light as a snowflake. I'm free!" Mamma's face had a soft glow from within. As she smiled, she looked radiant in spite of her bruises. The overhead light filtered through her thinning hair shining like a corona.

"Thank God you didn't break your hip. Is there anything I can get for you?"

"Don't need a thing. I'm tired," she said sighing deeply. "Just want to go back to my room and rest these old bones."

My shoulders were hiked up to my ears and my neck ached.

Mamma studied me. "Arté, you should see your face. You look as if someone just said you were adopted."

"Well, at least your sense of humor is still intact...I wasn't adopted...was I?"

Mamma quivered as she coughed up a great belly laugh. We chuckled as she beckoned me closer for Italian kisses.

* * *

I needed to bury myself in my work to take my mind off Mamma Mia. I rolled up in my old silver PT Cruiser, taking a moment to admire my quaint store-front studio. Originally it'd been a turn-of-the-last-century neighborhood grocery store. In front of the gray shaker-shingled building stood an antique park bench, which I'd painted teal with turquoise trim and flanked with gray weathered-wooden barrels spilling over with coral geraniums. A stained-glass artist, Patrick, owned the building. His studio was opposite mine and he'd created a stained-glass border around the massive windows, which received North light. It reminded me of a church, adding to the sanctity of my creative space. I was fortunate to have a commercial studio where I could teach, hold open studio tours during the holidays, and create my large Angels of Peace. Patrick gave me a huge rent discount, he said because I also rented the upstairs apartment, but really because he was a kind fellow artist. My tiny apartment "was nothing to write home about," as Mamma would say. She'd never seen my apartment because she couldn't climb the stairs. I told her it was nicer than it actually was so she wouldn't worry so much about me.

Opening my door, I drew in the perfume of my oil paints and turpentine, my elixir. Prisms of sunlight pierced the colorful leaded-glass windows, casting rainbow shadows on the walls. Merlin, my cat I'd rescued seventeen years ago, brushed against my leg begging for a treat.

"Hey, Fuzzy Buddy, Mamma Mia is okay, so don't worry about her."

Merlin purred like he'd swallowed a motor. He gobbled three treats and retreated to the bay-window seat where he licked his silver-gray paws as he settled into his sunbathing position.

I retrieved the paint-loaded hog-hair brushes from the sink and cleaned them before they became crusted with dry paint.

Artist's studios are interesting. When you visit them it's like touring inside the artist's mind. Once my art history professor had shown a film on Picasso working in his studio where I noticed the bicycle seat and handlebars on the floor that later became his famous bull's head. I was surprised to see Picasso painting so rapidly—it was actually sloppy. During his lunch break, he devoured a whole fish, leaving the perfect skeleton. He fascinated me when he inked the fish bones and made a monoprint, stamping it onto heavy-weight paper. Picasso created art out of everything, including his lunch. I could make a monoprint out of my lunch, but it'd be messy because I'd been eating beans and rice for days so I could afford twenty-three-karat gold leaf for my angel's wings.

If you were to visit my studio, you'd see signs and posters on the walls: *Make Art, Not War* (Shepard Fairey), *Give Peace A Chance* (John Lennon), *Follow Your Bliss* (Joseph Campbell). My friends called me an old hippie...well, I was a holdover from the '60s, which was a generation steeped in high ideals. I graduated from high school in 1966, still wore the same Birkenstocks (which have been resoled four times), still wore my peace-sign jewelry, still had my Beatles sweatshirt, still missed Michael who'd returned from his second Viet Nam tour of duty in a body bag. That sounded harsh, but I forced myself to say it that way as a reminder to always work toward peace. I told Mary I was over Michael, but in truth a piece of me died in Viet Nam.

I resumed work on my eight-foot Angel of Peace. I'd done a detailed graphite sketch on wood and hired a carpenter to cut it out and build a standing brace for it. Angels were messengers of peace, and for centuries they'd tried to deliver the message of peace, but mankind refused to accept it. I envisioned an exhibit where I filled an entire gallery with over-sized Angels of Peace. Think of that impact!

I'd initiated a peace movement and saved money for two years to self-publish my book, *Weeping Angels*, which had full-color illustrations of my work, poetry, and essays on peace. I had several book signings and actually made a profit. I dedicated my book to the memory of John Lennon, who'd encouraged us to live in peace, and to Eleanor Roosevelt, who'd written, *"It isn't enough to talk about peace. One must believe in it. And it isn't enough to believe in it. One must work for it."*

I'd been captivated by angels since childhood. I used to get into trouble during Mass because I always stared upward at the heads of the *putti* supporting the Ionic columns in our church.

The nun always swatted me on the back of my head and hissed like a viper, "Pay attention!"

But I *did* pay attention. Astute attention. Just look at my angels today.

I listened to John Lennon's peace anthem, "Imagine," while adding more colors to my palette. I applied multi-layers of thin acrylic paint to my angel to build up the color, which reminded me of stained glass, and deliberately allowed the sketch to show through.

My cell phone trilled. *Oh no! Mamma.*

I smeared my brushstroke.

"Credo Art Studio…Already mailed it…all-righty then, just mail it back and I'll sign the check." My cheeks puffed out with air.

Pity, Joseph Campbell didn't tell me how to follow my bliss *and* pay my utilities.

I worried about Mamma as I tried to paint. Mamma Mia loved art and read art-history books as if they were novels. She named me after a brilliant Baroque painter, Artemisia Gentileschi, who'd painted in the style of Caravaggio—Mamma called her a *Caravaggista.* She was an anomaly of her time as she was a successful painter who'd studied in her father's *bottega.* Her subjects were female biblical heroines, such as Susanna and Judith Beheading Holofernes. Depicting women overcoming male domination, she championed her cause of in-structing women to be strong. I believed her body of work to be more interesting than Caravaggio's, certainly as theatrical… and bravura, but had more emotional content. While in college, I'd written my thesis on Artemisia. She'd been raped by her father's colleague and her father took the criminal to court. It was a sensational *'he said-she said'* trial. The transcripts are extant. Artemisia had to consent to testifying under torture of the thumbscrew to prove she'd told the truth. *Imagine!* Made me livid.

When Mamma had retired, she was in excellent health and we traveled to Italy. What a wonderful treat for an art history nerd like me. To stand before the *actual* master paintings that I'd studied! Misty eyed, I stood up close to view the brushwork, vivid colors, daring compositions, and figured out how the artists actually worked.

While in Florence, Mamma and I walked all over the city and visited every church, lingering over the artwork. We lit candles as we inhaled stale incense and damp, musty air of the dark, limestone and marble cathedrals. We spent time in the Uffizi, viewing Artemisia's paintings. In Rome on the Ponte Sant'Angelo, I froze, in what Joseph Campbell described as *aesthetic arrest*, in front of the twelve Bernini's angels, which held emblems of the crucifixion. Camera in hand, I forgot to take pictures! How did Bernini manage to give such movement and airiness to stone statues? Some kind of angelic alchemy transformed me on that bridge as I contemplated the role of angels and discovered they were symbols for messengers of peace.

Inside the Vatican Museums, we rushed to see Michelangelo's masterpieces and were among the first visitors in a small, dark chapel before it instantly filled up like a rock concert. Embedded in a mass of humanity in the Sistine Chapel, my mother—using her full lung capacity—screamed, "Get your hands off my *ass!*"

Worried my feisty mamma would clobber some randy Italian guy in a holy place, I glanced behind her. A gnarled old woman, dressed entirely in black—wool scarf knotted under her chin, from which a purple mole sprouted dark wiry hair, buttoned-up sweater, long skirt, wrinkled hose and scuffed shoes—grunted.

Puffs of garlic fumes emitted from her as she pushed hard on Mamma's butt, trying to move her along.

"*Basta!*" Mamma bellowed as she pivoted around.

They faced off like wrestlers, narrowed their eyes, and simultaneously flashed Il Malocchio hand signals. The grumpy Italian ninjas waved their bull-horned hands inches from each other's faces. It was an Evil Eye Standoff. Fearful of what might happen, I searched for an exit, but we were trapped in a sea of art lovers. Would Mamma Mia cause a riot in the Papal Palace?

Then Mamma and her foe burst out with hearty laughter, admiring each other's moxie.

The phone buzzed again, interrupting my painting. My stomach lurched. *Oh, no. Mamma!*

"Hello, may I speak to Artemisia?"

"Yes, sir, speaking."

"This is Sister Xavier."

Oh noooo. A nun!

"Hello, Sister. Is Mamma okay?"

"Yes. Don't worry. Your mother's fine. She's resting comfortably. I'm calling regarding St. Anthony's centennial. The Foundation would like to commission you to create a painting of the seven founding Sisters of St. Anthony's."

Paint *nuns*? My stomach flip-flopped. I needed the money and hoped my nun-o-phobia wouldn't get in the way. Buckets of sweat poured out of me.

"Thank you, Sister. I'd be happy to." I almost choked on the word *happy.* "Also, thank you for taking such good care of my mother. She loves living at St. Anthony's."

"Your mother's a piece of work. Years ago, I worked with her on D-2 and she always made me laugh. She often talks of her thirty-year nursing career at St. Anthony's."

I chewed on the tip of my nubby thumbnail. "Um, before I begin the painting, may I do some research in the hospital's archive? I need to learn the history of the founding nuns—really get to know them. Wouldn't want the painting to look stiff, you know, like a replica of a photograph."

"Of course. How about tomorrow morning at 9? Stop by my office and I'll show you to the archive room and give you a key. I can also put you in touch with the Motherhouse for more information."

"Thank you, Sister Xavier. See you at 9. Peace Out."

* * *

As I entered the archive room, which was surprisingly disorganized, a shiver of excitement traveled through my body... because, well, I'm a research nerd. There, that's out in the open.

Narrow and windowless, the room had musty ledgers and a bank of gray filing cabinets bulging with records of St. Anthony's School of Nursing. I was tempted for a moment to look up Mamma's nursing-school records, but was too eager to learn about the seven nuns.

I found purchasing orders, surgical notes, admitting records—written with a fountain pen in perfect Palmer-method handwriting—and yellowed newspaper clippings reporting the opening of St. Anthony's Hospital in 1908.

What? Wait. Here was a picture of the seven nuns standing on the steps of Miller's Groceries and Dry Goods store...hey, it was *my* studio! Was that some kind of a sign or something?

I leafed through piles of purchasing orders and found several from Miller's, all signed by Sister Ignatius. Looked like the nuns ate a lot of beans.

Then I saw an eight-by-ten, sepia-toned head-shot of a young nun. My hands trembled—you know, because of my *nun condition*—as I examined the fine photograph. I was a grown woman and nuns could no longer control me. Even though it was a little scary to look at a photo of a nun, my artist-self admired the beauty of the silver-print, which had rich darks, subtle mid-tones, and striking highlights.

Looked familiar...Oh, she resembled that mysterious nun who smelled like a lavender sachet. Couldn't possibly be her... must be a relative. What a great face! Bushy eyebrows, light eyes—probably blue—fair skin and a turned-up nose. She looked more Irish than corned beef and cabbage. I looked at the back of the photo and the same stylized writing said, "Molly O'Shea. Sister Ignatius, administrator, age 32." Wow. She was head of a hospital. A young female administrator in 1908, well before Women's Liberation was even a movement. Impressive! Here was another one. "Roisin O'Shaughnessy. Sister Augustine, Head of Operating Room, age 32." Her face, not as handsome as Sister Ignatius's, was interesting. A prominent nose cast a strong shadow over her upper lip.

I spotted a sterling-silver St. Anthony medal on a simple silver chain in a box near the Sister Ignatius photograph. *How odd.* The medal was gleaming with a highly polished finish on it. Wait. Shouldn't it be tarnished? I mean, I found it inside the box that had a couple inches of dust, so how could someone shine it and not disturb the layer of dust on the box? The elegant oval medal had an image of St. Anthony with emblems of a book and lilies. St. Anthony held the infant Jesus, who cuddled with him. On top of the oval were the words, ST. ANTHONY and on the bottom, PRAY FOR US. I turned it over. The back was engraved with the name *Molly O'Shea.*

The medal reminded me how Mamma Mia constantly prayed to St. Anthony to find lost items—she called him "my friend Tony." *"Tony, Tony, come around. Something is lost and cannot be found."* It worked every time!

I swiped the sweat off my forehead and absentmindedly looped the St. Anthony medal around my neck. As I continued on my treasure hunt, another wave of electricity buzzed through me, followed by a comforting warmth radiating from the medal.

I found another sepia photo, depicting a full-length image of a younger nun, who stood yard-stick straight and was too thin. She wore thick rimless glasses which magnified her eyes. Her big dark eyes smiled along with her full lips. The back read, "Mary Margaret O'Reilly. Sister Gertrude, student nurse and historian."

In a filing cabinet under all the boxes of photographs, I unearthed a thick book. At first, it looked like a missal for following Mass. I grabbed it and blew a big puff of air, as powdery particles drifted to the floor like pixie dust. No. Wait. A diary! Cleaning it off with a Kleenex, I held the black, pebbled-leather bound book to my nose and inhaled deeply. A woody scent and faded vanilla mixed with mildew arose from the tome. I loved the smell of old books—if they could bottle the scent, I'd wear it as perfume. Leafing through the tissue-thin pages, I felt as if I were on an archaeological dig. It'd been authored by Sister Gertrude. *Bingo!* Another deep sniff. Ah, lavender. Bet she hid it in her underwear drawer. I hadn't been this excited since winning $200 in a greased-pig contest Mary had entered me in.

FIVE

I triple sneezed due to the dusty archive room. I'd been re-searching four hours, but it seemed like a few minutes. Oddly, the nuns' history fascinated and frightened me simultaneously. I physically shook with nervousness due to my nun-o-phobia, but was attracted to their artifacts and stories.

Locking the archive door, I met up with Sister Xavier in the hallway. This tall, broad-shouldered nun didn't frighten me as much as my childhood nuns, probably because she dressed in a black suit, white blouse, and mini-veil, which wasn't as menacing as the long habits. But, she still managed to make me uncomfortable.

"How's the research going?" Sister asked.

"Fine, Sister. The archive room is quite disorganized, but interesting."

"Yes. I've been meaning to hire someone to organize it. Would you be interested in the job? Pays $400."

"Of course. I'll work on it as I'm researching. By the way, Sister, look at this St. Anthony medal I found in a box." I removed it from around my neck and handed it to her.

"Oh, Artemisia, we have *boxes* of St. Anthony medals!" she said, waving her hand. "You may keep it if you'd like."

"Thanks, maybe it'll help me with my commission." Securing it around my neck, I felt a tingling sensation, followed by a warmth radiating from the medal.

* * *

I breezed into Mamma's room and planted Italian kisses on her velvety cheeks. The color of her room reminded me of the French lilacs she'd cultivated at our home. I sat on her bed and settled in for a nice visit. The bruises from her fall had faded to pale ocher mixed with magenta and peacock-green. She resembled a Picasso portrait from his Blue period.

"Mamma Mia, come stai questa bella giornata?"

My tired little mother shrugged. *"Non ć male."*

"Not bad on this beautiful day, huh? Well, it's good to see you."

"It's good to be seen," Mamma said with a Henny Youngman delivery. "Did you bring me something tasty?"

"Yep. Made your special oatmeal-raisin-pecan cookies. To help with…you know, your *constipation* problem."

"Oh, good. I'm plugged up like the Hoover Dam."

I placed the large zip-lock plastic bag on Mamma's tray-stand.

"Pardon my boarding-house reach," she said, chuckling as she snatched the bag. "This week I had two pieces of lemon meringue pie, homemade pasta from that nice Wally guy, and Bar-B-Q ribs."

My eyebrows arched upward. "How'd you manage that? I know for a fact St. Anthony's kitchen doesn't serve Bar-B-Q to the senior residents."

"I have friends in high places," Mamma said, fluffing up her hairdo.

"Dang! Everyone loves my mamma."

"What's not to love? Forgot to tell you. I'm getting a new roommate named Belva."

"That'll be good company for you," I said, "and I know you'll be on your best behavior."

"I guess that means I shouldn't short-sheet Belva's bed?"

I tried to hide my smile, but it crept on my lips anyway. "Hey, Mamma, good news! The foundation of St. Anthony's asked me to paint a large canvas of the seven founding nuns for the upcoming centennial. A $5,000 commission! And a little job on the side of organizing the archive room. I can run my studio for a year. I'm researching the nuns' history and it's captivating." I reached for a cookie. "St. Anthony's opened in 1908. The poor sisters worked like farm animals! Now, you trained at St. Anthony's—I'd love to interview you."

Mamma bit into a moist cookie. "Yep. I was in training back in 1934. Was twenty years old."

"Do you remember Sister Ignatius, the first administrator?"

"*And how!* Anyone who ever met Sister Ignatius would remember her. She was the real McCoy. A hard worker...she rolled up her sleeves and worked right alongside the nurses and students. She visited all the patients every day to see if they needed anything and to offer them words of encouragement."

"From what I've learned so far, Sister Ignatius was a noble woman."

"But she could give you *the-what-for* if you got into trouble," Mamma said, snatching another cookie.

"Tell me all about your training. Wow! An eye-witness account of the very nun who initiated St. Anthony's Hospital!"

"Well, lemme see ..." Mamma talked around her mouthful of cookie. "Sister Ignatius would make unexpected visits to the students in the evening. Usually found us making fudge. The students always recited the rosary as a group before bedtime and we asked God to help us with our medical work. Oh...I remember how Sister Ignatius loved the poor!" Mamma became misty with her memories and reached for her handkerchief. "Sister was strict, but always fair." She brushed some cookie crumbs off her ample bosom. "Sister Ignatius had an Irish accent, which I mimicked and one time she caught me." My mother laughed roundly. "I did a funny impersonation of

Sister Ignatius—talk about laughing! The students howled. One day I was really hamming it up, laying on a thick brogue and Iggy—"

"*Iggy!*" I choked on my laughter. " You called Sister Ignatius, the hospital administrator and head of the school of nursing, *Iggy?*"

"That's what I called her. It really made the girls laugh. So Iggy walked up behind me and stood there for a minute. I was saying things like 'Tis a splendid day for a bowl of spuds,' and 'Saints Preserve us,' and 'Now, girls, I will not have you painting your faces—I have had enough of that rigmarole.' The student's laughter froze on their faces—they looked like they saw Marley's ghost! 'Uh…Sister Ignatius is behind me, isn't she?' I said in a raspy whisper. So I turned around to see what they were gawking at and thought, *Ye Gods, I'm up the creek without a paddle.* Talk about scared! Thought my head was going on the chopping block."

We laughed.

Mamma's belly quivered. "And you know what Sister Ignatius said?"

"I cannot imagine. You better tell me."

Mamma said in a perfect Irish accent, "Next time, roll your Rs more."

"Sister Ignatius had a good sense of humor too."

"Yeah, lucky for me. I was one of her favorites, you know. What else do I remember?… Oh, yeah. Sister Ignatius was fond of Horehound drop candy—she had a big glass jar of them on her desk and always had some in her deep pockets…I haven't thought of Horehound candy in years. Wonder if they still make them?" Mamma choked a little on her cookie and took a sip of water. "When I was a kid, I used to buy a bag of Horehound drops for a penny. My grandfather would send me to the store to cash his check. He'd spit on the sidewalk and say, 'If you get back with my money before the spit dries, I'll give you a nickel.' I ran like the wind. Then I'd return to the store lickety-split to buy a bag of Horehound drops."

"Horehound sounds interesting," I said. "I'll see if I can find some for you. Tell me more about your training."

Mamma pulled her shawl around her shoulders. "If a student showed up on duty wearing makeup, Sister Ignatius would escort the girl to the sink and scrub it off. Even if it was only a little powder! Then Sister would say, 'There, you look so much better'...of course, I know that only from hearsay."

"Hearsay? As in you *heard* Sister *say* it to you?"

When she fibbed, my mother had a *tell*—pretended to be acutely interested in trivial items. Mamma Mia took a sharp interest in her plastic water pitcher, studying it as if it were a Ming vase. "Isn't this a beautiful water pitcher?" She poured a glass of water and took a huge gulp. "We students were closely supervised by the nuns—I called them Nazi Nuns. Why, if we missed our curfew, we'd be crucified! On weekdays, we had to be in by 9 PM, but on weekends, we could stay out until 11."

"Did the students ever have any fun?"

"We had lovely dances in the community room of the nurses' residence. Of course, the nuns always chaperoned—I called them *fire extinguishers*...if you get my drift. When we danced with a young man, we were told to 'make room for the Holy Ghost.' One time, I had a date and he was so fresh! He tried to kiss me goodnight and had his *meathooks* all over me, probably because I was wearing *Gay Deceivers.*"

My brows scrunched in confusion.

"Gay Deceivers...you know, falsies! Back then, I was a skinny-marink! So I pushed him away, reached into my brassiere, removed the falsies, handed them to him, and said, 'Here, you like them so much take them home and play with them.'"

"Mamma Mia, I believe you missed your calling as a stand-up comic. So what happened if a student missed her curfew?"

"Well, she'd have the devil to pay. Sometimes the student

could get off with K.P. duty, you know, scrubbing pots and pans in the kitchen for a week, but if it happened again, she could get kicked out of training. At least that's what I heard."

"Ouch! That's harsh," I said, imaging a twenty-year-old girl trying to have a little fun. "Would she have been locked out all night?"

"If a student missed curfew, she'd try to sneak into the dorm through the hospital's boiler room, which was connected to the main residence by a damp, dark, cobwebby, smelly, rat-infested— " Mamma shivered, "underground tunnel. And every time the boiler would hiss, I'd...er, *she'd* jump out of her skin. Once inside the student nurses's residence, she'd never dare to take the elevator because it made too much noise, so she'd remove her shoes, being extra careful near the first floor where the nuns lived, and taking care on the third step that always squeaked— not that I ever did that."

"Well, that was certainly detailed," I said, laughing. "I'm intrigued by those nuns and their hardships. I feel as though they're present, like I know them and should help them in some way. But, they're...you know, *dead*. They have a strange hold on me. Surely you know about my fear of nuns, so why am I spending hours and hours researching them when I should be painting them? Speaking of that, I'd better get back to my studio and start working."

Mamma yawned widely. "Okay, honey. Thanks for the cookies—they were *de-lish!* Now get some rest and don't work so hard. Oh, don't forget to take my pocketbook with the Lorna Doones."

SIX

Entering my sun-filled workspace, I sucked in the air, heavy with linseed oil and turpentine, and let out a happy sigh. I had a quick lunch of a garden salad loaded with garbanzo beans for protein. I'd sketched a few compositions of the nuns when the bell atop the door jingled. A possible customer!

A paunchy, middle-aged man wandered in and perused my work. He bought my book, *Weeping Angels*, along with a fused-glass Angel Amulet for his wife's birthday. I was flattered when he asked me to sign my book.

He reeked of English Leather aftershave, which transported me back to my miserable marriage to Richard, who'd bathed in that cologne. I used to enjoy the musky scent of leather, citrus, and cedar. Now it nauseated me.

In my thirties, I'd longed for children, so I married Richard. Mamma couldn't stand him. I'd given up my studio and my artwork to augment our married income and went to work as a dental assistant. Joseph Campbell—I had an intellectual crush on that man—would have said I led an inauthentic life. Looking inside of people's mouths all day wasn't my idea of "following my bliss." I stuck it out *six long years,* but when he reneged on his promise to start a family, I bolted. I took back my maiden name because I didn't want a constant reminder of my misery. Besides, he was a lousy lover—not generous, if you get my drift. Jeez, his name should have tipped me off—what a dick!

"Can you write a personal note to my wife, Jennifer?" the balding guy with smiling dark-brown eyes said. "She loves angels. Just *loves* them."

Now, there's a good man. "For a nice customer like you, I'm including a handmade Angel of Peace-card—my compliments. Here, let me gift bag the necklace," I said, as I slipped the amulet into a turquoise organza pouch. "If you'd like to sign my guest book, I'll put you on my mailing list. I'll be holding Open Studio soon—that's where I demonstrate my painting techniques." I smiled as I handed him his purchase. "Hope to see you again."

"Will do. I'll bring Jennifer to see your beautiful big angels," he said.

After he left, I read Sister Gertrude's diary.

September 6, 1908

Dear Diary,

Today St. Anthony's Hospital was born. Dr. Eamon Rooney had petitioned Bishop McCabe for seven nuns to help run the hospital and initiate a school of nursing.

Even though I entered a teaching order, here I am training to be a nurse!

Dr. Rooney gave a wonderful talk to us after dinner. He said, "We will not allow any more suffering of the poor. That would be a sin of omission. Our motto of St. Anthony's is 'misericordia ut infirmus.' He instructed us to begin each day reciting, 'Mercy to the Sick.'"

Dr. Rooney is a splendid surgeon and so kind to me and the sisters. His wonderful sense of humor makes us all laugh. He has only one wee flaw. Cursing! He doesn't mean to curse and tries very hard not to, but wayward words slip out like hiccups. Sister Ignatius has spoken to him, many times, and she's 'not having it!' He had a severe 'case of hiccups' the other day and I had to cover my ears with my veil.

I did a few more sketches of the nuns, trying out different compositions and playing with the graphic patterns of the black and white habits. Again, the bell jingled.

A tall, willowy, young woman ambled into my studio. As she removed her headphones to turn off her music, her multiple bracelets clanged along her wrists. "Mind if I come in and take a look-see?"

"Welcome to Credo studio. Take your time. I'd be happy to answer any questions," I said, straightening up my messy countertop.

"You do all these paintings?"

"Yep."

"Is that real gold on the angel's wings?" she asked, pointing to a small painting.

"Afraid so. I mean, yes. Twenty-three-karat gold leaf. Costs a fortune!"

"Wow! All these angels. You must be very religious," she whispered as if she were in church.

"Not really."

"You should name your studio *Angels R Us*," she said.

I couldn't help but stare at her swimming pool-blue eyes. I'd never seen that eye color before. She had pale translucent skin, like fine porcelain, and a swan-like neck. Her long, auburn corkscrew curls were thick and a bit wild. Often, I mentally sketched interesting-looking people as I spoke to them and studied their features—not in a creepy way, rather, more in an academic manner— noting facial relationships. It was kind of my hobby. For example, the relationship of the tip of her nose to her upper lip was delicate and her philtrum—the vertical groves above the upper lip— formed a perfect Cupid's bow. She looked as if she just stepped out of a Pre-Raphaelite painting.

"I *always* wanted to learn to paint. It's so cool to be an artist. Do you give lessons?" She handed over an Angel of Peace Amulet. "How much is this?"

"Yes, to the lessons. That fused-glass amulet is fifty dollars."

"I really like your studio," she said.

"Why, thank you. What's your name?"

"Lily."

"My friends call me Arté." I extended my hand.

She shook it vigorously. "I get it! Arté... sounds like art and you're an artist."

I smiled. "You know, Lily, you'd make a perfect model for my angels. Ever done any modeling?"

"You don't mean nude, do you?"

A low throaty chuckle burst out of my mouth. "Good heavens, no! I'd give you free art lessons, including supplies, in exchange for modeling for my large Angels of Peace .. if you're interested."

"You mean like these giant angels?" she said, pointing to the large angels in the back of my studio.

"That's right."

She did an uninhibited happy dance. "I'm going to be famous! I'm going to be famous!" she sang in a charming, childlike way. Then she burst into "Amazing Grace," as she clasped her hands together in prayer and looked skyward. Her voice was lilting.

"How old are you, Lily?"

"Thirty."

"You're very funny. Love your outlook on life."

I gave her my business card, as she wrote *Lily*—with great flourish and accented it with stylized flowers— in my guestbook along with her cell number.

* * *

I headed to St. Anthony's archive room to clean and organize. It looked as if a bomb had exploded inside. I attacked the closet first, which was crammed with admission books, photographs, boxes, and loose papers.

45

The doorknob turned as Sister Xavier's deep voice said, "We can talk privately in here, Governor."

I switched off the light and hid in the closet.

I heard scuffling noises. What was going on? Sounded like serious groping. I peeked through the old-fashioned keyhole. Governor O'Shea was *kissing* Sister Xavier! It was hot and heavy with lots of lip-sucking sounds and labored breathing. His hands were all over her.

My mouth gaped open like a Venus Fly Trap. This had to be worse than a kid seeing her parents having sex. *Sex!* Oh no, what if— Afraid of making a sound, I held my breath. Rigor mortis had set in me.

Should I try to help her? Does she want to kiss him?

A hic-cup squeal and then a loud thud. She karate-kicked him—like a ninja— in his groin.

Well, I guess she can take care of herself!

He doubled over holding his crotch and gasped in a helium voice, *"My nuts!"*

I shoved my fist inside my mouth and bit it.

Sister Xavier squared her broad shoulders and straightened her mini-veil. In a deep, gravely voice, as if her vocal cords were rubbed with sandpaper, she said, *"I am a nun!"*

Oh, sweet Jesus! I felt a sneeze coming on from all of the dust in the closet. *Please, please, please,* do not let me sneeze! I pinched my nose hard and concentrated on the pain. I closed my watery eyes and pretended to be invisible. I stifled my sneeze by the sheer power of positive thinking.

"I am so sorry, Sister Xavier," he said in a husky tone, "I had no right to do that. Can you forgive me?"

"What was it that you wanted to ask me?"

"I need your help locating a St. Anthony's document from 1908...for a friend...who's researching his genealogy. But, frankly, I don't know how you'd find anything in this mess. It's a disaster!"

"Well, you could have asked me that on the phone. I suggest we leave and forget this ever happened."

I heard the door slam shut, but waited a good ten minutes before I came out of the closet.

A knock on the door. *Oh, no!* Are they coming back? The door creaked open and the mysterious, lavender-scented nun stepped in with a stack of old charts.

"Excuse me, but these records belong in the archives," she said handing them over to me. "You know, back in Ireland we have a saying, 'the lawmakers are the law*breakers.*'" She peered at me knowingly. "Also, we say, 'Ye can tell when a politician is lying because his lips are moving.'"

I shrugged and said, "Thank you, Sister." What was she, the queen of non sequiturs?

I had enough of that archive room, left, and made a restroom stop in the lobby. Sitting in my stall, trying to erase from my psyche the sight of a nun making out, I heard the unmistakable squeaky sound of Sister Xavier's rubber-soled orthopedic shoes. Reflexively, I stood on top of the toilet seat so she wouldn't see my feet.

"Anybody in here?" Sister X called out. She waited a beat. "Fair warning, the janitor is going to clean the bathroom now."

I remained quiet as a corpse, as I peeked through a crack in the partition.

I saw Sister Xavier peeing...*standing up.* Sister X had a *weenie!* That indelible image will be forever seared into my mind's eye. I was scarred for life.

Hyperventilating and wringing my hands, I couldn't wait until she/he left. I was frozen in a crouching position on top of the toilet seat for twenty minutes. After finishing my business, I ran out of the bathroom and didn't stop until I reached my car in the parking lot. My shaking hands reached for my phone and managed to dial Mary.

SEVEN

"**M**are, drop *everything* and meet me at my studio. *Now!*" Mary came storming through my door. "It's a good thing I wasn't holding a baby! This better be good. I had a soufflé in the oven and now George is having a giant pancake for dinner."

"How about this: Sister X and Governor O'Shea making out in the archive room? That good enough?"

"Hot damn!" Mary wiggled her over-penciled eyebrows like fury caterpillars.

"With me hiding in the closet. Heard everything. Can you imagine? Jeez, remember all the lectures by the nuns in school about kissing? And here was a nun swapping spit with a politician!"

"No shit, Dick Tracey! I had Boston nuns—they were the toughest." Mary swayed back and forth. *"Wicked Pissa!"* She twitched. "Did they do *the deed?"*

"Nope. Just one kiss. It sounded like the governor kissed her—what the hell is he up to?"

"Dunno, but you can bet it's not good," Mary said.

"But, wait," I clutched Mary's arm, my fingernails digging into her flesh. "There's more." With an expression of a shell-shocked soldier, I stared straight ahead, wide-eyed. I whispered, *"Sister X has a dick!"*

"What the *hell* are you talking about?" Mary asked.

"Sister is a *mister!*"

"Huh?"

"I saw her...*him*...taking a wiz in the ladies bathroom." I shook my head, trying to remove the permanent image from my mind.

"Are you sure?" Mary asked.

"I think I know a penis when I see one."

"But...but, how could she hide a wiener while living in a convent? I mean, she lives with a bunch of nuns."

"Um...probably feigned modesty, you know, pretended to be extra shy."

Mary said, "Sister X is my boss—I'll never be able to look at her again!"

I stared off into middle space, "I'll never be able to look at sausage again."

For the first time, Mary was speechless. She just wandered out of my studio like a sleepwalker. She couldn't process the information either.

* * *

I took a long walk along the river and returned to my studio totally spent. I stretched out on the cot with Merlin curled up against my head and read Sister Gertrude's diary late into the night.

September 12, 1908

Dear Diary,

When we arrived at Verdant Valley, our first glance at the new St. Anthony's Hospital was shocking! We sisters had much work to do. There was a jungle of grass and weeds, discarded lumber and debris all around the building and the unpaved road was a mire of mud. We rolled up our sleeves and secured them with straight pins from our wimples and got to work. Then we discovered the new electric elevator was broken. Last evening's

49

thunderstorm had burned out the motor and we are having our grand opening next week.

Sr. Ignatius calmly stated, "God and St. Anthony will provide."

Then we climbed the stairs to the operating room and Sr. Ignatius exclaimed, "Saints preserve us! I cannot conceive how our work can be done in this tiny room. Why, there is more room in a matchbox!"

Later, we toured the patient wards and saw an ornately-carved mahogany bench in the hallway. Sr. Ignatius marched over to examine it and spotted the attached price tag. She cried, "Thirty-five dollars! Holy Mary Mother of God. How does Reverend Mother Euphemia think I am going to pay for this? She gave me an entire budget of fifty dollars. I will have to stretch my money tighter than the paper on the wall."

Sr. Augustine said she'd move it to the maternity ward because it would make an excellent 'agony bench' for the expectant mothers.

Next, we inspected the basement and discovered an unkempt cellar. Sr. Ignatius tried to start a fire in the coal furnace so she could boil water for our massive cleaning job. She had considerable trouble getting the fire started and her face turned red as a beet.

Sr. Augustine motioned me to join her. "Excuse us, Sister, we need to check on something."

We searched out the chapel and Sr. Augustine prayed aloud. "St. Anthony, now, you know Sr. Ignatius is a cyclone in a veil, but she is completely overwhelmed. Why, she doesn't know if she's on foot or horseback! Please help us to prepare your new hospital for the grand opening."

We returned to find Sr. Ignatius slumped over the stove. Weeping!

Sr. Augustine said, "Our dear Lord and St. Anthony have a grand job ahead of them and Iggy"—I was shocked to hear that nickname! Were we even allowed to do that ?—"it would be a big help to them if you would not sit here crying." She handed her a handkerchief.

"Right you are." Sr. Ignatius honked her nose loud like a goose. "I do not know what came over me. I will offer it up."

Then Sr. Augustine said, "Here, I will start the fire. Back on the farm in Ireland, 'twas me job to keep the furnace going. You rest a wee bit."

Sr. Ignatius upended a bucket and sat upon it as she blotted the perspiration on her face. She said, "We should walk downtown and introduce ourselves to the merchants and tell them about our mission. If we play our cards right, they will think it is their idea to donate the mops, pails, brooms, soap, and supplies."

I'd fallen asleep on the cot in my studio and dreamt that the St. Anthony nuns talked to me. I wasn't sure it was a dream. You know how scary that is? Think of the *"filthy mouths and bad attitude"* scene from the *Blues Brothers* when they went to visit *The Penguin.* It was the scene where Kathleen Freeman beat the stuffing out of the brothers with a metal yardstick like a Kendo master. That nun was a pussycat compared to my third-grade teacher, Attila the Nun. I wonder if there's a support group for nun-o-phobia sufferers?

I startled awake to the strong scent of lavender. Bolting upright, I felt the gazes of seven nuns stab me. Their expressions relayed a message: Remember the mission. I wasn't exactly sure what that meant. A sign to be mindful of their hardships and the importance of St. Anthony's Hospital? Anyway, it was a good title for the painting.

I ran upstairs to brush my teeth and grab my swimming gear, then headed to the Y.W.C.A. to swim laps. In addition to painting, swimming continuous laps was therapeutic to me. As I pulled my body through the silky water, I'd think about my paintings, work out compositions, and in general, figure out my life. After swimming, I had my morning dose of McDonald's coffee followed by a visit to Mamma Mia.

I strode into Mamma's room carrying a basket with my art supplies and two perfect long-stemmed red roses—Mamma's favorites. We traded Italian kisses. My mother smelled like Lily-of-the-Valley dusting powder, which reminded me of the swath of lilies that'd edged our white bungalow. Mamma had also cultivated antique moss-roses in our backyard among the lilac, hydrangea, and peony bushes. She sure had a way with flowers.

"*Ciao Bella*. How are you today, Mamma? Ready for Arts and Crafts? I'm teaching today and you're my assistant."

"You bet'cha. What beautiful roses! Arté, give one to Belva. She fell out of bed. Again."

"How sweet you are, Mamma," I gushed like a proud parent.

Mamma rolled her eyes and I thought for a moment she was having a seizure. Nope, she spied Lola.

"Uh-oh…here comes *Flash Gordon,*" Mamma said, curling her lip like Elvis.

A petite lady with a halo of tangerine hair and strands of faux pearls around her wrinkled neck approached us. She was strapped into her wheelchair, clutching her pocketbook close to her chest like a teddy bear. She inched her way toward Mamma's room. Using her feet, she took baby steps to propel herself forward. She moved slower than Tim Conway doing his old-man routine. She looked fragile, like she'd snap in two if she sneezed. "Which way to Bloomingdale's? Which way to Bloomingdale's?" the feeble-minded woman chirped.

"Don't talk to her now," Mamma whispered, "talk about slow! She's slower than molasses in January. We'll never make it to class in time."

"Which way to Bloomingdale's? Which way to Bloomingdale's?" Lola repeated mindlessly.

Mamma said loudly, "Lola. Turn around and go out the

door. Turn left. Then go *all the way* down the hall, that's Maple Avenue…and turn right at the light on Main street. You'll see Bloomingdale's. Can't miss it."

Lola obeyed, moving like an inchworm, chanting, "Which way to Bloomingdale's?"

"Mamma Mia, was that nice?" I scolded.

"What?" Mamma shrugged. "That's how I always get rid of Lola."

I handed Mamma the basket as I wheeled her into the craft room. She helped me set up. Today we were making painted birdhouses and decorating them with miniature picket fences and flowers. Mamma selected dark-chocolate brown for the house with robin's-egg blue for the trim. When finished, her birdhouse was neatly painted.

One resident with lavender cotton-candy hair must have scratched her head with glue on her fingers because there was a tiny bird stuck in her hair. Mamma got my attention. "Her bird flew the coop."

Another lady, who wore a wig, had red paint on her nose and looked more confused than a failing student taking an algebra test. With scrunched eyebrows and tilted wig, she violently shook her hand to remove the flowers that were glued to her fingers.

"You'd better help her before she has an epileptic fit," Mamma said.

The peppy social director, the same one who taught stretch exercises, said in a booming voice, "Okay, ladies, while your paint is drying, let's gather around the piano and have our song circle." She played "Don't Sit Under The Apple Tree With Anyone But Me."

Mamma's voice was round and full, she sang mid-tone and sounded much younger than her eighty-nine years. She could have been a professional singer. Then the social director selected "The White Cliffs of Dover" and Mamma's singing made me misty. I thought of the *fly boys*, as Mamma called them, during World War II...and that led me to think of Viet Nam and Michael.

After I washed the brushes and cleaned up the community room, I wheeled my mother back to her room. I helped her out of her wheelchair and into bed.

"That class was fun. Mamma, your birdhouse was far and away the best."

"No kidding, Sherlock."

"Are you tired?"

"Nah, stay awhile and visit. How's the commission coming along?"

I drew in a sharp intake of air and blew it out in a puff, lifting my bangs off my forehead. "There's something weird about that commission. When I was a kid, surely you remember how frightened I was of nuns?"

"And how!"

"Especially my tormentor, Sister Attila the Nun. One time when I had a nasty cold and sore throat, you sent me to school with Aspirin gum. She caught me chewing it and made me stand in front of the class, take the gum out of my mouth, and stick it on the bridge of my nose. She made sure it had a long drying time before she *ripped* it off my little face. It's a wonder I didn't need a skin graft! *Aspirin gum, for godsake!"*

"But I took care of that *baccalá,*" Mamma said as she flattened her hand and bit it, her Italian gesture for *Don't mess with Mamma!* "When that no-good nun locked you in the cloakroom because of the '*coolie*' incident," Mamma said, unable to hold back her laughter, "I didn't let her get away with it. I called her and told her in no uncertain terms to *never...ever* do that to my child, or any child, again or I'd kick her *coolie* across the room!"

"You know," I said, " we had a loving nun in kindergarten. In first grade, a kind, cheerful nun taught our class. Second grade was relaxing and quite easy as it was a review of everything we'd previously learned. Our second-grade nun was young and gave us encouragement, even doled out hugs and pats on the head—she actually loved children. I'd been suckered in to a false sense of security. Third grade: *Bam!* Attila the Hun. I'd been conscripted into the holy hell of Sister Attila the Nun's gulag. Her mission was to traumatize kids for their lifetimes."

Mamma scowled. "I *spit* on that rotten nun's grave. *Pa-Tooey!*" She reached for a Kleenex to wipe the spit from her chin.

"I still have nightmares about her," I said. "She's the reason why I'm so introverted, so fearful of public speaking. That nun reduced me to a cipher with her cruel words and punishments. Sure, I had a good education and beautiful Palmer-method handwriting—she engraved that into me—but she did a number on my self-confidence."

Mamma's jovial mood changed like quicksilver. "Artemisia! Why am I not your role model? Haven't I set a good example for being strong and outspoken?"

"Yes. But you're also kind. I don't fear you."

"Arté—you're sixty years old. Do *not* let a third-grade nun define your life. When the horse you're riding dies, get off! Snap out of it," she said, snapping her fingers loudly. "That's *it! Capisce?*" She took a sip of water. Then a deep inhale, which she expelled with great force. "When you became ill with hepatitis and vomited all over Sister Attila's shoes and she made you clean it up and then sent you home without *notifying me,* that's when I took action. You know, I was so worried about you. Your illness could have been life threatening. Thank God we caught it early. Of course, I demanded a meeting with that nitwit nun."

"I often wondered what you said to her. She never bothered me again after your meeting."

"Well, besides swearing at her in Italian, I cast *Il Malocchio* on her," Mamma said, narrowing her dark brown eyes and flashing her famous sign. She held down her two middle fingers with her thumb, leaving her index and little finger straight up, like the Hook 'em Horns sign of the Texas Longhorns. She waved her calamitous Italian symbol menacingly.

"Oh no, The Evil Eye!" I had a clear visual of my feisty Mamma and Sister Attila the Nun at a show-down, like in a Western where two lone gunslingers faced off as a giant tumbleweed scuttled across the dirt road accompanied by haunting Pan Flute music.

"Why didn't you pull me out of Catholic school like Fearless Freddy the Finger's mother did?"

"Artemisia. The Catholic education was the very finest and you know how I felt about a good education. So I made sure that noxious nun would never mistreat my precious little girl again…or any defenseless child. That *bully*! I wasn't the only mother who'd complained about her, but I bet I was the loudest. I had serious words with her supervisor and the Mother Superior placed her on probation. If she acted out one more time, they were going to commit her to a mental institution."

"I always thought she was certifiable. Wow, Mamma, you saved my *coolie!*"

EIGHT

"Lily, tilt your head slightly toward the window and fix your gaze on that red dot above the door."

"Like this?"

"Perfect," I said as my camera clicked like a machine gun. If only I could capture the other-worldly quality of Lily! Dressed in a long, white, satin robe with a gold braided-cord cinched around her waist, she shimmered from within as the natural light from the north window bounced off her cork-screw curls.

I grabbed my sketch pad and conté crayon and scribbled some quick gesture drawings, hoping to render the beauty before me. The red conté on buff-colored paper had an old-world look, which I punctuated with turquoise for her eyes.

"Okay, Lily, take a break."

In her angelic getup, she broke out in a Michael Jackson dance singing "Thriller."

* * *

I stopped at the gas station to fill my P.T. Cruiser and had a major fit. Stomping my feet and yelling, "*Double crap!* The price of gas! You're killing me!" I kicked the gas pump and stubbed my toe. Okay, my Italian temper got the best of me. Some people loved the smell of gasoline fumes, but the odor of petroleum nauseated me. The eighty-degree temperature caused the liquid vapors to produce wavy lines before my eyes. My cellphone chimed. Mamma Mia cried so hard, I couldn't understand what she'd said.

"Slow down. Take a deep breath and speak slowly."

"Arté! Come quick. *Subito!* They're taking me to surgery."

* * *

I raced to St. Anthony's. On the elevator I overheard two orderlies discussing the closure of St. Anthony's. That was so ridiculous—didn't they know St. Anthony's was preparing for its centennial celebration? ...Still...what *if* St. Anthony's closed? What would happen to Mamma? I pushed that uncomfortable thought out of my mind.

I rushed into Mamma's room. A doctor dressed in Cerulean-blue scrubs examined her with his stethoscope. There was something familiar about his eyes, which matched his O.R. garb.

Oh...that cute Donald Duck-doctor! He was so kind to that little girl.

Mamma rubbed her tummy and softly moaned in Italian. She stopped whimpering long enough to say, "Doctor Goodman, this is my daughter, Artemisia. Arté, meet the finest surgeon at St. Anthony's." Then she resumed her writhing.

I nodded. "Doctor Goodman, how is she?"

"Well, your mother appears to be in a great deal of pain. And the symptoms she described are conducive with an acute appendix."

"*Acute* appendix? My appendix is cute? Why, thank you, Doctor," Mamma said, and returned to groaning.

Dr. Goodman laughed.

Mamma motioned for Dr. Goodman to come closer to her. "Can I ask you something, Doctor?"

"Of course, Mrs. Credo."

"Do you mind if I run my fingers through your gorgeous hair?"

"Have at it," he said, bending close to her. He smiled and one dimple appeared.

Mamma used both her hands to thoroughly examine his thick silver hair. She rubbed his head vigorously, like a beautician shampooing a client. "What thick hair!" my mother said, enjoying herself a little too much, "just like my Giuseppe's."

Horrified, I said, "Mamma! *Basta!"* I squinted, beaming laser rays straight through Mamma.

"I get this a lot—especially from the geriatric crowd," Dr. Goodman said with a lopsided grin.

I said, "Appendicitis? *My mother* has acute appendicitis?"

"Yeah. An inflamed appendix," he explained, as if I were a little dense, as he combed his hair with his fingers.

Mamma rubbed her belly harder and cried, "Oh, *Dio!"*

"Um…Doctor Goodman, may I talk to you in the hallway?"

We moved to the hall. I studied my feet and curled my toes, not sure how to begin. "Doctor Goodman, I …ah, think Mamma Mia is trying to pull a fast one on you. She delivered me by C-section—sixty years ago—and she told me…many times that her appendix had been removed during that surgery."

"So, you're sixty?" he said, studying my face. "I'd have guessed younger—I'm sixty-one. Never met a woman who volunteered her age before." Leaning against the wall, Doctor Goodman narrowed his eyes and said, "Are you positive she had her appendix removed? Why would she make this up?"

Oh, great! I was *not* telling this cute doctor that my mother was trying to fix us up. Jeez, how embarrassing. "Um…I dunno—maybe for attention? …Munchausen syndrome? Her sister also told me about Mamma's appendectomy. I'm sure of it."

"Well, that explains why her abdomen isn't rigid. Your mother is very funny—a real piece of work."

"I get that a lot," I said, rocking back on my heels.

Scratching the back of his neck, he said, "We should have

some fun with her. Let's make her think she's actually going to surgery. You game?"

Oh, good Lord! How far would Mamma go to fix me up? Would she allow herself to be cut open?…Maybe…after all, he was a doctor. "Yeah. Mamma needs to learn a lesson."

We entered her room and he picked up the phone and dialed. "Is this the O.R.? Oh …hi, Peggy. Tell the girls to prep room three for an emergency appendectomy." He glanced at Mamma, who'd abruptly stopped moaning. "How old are you, Mrs. Credo?"

"Eighty-nine."

"Any allergies?"

"Yes. I'm allergic to surgery."

"Don't worry, Loretta, I'll take good care of you. I'll make sure I don't use the rusty scalpel."

"Let's not be hasty here," she said, "maybe the appendix will get better on its own."

"Oh, no," Dr. Goodman said in a hushed tone like an undertaker. "That *never* happens. We must operate before the appendix ruptures." He took her hand and patted it. "Loretta, you're a nurse, *surely* you know that."

Mamma's facial expression changed like a slide show. Panic was a new emotion for my mother. Her eyes widened, showing all the whites and her head jerked unevenly. For once in her life, Mamma Mia was speechless.

Dr. Goodman examined Mamma's bumpy legs. "These varicose veins are quite pronounced. I'll have the nurse come in and put anti-embolism stockings on you. She'll prep you for surgery too."

Mamma's mouth moved, but no words came out.

Doctor Goodman said, "Artemisia, I'll walk you to the elevator."

By the elevator, he burst into a rich, deep laughter. "How long should we let her squirm? Haven't had this much fun since

I exchanged signs on the Women's and Men's dressing rooms." I checked my watch. "Twenty minutes should do it. Doctor, I want you to know I dearly love my mother—she's all I have in this world, but sometimes she can go too far. Thanks for teaching her a lesson."

"My pleasure. I'll go back in a few minutes to cancel…I'll tell her I have another emergency surgery before hers—can't wait to hear what she'll say."

"Bet she has a miraculous recovery."

The elevator doors slid open and Dr. Goodman stepped on, still laughing. "See ya later, Arté."

"Peace out," I said. Did he say he'd see me later? Wait till Mary heard about this!

NINE

I returned to my studio, delighted to have a large block of painting time to work on my commission. As I squeezed blobs of oil paint onto the palette, I thought about the brave posse of nuns and their hardships and sacrifices they'd made for St. Anthony's Hospital and the poor of Verdant Valley. This much I knew: It was the nuns' manifest destiny to have been missioned to St. Anthony's Hospital and there was *something* greater than my little existence—like a Higher Power—at work here. After awhile, I switched gears to create my notecards.

A rapping came on my window. I glanced up to see Lily's pretty face and wild curls slowly lowering as if she were riding down an escalator. That girl always put a smile on my face.

Lily breezed in. "Hiya, Angel Lady."

"Hey, Lilypad!" I smiled warmly.

"Whatcha doin'?" she said, unplugging her headphones.

"I'm making a big batch of Angel of Peace notecards. Would you like to help?"

"Sure."

"Here, let me show you how to stamp. These are fine-art stamps of Renaissance angels. See how detailed they are? Load them generously with this sepia-toned ink and carefully position them on the card. Press down hard, but take care not to move the stamp, because that'll blur the image. Then, carefully lift the stamp straight up from the paper. Here," I said, handing it to her, "give it a go."

Lily concentrated heavily, slightly biting her tongue. She held her breath as she lifted the stamp from the card. Her face brightened. "*There!* How's that?"

"Perfect! Let it dry a few minutes and then take that fine-tipped brush and paint the wings with glitter glue. And then let that dry too."

Lily worked slowly and deliberately. After it had dried, she asked, "What's next?"

"To finish, use the colored pencils." I handed her a large wicker basket filled with *Derwent* sharpened pencils in various hues and shades. "This is the fun part. A trick I use to soften the color is to buff it with a Q-tip."

Lily became lost in her work as I stamped several cards. "We make a good team," I said.

"Like Laverne and Shirley," she said, giggling.

When Lily finished, she beamed like a preschooler showing off her artwork. "Can I keep it?" she asked, with a big grin.

"Of course! Don't forget to sign the back."

"Thanks, Arté. It's for my dad. Well, I'm going to make like a fetus and *head out.* Toodles." And off she went, singing "Amazing Grace."

I reached for Sister Gertrude's diary, which read like a novel.
December 20, 1918
Dear Diary,
I mop and wax the lobby floor every day until I can see my reflection in it. It's my pride and joy! And every day Dr. Rooney runs up the front steps, bursts through the door, runs down the hall and skids to a stop in front of Sr. Ignatius's desk. It is his routine. He looks at Sister with great surprise and says, "Why didn't you tell me the floor was so slippery?" Sister Tomasina, our receptionist, tries to hide her smile, but it doesn't work. Without looking up from her paperwork, Sr. Ignatius always

says, "Good morning, Dr. Rooney, I trust you will watch your language in the O.R. this morning."

Our census was low. On my morning rounds, I commenced to planting St. Anthony medals under the mattresses of the empty beds. And, sure enough, St. Anthony answered my prayers by filling up every bed. What a saint!

We hit another dry spell in our accounts receivable, but I know St. Anthony will help us. Mr. Sperduti, the carpenter at the hospital, has been so kind supplying us with bushels of apples and his homemade cider. And dear Mrs. Sperduti sent along dozens of her canned tomatoes. God bless them! The painter was unable to pay for his operation and Sister Ignatius forgave his bill. He responded by painting every hall-way in the hospital and old Mr. McGreggor paid his debt with jars of pennies!

Sister Ignatius assigned me the task of filling a dozen bushel baskets with coffee, tea, sugar, butter, eggs, flour, cere-al and fruit for the poor of V.V. When I finished, the store room was bare and so was the ice box! I hope we don't have to eat potato-skin soup again. Sister instructed me to go to Miller's and purchase fifty pounds of mixed candy for the children for Christmas—peppermint, Horehound drops, spearmint, lem-on drops, and licorice. Okay, I confess. I ate some candy while packaging it in small boxes. Mea culpa!

Mr. Houlihan, the butcher, had delivered a big ham to the convent as payment of his wife's maternity bill. We were in Hog Heaven! We made it last a long time. We feasted on glazed baked ham, scalloped potatoes and ham, ham chow-der, ham and eggs, ham and cheese sandwiches, and chopped ham salad. We made sure to save the bone for ham and split pea soup. Now that the ham is gone, I'm praying a novena for Mrs. Houlihan to have another baby soon. Maybe we'll dine on a leg of lamb!

Sister Ignatius appointed me secretary to take notes

*during the Welfare Board meetings. We had a very impor-
tant meeting this morning and Sr. Ignatius was not nervous
at all because she was on a mission of mercy. She fought for
the rights of Mr. Goodman. The Commissioner said if Mr.
Goodman stopped drinking and had a job, he wouldn't need
assistance, whereas, she informed him to attend the meeting
unbiased. He was so pompous. Sister said, "Mr. Commissioner,
sometimes I forget you're so perfect. For your edification, Mr.
Goodman is head of maintenance at St. Anthony's Hospital.
And he does a splendid job, but he has fallen on hard times.
His son suffers from a serious medical condition and desperately needs surgery." Sister's gaze pierced every man directly
and they cleared their throats. "Gentlemen, it is not our job
to judge and we are not here to be carrying tales. We all have
enough dirt on our front porches—let us sweep off our own
porch first. I hereby approve Mr. Goodman's application. Next
case." Sister Ignatius is afraid of no man!*

* * *

St. Anthony's had taken on a new meaning. It became more
than Mamma's beloved home. Standing before it, I viewed the
hospital through educated lenses. The Latin motto, *Misericordia
ut Infirmus*, was carved into the lintel across the top of the
door. Never noticed that before. The maroon-brick façade was
topped with a massive stone Celtic cross sculpted out of green
Connemara marble—a nod to the mostly Irish staff. For one
hundred years, the anthropomorphic building had witnessed
life, death, pain, and joy. If one studied it long enough, one
could almost perceive the structure breathing. A hub of humanity, inhaling and exhaling.

Inside the lobby, I perused the glass display cases hous-
ing the antique surgical instruments and photographs of the
school of nursing graduating classes. Hey, there was Mamma!
How beautiful in her starched, optic-white uniform. Her cap

contrasted against her thick, dark, wavy, '30s hairdo. A sepia-toned photograph of Dr. Eamon Rooney's rugged face with his mane of black hair, chiseled nose, and square jaw smiled at me. I nodded back at him.

Standing before the over-life-sized statue of St. Anthony holding the infant Jesus, it was easy to imagine his infallible protection over the charity hospital.

I admired the large oil painting of Sister Ignatius, which hung opposite the elevator. She bore a striking resemblance to the mysterious nun I kept on running into at St. Anthony's. A strong sensation of déjàvu overcame me, accompanied by a whiff of lavender. I couldn't stop staring at her. Puzzled, I tried to figure out the important information the portrait held. The elevator pinged, snapping me out of my trance.

*　*　*

I visited Mamma and found her in the activities room, participating in the Song Circle. The residents were gathered around the piano, swaying to *Sentimental Journey.* Some sang brightly and snapped their fingers in time to the melody, while others had far-away expressions. Mamma called out, "Hey Pianoman, play *Can't Take That Away From Me.*" Her clear voice sang, "*The way you sip your tea . .*" I joined in and later returned my mother to her room.

"Arté," Mamma said, "how's the commission coming along?"

"There's something strange about it." I rubbed my forehead in an effort to clear my thoughts. "So here I am, a nun-o-phobe, and I feel like the seven founding nuns are my friends, but at the same time, I'm sort of afraid of them. It's so …eerie…I mean, I actually worry about them, especially Sister Ignatius… and she's been *dead* since 1939! Sometimes it seems as if the nuns are watching over me and guiding me while I'm painting their portraits. It's the strangest feeling."

Mamma rubbed my arm and frowned. "It's probably because you read about them every day and you spend a lot of time here at good old St. Tony's."

"Maybe…still it's odd. I mean, I even get mad because the nuns were discriminated against and mistreated by the uppity surgeons who thought it was beneath them to step foot inside St. Anthony's Hospital…and that was one hundred years ago."

Mamma handed me a glass of water. "Here, this will make you feel better. How do you know the nuns were mistreated?"

"Because," I said, "Sister Gertrude left a fabulous diary. You remember how women were treated in the first half of the twentieth century. They were devalued. And there was Sister Ignatius, the thirty-two-old female administrator of a thriving hospital. I doubt there were any women executives back then. She was an anomaly of her day. *And* she was a nun, so there probably was religious discrimination too. It was impressive that she steadily grew St. Anthony's with grace and grit."

"I never thought of her that way." Mamma looked like a guilty child with her eyes downcast as she inspected her fingernails. "Shouldn't have called her a Nazi Nun."

"Sister Gertrude's diary is priceless—very detailed," I said. "It sounded like she was a nervous ball of energy and so funny! Do you remember her?"

"And how! Talk about cleaning! She was forever cleaning the halls. Dusting, mopping, and waxing—always in perpetual motion. That was her trademark. I called her Sister-Mary-Mops-A-Lot." Mamma giggled and then laughed out loud. "She was so excited about the brand new electric floor waxer and couldn't wait to try it. Gertie weighed about ninety-five pounds—the machine was tall and when she turned it on, it spun her around and around like a rag doll. She got caught up in the cord. Her veil was flying and her rosary beads rattled—looked like a whirling Dervish. She was my favorite nun…a Nervous Nelly. Gertie never walked, she always hustled down the hall, half-running.

She wore thick glasses and knew all the latest lingo—taught her some myself. She said things like, 'What a riot!' and, the one she always said to me, 'Well here's another fine mess you've gotten me into.' We became good friends." Mamma had another laughing fit. "One time, Sister Gertrude and I were assigned to bathe the newborns. She loved babies! After she'd bathed one, she held him up cooing at him and saying, "What a good boy you are! Time for your diaper now." And he sprayed an arc of pee right in her face. For the next little baby boy, she donned a surgical mask and goggles. We sure had fun together."

I said, "During the first three years of St. Anthony's, Sister Gertrude wrote that only three doctors, two Jewish and one Catholic, would patronize St. Anthony's. She stated that the other doctors would not admit patients to St. Anthony's unless the patient insisted upon it. And when the opposing doctors *did* work at St. Anthony's, the nuns 'had to take much by way of criticism and unkind remarks.' She said Sister Ignatius reminded the nuns they were doing God's work and to offer it up."

Mamma yawned and tried to keep her eyes open.

"I'll let you rest," I said, leaning over to kiss Mamma's olive-oil-cheeks, which made me crave a garden salad, "see ya later."

"Tomorrow I'm cooking in the community kitchen for the residents," Mamma said. "Making eggplant parmesan. Take some of my personal-care money and buy a dozen little eggplants, you know, the beautiful baby ones with the shiny smooth skin and less seeds. Oh, and a bottle of good olive oil—*extra virgin!*" She waited a beat. "How can we be sure those little olives are virgins?" She laughed. "Wait! Take my pocketbook with the Lorna Doones. And don't forget to return it for the next exchange."

"*Ciao Bella,*" we said to each other.

* * *

Lily and I hunched over the counter in my studio, examining the gold leaf booklet.

"This is genuine, twenty-three-karat gold leaf. It's pounded into thin sheets."

"Cool beans!" Lily said.

"It costs a stinkin' fortune. Fifty dollars for this little bit!" I said. "So, see this rabbit-skin glue?"

"Eeeww! Not real rabbits? What is this? *Fatal Attraction?*" She narrowed her eyes, "Did you boil a bunny?"

"Afraid so. I'm following the Renaissance recipe for applying gold leaf and that's what they used." I stirred a small pot of viscous material on the hot plate. "You need to warm it slightly and apply a thin coat to the area to be leafed. Let it dry—just until it's tacky."

"You mean crude and tasteless?" Lily said, smirking.

I chuckled. "Tacky, as in sticky. Now, pay attention."

"Yes, Master," she said, saluting.

"Then you take a big brush, and using static electricity, pick up a gold-leaf square and gently lay it down on the glued area. You have to be very careful not to breathe on the gold-leaf because it'll fly away—very friable—like butterfly wings. If you touch it with your fingers, it'll dissolve. Sometimes I wear a mask."

"Wow!" she said.

"I know! There's a lot of waste because it's difficult to handle. One time, I sneezed and wasted twenty dollars worth of gold!"

"*Day-um!* That was one expensive *ha-choo,*" she said.

TEN

I stopped by the grocery store to buy Mamma's eggplants and extra-virgin olive oil. Also I needed toilet paper, which reminded me of my miserable marriage to Dickk. Not only for obvious reasons, but because we constantly argued about how to place the roll on the dispenser—over or under. Dickk, in his dictatorial way, pontificated that the paper *must always* roll over—like some toilet paper manual stated that and to do otherwise would cause a seismic catastrophe. He lent new meaning to the term *anal retentive*. But, don't worry, I always changed it to roll under. And when he questioned me about it, I swore I did not touch it and was quite convincing—could have been an actress. Just for giggles, I'd change it back his way, my way, and then his way. I had a special brochure printed, *Signs of Early Onset of Alzheimer's Disease*, which stated "Forgetting which way one placed the toilet paper on the roll was a sure sign of Alzheimer's disease." I left the brochure where he'd see it and Dickk thought he was losing his mind. My inward amusement was so intense, I nearly ruptured my spleen.

* * *

I returned to my studio and worked on my commission until hunger twisted my stomach. My legs ached too because I always stood while painting. I'd been working for hours, but didn't remember adding oil paint to my palette or mixing colors.

I sat down and looked at the canvas on my paint-stained easel. I blinked. The painting was well executed. Quite good. The nuns stood erect on the stone steps of St. Anthony's Hospital and were as architectural as the building. Their countenances arrested the viewer. I stood to the left of the painting—they looked at me. I stood to the right of the painting and they still looked at me. Don't know how I did that. The black and white patterns of their habits depicted a strong graphic design. The brushstrokes were descriptive and lively. While I'd painted, the nuns' history filtered through my psyche and traveled down my arm to my hand, which held the paintbrush and registered on the canvas. Finally, at least *something* in my life was going well.

I sighed deeply and slumped my shoulders. I dreaded the next four hours because I had to report to another kooky job Mary had landed for me—why did *I* have all the fun? Have you noticed Mary was absent when the jobs were whack-a-doodle?

* * *

I rolled up in my old PT Cruiser in front of the SUBWAY Sandwich Shop and went inside to change into my giant SUBWAY-sandwich costume. The store manager, a pudgy guy in a dirty white t-shirt, instructed me to dance as exaggeratedly as possible. If I could hook in fifty customers, I'd get a fifty dollar bonus! A small packet of twenty-three-karat gold leaf for my angel's wings sold for fifty dollars, so that was my goal.

Coming of age in the 1960s had its advantages. On the corner of Main and Church streets, I performed my zany rendition of the Hustle, Swim, Twist, Watusi, Frug, Hully Gully, Locomotion, Boogaloo, and Jerk. I was eternally grateful that I could dance with wild abandonment under the guise of the goofy costume, which was top-heavy.

I got clammy and a little winded as I began a particularly ambitious Mashed Potato-dance when my feet got tangled and I fell onto my back.

My arms and legs wriggled like a turtle flipped over. I thrashed as the fake tomato slice and floppy lettuce slapped my face. I sweated like Nixon.

The comic scene drew a large crowd as I struggled to flip over. Cell phones whipped out to film my fiasco—it had probably already gone viral on YouTube. Someone called the local TV news station and they arrived faster than a fire truck answering a five-alarm fire.

Hope the manager was happy now. This costume was so heavy. Why the hell didn't someone help me up?

I felt helpless like those pathetic live lobsters in the fish department of my grocery store—you know the ones, sunk to the bottom of the tank with rubber-banded claws.

A newscaster leaned over me. Even though she was young, she had so much botox injected into her forehead, her eyebrows couldn't move.

She looked like a plastic Barbie doll. The insensitive chick stuck the microphone in my giant submarine-sandwich face. "Is this a gimmick to get customers?" she had the nerve to ask.

I disguised my voice by lowering it a few octaves. "No, dude."

I tried to swish the faux limp lettuce out of my eyes as a strong hand grabbed my arm and pulled me upright.

The newscaster interviewed the kind stranger. "Are you part of the act to attract more customers?" she asked in her phony TV-voice.

Joe Goodman replied, "No act. You should cut this guy some slack. Give him some water, he's probably dehydrated."

Doctor Donald Duck? *Mary McKee!* She was not long for this world.

Pure panic gripped me. In a deep, raspy voice, I said, "Uh,

thanks, dude. Time for my break." I ran faster than Usain Bolt into the sandwich shop and hid in the bathroom.

* * *

I returned to my apartment, took a long shower and slipped into my comfortable clothes—well-worn jeans and Beatles tee-shirt. Snacking on organic yogurt with my feet propped up, I read Sister Gertrude's diary.

October 20, 1935
Dear Diary,
Oh, Catfish! That darn Dr. Richard Heade! That's right, I said darn. He dislikes working in our hospital and I got stuck with him today. He was in a malicious mood. He complained bitterly in the operating room and had the audacity to throw a surgical instrument! Sr. Augustine, who administered anesthesia, was livid! I thought she would box his ears!

Then I had to make rounds with him on the ward and assist him in changing dressings. I could do nothing right for him. He found fault with everything I did. He dropped the suture scissors and yelled at me! Called me an idiot. Then he didn't think the forceps I handed him were fine enough. I told him they were Dr. Rooney's favorite forceps and he bellowed at me. "How dare you talk back to me! Get out of my sight, you silly penguin." Sr. Ignatius stood in the hallway and heard everything. Dr. Heade stepped into the elevator and Sister stopped the door from closing. "I need a word with you. You cannot treat me Sisters in such a disrespectful manner. I will not have it!" He looked at Sister with pure disgust, with his nostrils flared, as if he smelled rotten garbage. Sr. Ignatius said, "I have seen and heard enough of your shenanigans. St. Anthony's has survived years without your patronage and we do not need a prima donna dripping with sarcasm now. And we most certainly can do without your autocratic attitude. I will have you know, you can keep your churlish remarks to yourself!" Sister's face turned red as blood. "If you ever think of acting so shamelessly again to one of me Sisters—make no mistake—I will personally lay you out in lavender."

Dr. Heade straightened and set his jaw. His lip curled. "Now, see here— "

Sr. Ignatius pushed the 'close' button and the door sealed him up like a tomb.

Sister told me to take the remainder of the day off. Said I deserved a rest and go to her office and take a nap on her divan. "Help yourself to me Horehound candy," she said kindly. So I took a whole pocketful! In case we had potato-skin soup tonight, again.

Rhett had her eyes all dolled up and Sister Ignatius took her to the sink and washed her face. Gave her a lecture about wearing "so-called make up" on duty.

Dr. Heade was the topic of our dinner conversation. Sister Augustine said, "I simply will not tolerate that man in my operating room! He may be a surgeon, but that does not give him permission to throw instruments." Sister Ignatius said we must pray for him because apparently he is handicapped in the personality department and, for all we knew, his mother may have dropped him on his head when he was an infant. She said, "He is socially constipated. Let us pray for a spiritual laxative for him."

Rhett and I got in a peck of trouble. We got called on the carpet in Sister Ignatius's office.

Wonder what they did? Who was Rhett? Wait a minute... she was talking about *Loretta!*

ELEVEN

I had questions for Mamma about Sister Gertrude and her diary. Eager to visit with her, I hurried over to St. Anthony's and skidded to a stop just outside her door because I overheard Mamma and Tess, her emissary, whispering loudly. Tess, a stout redhead, adjusted her thick bifocals.

"*Jesus, Mary and Joseph*, Tess! We'll be boiled in oil if they catch us again," my mother ranted in an undertone.

"*Jeez-Louise*, Loretta! You look more worried than a turkey in November."

"Why the hell did you bring the *whole platter* of doughnuts?"

"Didn't know what kind you wanted. So, sue me!" Tess said in her gravely smoker's voice.

"*Quick!* Don't stand there like a bump on a log. Give me a jelly…and a glazed—is that a chocolate one? *Make it snappy!* Hide them in my underwear drawer under my brassieres. Judas Priest, is it hot in here? Feel like we're dealing drugs," Mamma said.

"For *Chrissake*, don't have a coronary. I'll return the platter before they notice," Tess said in a raspy whisper.

A pudgy nurse hustled into Mamma's room as I pretended to wait for the elevator.

The nurse said, "Oh, *there* you are, Tess! Been looking for you. Have to put your compression stockings on you."

75

"Is that a mouse in the corner?" Tess hollered in her gritty voice, as she hid the platter of doughnuts behind her back.

I stood unnoticed in the doorway, watching.

Jumping up onto the bed in one swift movement like a gymnast, the nurse let out a high-pitched scream. She moved fast for a big woman. "Oh my God! Where?" She hyperventilated and clutched her chest.

Tess quickly placed the platter of doughnuts on the chair behind her and threw Mamma's afghan over it. "Oh, my damned eyes are so bad. Guess I'm seeing things."

The nurse carefully climbed off the bed, stopping to check her pulse. "Tess! You nearly gave me a heart attack. Have a seat in the chair so I can get these stockings on you."

"What? *This* chair?"

"Yes, of course. It's the only chair in the room," the nurse said, slightly annoyed.

"How about I sit on the bed?" Tess said.

"*No-oo*, it's easier in the chair. Tess, what's *wrong* with you? I have to hurry and hand out meds. I have a lot of work to do and you're not my only patient."

Tess shrugged and looked to Mamma for help.

Mamma doubled over, holding her belly. "Ow...ooh! Nurse. Quick! My bowels are in an uproar. Hurry, get me to the commode—my suppository just kicked in."

The nurse helped my mother to the bathroom as Mamma wildly waved her hand behind her back to signal Tess to get rid of the platter of doughnuts.

The nurse left the room, mumbling to herself. I waited a few minutes before I went in.

"How are you, Mamma?" I said.

She quickly pushed something behind her back, as her gaze darted around the room. "What are you doing here?"

"Uh...the same thing I do everyday, visiting you." I grinned. "You know, I could go for a Dunkin' Doughnut—been craving one. Want a glazed?"

"*Artemisia!* You know I'm a diabetic."

"Right." I peered at her with arched brows. "Actually, I have questions about Sister Gertrude's diary," I said, as I retrieved it from my purse. "What the hell did you do to get a nun in trouble?" I waved it in front of her.

Mamma snatched the diary and opened it to the bookmarked page. She read silently and heaved up a belly laugh. "We were assigned to the dinner cart and were instructed to deliver the food while it was *hot* and Gertie and I were late—as usual. We ran down the hall pushing the huge cart and didn't quite make the corner. The dinner rolls scattered like flying saucers. Our eyes bugged out, like we were in front of the firing squad. I said, 'If we pick them up really fast, the germs won't have time to hop on them.' Sister Gertrude gave the bread a special blessing for extra insurance and we delivered the rolls to the patients. But, somehow Sister Ignatius found out. I think Sister Gertie spilled her guts because she was so holy—couldn't take the guilt."

When I stopped laughing, I said, "Do you remember Dr. Heade? Apparently he didn't like to work at St. Anthony's."

"Yeah. Mean as a snake. He was on staff at the other hospital."

"Was there a carved mahogany bench at St. Anthony's—maybe in the maternity ward?"

"A beautiful one…had carved cherubs on the arms and legs. We called it the 'agony bench' because the women in labor sat on it as they were waiting to be admitted. Over the years, they'd rubbed the arms smooth—for good luck and because they were in pain." She yawned a few times.

"Need a nap?"

"Been extra tired lately, see ya later," she said as she nodded off.

TWELVE

I attended Mamma Mia's monthly medical-review, which was in the conference room across the hall from her cozy abode. She liked that she was situated near the elevator too—and next to the supply cupboard, which housed the packages of Lorna Doones. She also was close to the nurses' station, which was excellent as Mamma didn't want to miss out on anything. Prime real estate.

Mamma's internist, dietitian, physical therapist, and nurses discussed her condition and we all voiced our concerns.

Doctor Higgins worried about Mamma's heart condition. It was not good. "Artemisia, we're not able to control your mother's atrial fibrillation. I had hoped her heart rate would convert, but it's constantly racing. It's quite a strain on her heart. And I'm afraid her asthma is worse."

"Also," the dietitian added, "her diabetes is out of control and the meds are not working. I know she's opposed to taking Insulin shots, but we don't have a choice. Especially after the *doughnut incident.* I'm worried about her blood sugar—it's off the charts."

"Loretta's spinal stenosis is becoming more advanced. Her nerve-block seems to be wearing off," the physical therapist informed me, "and that's why she's having more back pain."

"I have to treat her back pain with opiates, if she's to get any relief," Dr. Higgins added.

My poor Mamma Mia. "I'll talk to her about all of this," I said as I gathered up my notebook and shuffled across the hall to visit Mamma, surrounded by a wall of worry.

I gave her extra Italian kisses, so happy to still have my little doughnut-stealing Mamma.

"*Ciao Bella!* I'm still searching for the Horehound candy for you, but they have to be sugar-free. Not sure if they still make it because it's an old-fashioned candy. I did some research and discovered Horehound is a member of the mint family. The ancient Romans used Horehound to clear the mind and promote quick thinking. Pretty cool, huh?"

"No wonder I was such a smart kid—I ate a bushel and a peck of Horehound drops back in the day."

"So… I just came from your medical-review. There was talk of you and Tess and an incident with a *platter of doughnuts.*"

"Oh…*that.*" Mamma took a sudden interest in picking lint off her black pants. "I didn't tell Tess to bring an entire *platter* of doughnuts." She squinted. "Who spilled the beans about the doughnut caper?"

"Never mind that. Seriously, your blood sugar is uncontrollable and the medicine isn't working. Doctor Higgins said you must go on Insulin injections."

She sighed deeply as she slumped her shoulders. "How's my ticker?"

"I'm afraid it's not good."

Mamma took my hand in her soft, paw-like one. "Arté, look at me. Where are my joys in life?" She motioned with her palm up. " I have you—thank God for that! And, sure, my mind is sharp as a bayonet, but I can barely walk." Her priestess-like visage pierced me as her dark eyes unblinkingly gazed into mine. She moved closer to me, smelling of olive oil. "You know, when your body fails you, it's the ultimate betrayal." She sucked in a deep inhale and pushed the air out slowly. "I can't exercise.

Don't smoke. Don't shop. Don't drink. No sex…at least not with a partner. Food is my last joy." She jutted her chin. " I'm eighty-nine—if I want a *stinkin'* doughnut, I'll have one!"

I finished my visit, brushed her cheeks with Italian kisses, and collected her pocketbook for our illicit cookie exchange. I shuffled to the archive room to research my nuns. I know…*I know!* I should be working on my painting, but I was not the one in control.

* * *

Mary and I had signed up for the glass-fusing class at Community Arts. Our friend, Johnny Mae, joined us. She was our art companion who worked with Mary at St. Anthony's business office, and a painter who rented studio space at Community Arts. Johnny Mae created large paintings of Jamaican women, which were joyful and colorful. Her smooth cinnamon skin had lavender undertones and her high cheekbones were like that of a fashion model.

"Johnny Mae," I said, "I'd love to do your portrait. Wear your purple caftan with the flowered headdress."

She beamed a smile exposing straight, white pearlescent teeth. "Only if you pay me with one of your angel paintings!"

Drooling over the shimmer of the dichroic glass, we were like jewel thieves set free in Tiffany's. I was drawn to the aqua sparkle of the metallic pieces and designed a pendant in the colors of the Caribbean Sea. Johnny Mae chose saffron and purple glass, while Mary settled on red and orange. We sandwiched the small pieces together and they'd melt and blend in the kiln. Sometimes we'd see surprising results, always yielding one-of-a-kind artwork. I had some difficulty cutting the shapes I wanted.

Mary chirped away, trying to recall the name of an artist she wanted me to look up. *"Pissa!* I'll think of it later—shoulda taken more fish oil this morning."

"I used to take ginkgo biloba for a good memory," Johnny Mae said.

Mary said, "Yeah, that's good too."

"Only problem was," Johnny Mae said, "I would forget to take it."

"Take what?" Mary said. Then she chuckled. "Just kidding."

I filled them in about my commission and research of the nuns.

Mary sucked air through her teeth as she wagged her head. "Ooh, Arté, I don't know about *you* painting *nuns.* You and nuns don't mix too well."

"*I Know!* But I'm behind in my rent and desperate for money."

"But, remember when I told you a joke about nuns and you broke out in hives? Maybe you should borrow some of my Xanax."

"You take Xanax?...and you're *still* hyper?" I said.

Mary giggled. "Yeah. Can you imagine me without it? I'd be like Barney Fife on speed. So, you excited about your solo exhibit at Community Arts?"

With my head down, I concentrated on cutting the glass. "Turned it down," I mumbled.

"*Say what?*" Johnny Mae's voice pitched highly. "You turned down a big-ass solo exhibit? *Girl!* Which kinda crazy are you?"

"Whadda mean?" Mary shouted. "You can't give up a chance like that. A solo show is *wicked* awesome!"

"Not thrilled about giving a gallery talk," I said, pretending to shudder.

"*Aw, can it!*" Mary spouted. "*Cut the crap!*"

Blood spurted all over the gleaming glass as I'd managed to lacerate my index finger and thumb on the edge of the cut glass.

"*Damn it!*" I hissed.

"Ohmigod!" Mary shouted. "Don't panic! Don't panic!"

Her hyperactive actions looked like a cartoon character as she paced back and forth. "That's going to need stitches."

Johnny Mae's almond-shaped eyes grew bigger. "*Mercy! That's a lot of blood!*"

Mary raced into the bathroom like Road Runner for a bunch of paper towels and wrapped my hand. The towels turned beet-red. She ushered me to St. Anthony's emergency room, nattering on the whole time. Mary sat in the waiting room as Johnny Mae held a cold cloth pressed to Mary's forehead. The sight of all that blood was too much for her.

* * *

It was just my luck to get the new intern on call in the E.R. He was nervous and his hands shook. I'd deeply sliced the length of my index finger and my thumb. He tried to numb the area by blocking the digital nerve, which was more painful than the laceration—it felt like the needle went straight through my finger. He forgot to inject my thumb. The neophyte intern began suturing and I felt every stitch, which made me queasy. I was relieved when he was paged STAT because of a real emergency. Take your time!

Was Doctor Goodman around? Then he strolled into my cubicle. Spooky, right?

"How's it going? Let's see." He picked up my hand. "Wow, how the hell did you do this?"

"Cutting stained glass to make a pendant."

"Can you bend your finger?"

I bent it slightly.

"Very good. I can see the tendon, but I don't think it needs a surgical repair. Jeez, you look white as paste."

"I'm going to barf."

He shoved a stainless-steel kidney-shaped basin under my face, which I quickly filled with vomit. I made barking-seal noises as guttural retches heaved my body. The miasma made me gag even more. He held my long hair out of the mess and handed me a Kleenex.

"Well. That was real attractive," I said, wiping away the spittle. The sour tang in my mouth annoyed me. "Got any gum?" He reached into his shirt pocket and tossed a stick of peppermint gum at me. "Thanks." Chewing on a minty wad, I asked, " Would you mind sewing my hand? The nerve-block the intern gave me isn't working. The tip and base of my finger are numb, but the middle where he was stitching isn't. I've felt every stitch so far. And he forgot to inject my thumb."

"Sure," he said, scrubbing his hands and donning rubber gloves. "That's why you blew chunks, the pain caused an involuntary response. Are you allergic to Novocain? I'm going to anesthetize it properly and I won't forget the thumb," he said, filling the syringe. "A little sting here. And now I'll wait a few minutes for it to take effect." He gave me that killer grin. "You know, Arté, you're supposed to cut the glass, not your hand."

"Thank you, Doctor Obvious!"

The corners of his full lips curved upward, creating that single dimple.

The morbidly obese guy they'd wheeled into the cubicle next to me made a lot of noise behind the curtain. We heard loud belching followed by a train of farts.

Dr. Goodman said, "It's the Methane Express." We tried not to laugh, but it was impossible.

He whispered, "He's my patient and that's the most intelligent thing he's said all day."

I laughed out loud and my good hand flew to my mouth, trying to stuff my giggles back inside. I forgot all about my pain as Dr. Joe Goodman's nimble fingers placed twenty sutures in my hand.

The odor of liquor permeated the emergency room. We heard the nurse ask the inebriated patient if he knew what his blood type was.

Dr. Goodman said, "Pinot Grigio."

"You're killing me," I said as I held my good hand up like a stop sign.

"Just trying to take your mind off your pain."

"Thanks, Dr. Goodman, for taking care of me. I'm so thankful the tendon wasn't cut and it's my left hand, so I can still paint." I glanced at him shyly, "Mostly I'm glad you wandered in here."

"I think you should charge more for that pendant you were making." He held my hand as he wound an ace bandage around it.

An electrical charge surged up my arm to my heart and it had nothing to do with my injury.

THIRTEEN

I organized the archive room into two sections, St. Anthony's Hospital's records on one side and the school of nursing information on the opposite. I'd almost finished when I moved a filing cabinet and discovered a crumpled folder behind it. I recognized Sister Gertrude's elegant handwriting. The cover read, *Requiem for Doctor Eamon Rooney, 1920.* I sat crossed-legged on the floor and opened it.

Everything I know about nursing and healing the sick, I learned from Dr. Rooney. He taught me to be God's instrument of mercy.

I was the special-duty nurse to Dr. Rooney. It was inconceivable that our own Dr. Rooney was a patient! It was touch and go for a while, but we all believed he would make a full recovery. I spent many hours at his bedside as my fingers hiked along my rosary beads. I kept a perpetual hot water bag on his chest and a cold cloth on his forehead. I concocted my dear Ma's formula for catarrh made of boiled onions, honey and hot milk for him. Even added a wee bit of whiskey.

Dr. Rooney was puzzled as to how I always had a piping hot water bag for all of his patients. He would sneak into his patient's room on tiptoe at two o'clock in the morning to catch me unaware, checking the temperature of the bag. He asked, "How did you do it? It was supernatural, I tell you!"

"Well, you will remember the very first thing Sister Ignatius did was to have the main street of St. Anthony's paved. She took much criticism from Father Finkel for paving Divine Street. Father said, "I suppose the dirt road is not good enough for our highfalutin' neighbors." But it was a brilliant move on Sister's part, for it kept all the dust and dirt out of our hospital.

Doctor Rooney said, "I agree, Sister, but I fail to see what that has to do with the hot water bags."

I confessed that I listened for the click-clack of his horses' hooves on the newly paved road.

"Well, Sister Gertie, you pulled a good one over on me!" We laughed over that.

Sister Ignatius paid him a visit. "Good day to you, Eamon," she said, "Is there anything I can do for you?"

"You can pray to your buddy, Saint Tony, for me."

"Tis been done."

"Sister Ignatius," Doctor Rooney said, "I want you to know how sorry I am for my cursing. I always tried to edit myself, but the words slipped out. It was never intentional."

His chest heaved with every breath and he suffered a coughing fit.

Sister placed the emesis basin under his mouth and wiped the stringy saliva off his chin. "Hush...hush now, Eamon, save your strength. Everyone has vices—a little blue language is not so bad. Why, I learned a few new words! I believe in my heart," Sister said, thumping her chest, "all of your good works more than make up for any vices you may have. Just think of the children's clinic you initiated. Our head of maintenance, Mr. Goodman, and his son are most appreciative of the clinic. Why, Mr. Goodman's wee lad is walking now. 'Tis surely a miracle."

He spoke again, taking her hand. "Sister Ignatius, I want you to give my eulogy," he said fighting for each gulp of air, "And remember, no pious piffle!"

"You have me word, Eamon," she said, nodding.

Our Doctor Rooney smiled and closed his eyes and never opened them again.

When Sister Ignatius was able to recover her voice, she said, "The bright light of our polestar has burned out. May God have mercy on his beautiful soul."

Keening at a private Requiem Mass in our convent chapel, we huddled together to say farewell to our friend and mentor, who was the beating heart of St. Anthony's Hospital. Each too sad to speak, we found solace in the cadence of the Latin Mass and the familiar smooth beads of our rosaries.

FOURTEEN

In the archive room at St. Anthony's, I sobbed like a child with a skinned knee over the death of Doctor Eamon Rooney. Even though he died in 1920, on an emotional level, I knew him.

I pulled myself together and needed to visit his grave. Wanting to know where he'd lived in my hometown, I jotted down the address of his house from the obituary notice and set out to pay homage to my hero.

I blew my nose and locked up the archive room. In the hallway, I stepped squarely into Doctor Joe Goodman. I mean, rammed him—nearly knocked him over. How embarrassing!

"Whoa! Arté, where's the fire?" He scrutinized me like a medical student performing an autopsy. "You okay?"

My red-rimmed eyes and drippy nose were not attractive. "Hi Joe...Dr. Goodman...Dr. Joe Goodman. Yeah, I'm fine. Just doing more research in the archive room so my painting will be authentic. Getting ready for St. Anthony's centennial."

"How's the hand?"

"Good as new. You did a great job." I flapped it around like a drunken bird.

He grasped my hand to examine it and made me tingle all over. "Yep. Looks good."

"I ran across some information that mentioned Joseph Goodman and wondered if he was related to you?"

"That's interesting...Maybe. My family has lived in Verdant Valley for many years. I'd like to hear more, but I'm headed for surgery now. See ya later, Arté."

"Peace out," I said, wishing I looked more presentable.

* * *

I stopped by my studio, picked a few flowers and drove by Doctor Rooney's former address and was surprised to see that it was now McDonald's. That made me gloomy because I'd expected to see a grand Victorian house.

Then I drove to Holy Sepulchre Cemetery. I parked under a massive maple tree and listened to the distant whine of the lawn mower, which sounded like the never-ending cry of a naughty toddler.

I roamed around for thirty minutes, sniffing the sweetness of the freshly-cut grass and reading the headstones. Finally, I located a modest tombstone. I should have known from my research that Doctor Rooney's grave would not have been ostentatious. As in life, he was humble in death.

I knelt before the roughly-hewn, light-gray granite marker, crossed my chest, and talked to my dead friend, whom I'd never met.

"Hey, Doctor Rooney. I'm an artist and have been commissioned to paint a portrait of the seven founding nuns of St. Anthony's. I've researched and learned so much about you and the Sisters. You did such a noble deed for the poor of Verdant Valley. Thank you for initiating St. Anthony's. My mother trained there as a nurse, worked thirty years, and now is a resident on the skilled-nursing unit. It's her home and I'm grateful to you for that. You were a gifted surgeon and all that you did *mattered*—you made V.V. a better place. St. Anthony's is about to celebrate its one hundredth anniversary—you probably already knew that. I'll keep you in my prayers. Peace Out."

I placed a pink Rose of Sharon on Dr. Rooney's simple headstone.

* * *

I trekked back to St. Anthony's to visit Mamma. After I handed her the empty faux-leather pocketbook, she quickly filled it with Lorna Doones and grinning broadly, looped it over my arm.

"Mamma Mia, how's your appendix today?"

"I don't know what you're talking about," she said as her eyebrows scrunched together like two caterpillars mating. Fascinated with rearranging the box of Kleenex and water pitcher on her bedside tray, she said, "Arté, I heard more rumors of St. Anthony's closing. Are they true?"

"Who told you that?"

"I hear a lot when people are waiting for the elevator."

"Well, I doubt it. Nothing but gossip, why, good ol' St. Tony's has been around for one hundred years! Don't worry, Mamma, it might upset your appendix. I have to go now to work on my commission."

We said *Ciao Bella* and traded *baci*.

* * *

Inside the elevator, I reached into Mamma's pocketbook and took out a package of Lorna Doones. The elevator stopped on the fourth floor and Dr. Goodman stepped in. He wore crumpled blue scrubs and his curly hair was matted down from his surgical cap.

"We have to stop meeting this way," he said. "Lorna Doones! I *love* those."

I opened Mamma's pocketbook and offered him some cookies.

He grabbed two packages, ripped one open, and shoved a whole cookie into his mouth. "Thanks, I'm starving. Where'd you get all the cookies?" he said with cookie crumbs spewing from his mouth.

"My little conniving Italian mamma steals them from the supply cupboard," I said, as if everyone's mother was a cookie thief. "She thinks I can't afford food. Says for the amount of money she's paid to live at St. Anthony's, she *owns the damn Lorna Doones!*"

He chuckled. "Have you eaten yet?"

"Nope. Not since I saw you this morning by the archive room."

"You mean when you nearly knocked me over? I haven't eaten since then either. Wanna grab a burger with me? I'd like to hear more about your research and Mr. Goodman."

"I could go for a burger," I said, contracting my stomach muscles to quiet its rumblings. The thought of a hamburger made my mouth water.

"I'll change and meet you in the lobby in ten minutes."

Jeez…I didn't think this was a date. But still. Wait till I told Mary. I scurried to the Ladies' Room to spackle my face.

FIFTEEN

Joe Goodman and I sat in a red-Naugahyde booth at The Burger Shack, as juicy bacon-cheeseburgers were set down before us. We'd ordered chocolate milkshakes and shared a large platter of fries, which was kind of intimate.

I took a huge indelicate bite of the burger and an orange mixture of ketchup and mustard dripped down my chin. I quickly blotted it with a napkin, hoping he wouldn't notice.

"You missed a spot," he said with a crooked grin and pointed to my chin.

Strange how comfortable I felt with him. No pressure—well, why would there be? It wasn't a date. Didn't feel shy—at all—about diving right into a fat burger with a cute guy sitting across from me. Giggling, I said, "I'm starving like a Hollywood starlet on Academy Awards night."

He chuckled as he squirted a well of ketchup on the fries. "A lot of the movie stars look emaciated. They look like walking X-rays."

"That's a problem I don't have to worry about. I mean, *fat chance* I'd be emaciated," I said as I slurped my thick shake. "The implanted, veneered, worm-lipped chicks look like plastic Barbie dolls. Kinda feel sorry for them." I knew I was nattering on, but couldn't seem to stop. Okay, Artè, *focus.* I cleared my throat. "So, Doctor Goodman, I came across—"

"Hang on, name's Joe, okay?"

"So, *Joe Okay,* I found this—"

"My name is just Joe," he said as his Aegean Sea-blue eyes crinkled at the edges and his lopsided dimple appeared.

"Okay, *Just Joe.* Jeez, make up your mind."

"Very funny…you must get your humor from your mother."

"As I was saying, *Just Joe,* I discovered this document, a transcript of a Welfare Board meeting, in which Sister Ignatius—she was the first administrator of St. Anthony's—totally went to bat for Joseph Goodman. He was a fine man with a large family and his son suffered from a medical condition. Anyway," I said, scarfing another portion of the patty and talking around a lump of meat, "Sister Ignatius made sure that Mr. Goodman had the surgery he desperately needed. And she hired him as Head of Maintenance. Also, his son was admitted to a special children's clinic to help him walk."

I paused to wipe the grease from my chin. "This part is good—Sister *royally* told off the Welfare Commissioner! Normally, I'm afraid of nuns, but you gotta love that one." Squelching a belch, I popped the remainder of the beef into my mouth. "So good! Must be angus beef."

Joe's lone dimple disappeared as his smile faded. "My family always highly regarded Sister Ignatius and St. Anthony's Hospital—that's why I became a surgeon and returned here after my training. My grandfather was Head of Maintenance at St. Tony's." He played with the salt shaker. "My father, who walked with a limp, spoke lovingly of the hospital…he was the little boy in the report. Hadn't known about the Welfare." He slowly shook his head. "Wow."

"Sister Ignatius should be canonized! She was a champion for the poor and disadvantaged." I reached for my creamy milkshake and took a big chug. "The research is fascinating. It's like detective work. Been reading Sister Gertrude's diary—what a hoot!"

He squinted his blue eyes. "Wait. You're afraid of nuns?"

Dipping a long fry into a lake of ketchup, I jettisoned it into my mouth. "I'm a nun-o-phobe."

"What the hell is that?"

I waved my hand as if shooing away a fly. "It's a long story."

I went on and on telling Joe about my research and how riveting it was. Of course, I didn't mention the part about the dead nuns talking to me in my dreams. Like when I thought they were actually in my studio. Didn't want him to think I was Looney Tunes.

"Joe," I said, salting the fries, "I'm dying to know what Mamma had to say for herself when you busted her about her *acute appendix.*"

"Well, I ordered a CT scan just to be sure. When I told her the appendix didn't show up on the scan, she feigned Alzheimer's." He did a spot-on imitation of my mother. "What appendix?... Who are you?...Where am I?" The comic surgeon looked to the left, then to the right, and with a perfect Clem Kiddlehopper expression said, *"Who am I?"* We laughed.

When I thought about Mamma losing her home at St. Anthony's, I grew serious.

"There're a lot of rumors about the possible closure of St. Anthony's. That's gossip, right? I mean, St. Anthony's has survived one hundred years! The nuns had saved it from closure many times...and the hospital made it through pandemics, floods...wars. The more I research, the more I'm convinced that a Higher Power is at work regarding St. Anthony's."

His face clouded over as he folded his napkin and threw it over his plate. "Afraid it's not a rumor."

"But...my mother *lives* there...St. Anthony's is her *home.*"

* * *

Back at my studio, I dialed up Mary.

"Hiya, Arté, how'zit going? How's your hand? Hey, listen

to me, ya gotta take that solo exhibit—it'll help your career. You need the money!" Another thing about Mary, she talked in run-on sentences.

"Uh, hand's fine. Don't want to talk about the exhibit. I need you to come to my studio. Want you to take a look at my painting of the nuns. Oh, by the way," I said casually, "I had a date…well, sort of."

"Oh no, did your mother fix you up again?"

"In a way…well, indirectly. But this time it was a good date."

"Who?"

"*Donald Duck!*"

"You had a date with a *duck*? Wow. Didn't know you were into that sort of thing."

"No—remember the doctor on the elevator with the adorable little-girl patient…he talked to her in the Donald Duck voice?"

"*Shuddup!* Doctor Goodman? You went out with Doctor *Good*—Man? *Wicked pissa!* Be there in a flash!"

* * *

Mary burst through the door vibrating with curiosity. She'd made record time getting to my studio. With her amber eyes glistening and her over-penciled brows hiked upward, she said, "Start at the beginning and do *not* leave anything out. Is he a good kisser? I bet he— " her gaze locked on my painting of the seven nuns. "Ooh…Arté, that's *wicked awesome!* Look at their expressions. Why, it looks as though they're about to speak and they have something very important to say. It's your best painting ever."

"Thanks, I don't remember painting most of it. I was in some kind of a trance."

"Enough about the painting," she said waving her hand, "spill your guts about your date." Mary, who always swayed slowly back and forth when she talked, looked like a back-up singer for the Supremes.

"First of all, stop swaying. You're making me dizzy."

"So sorry," she said, hugging herself as if she were confined to a straight jacket.

"Well, *technically*, it really wasn't a date. I bumped into him as I was coming out of the archive room—literally, almost knocked him over. Told him about my research because I'd uncovered some information about his relative. Saw him again later in the day and Joe asked me to go get a burger so I could tell him about it."

"*Joe!* My, aren't we *chummy*. Where'd ya go?"

"Burger Shack. And, for your information, he insisted I call him Joe."

Quiet for a moment, Mary chewed on her bottom lip. "Did he pay for your meal?"

"Yeah."

"That's a good sign."

"Lucky for me because I only had a few bucks on me."

"Maybe it wasn't a real date, but it was a good start. So I guess there wasn't any smooching involved?"

I rolled my eyes. "Listen. What's with all the talk about St. Anthony's closing?"

Mary ran her fingers through her fiery-red hair and slowly shook her head. "I'm scared to death about my job. Afraid it really could happen. I manage the business office and St. Tony's is in debt—*big time!* Did ya know the hospital employs 1,000 workers? Just think what a closure would do to our local economy. I'll tell you this—they'll have to haul me out, kicking and screaming."

"Mare. What about the residents who live on the skilled-nursing floor? Where would they go? Just thinking about it makes my stomach flip."

She shrugged. "Don't know. That's a good question." She

hesitated and started swaying again. "Listen, I have a good job for you at the college and it's in the art department! Only part-time, but pays big *moola*! Here's the phone number." She handed me a slip of paper.

Relieved to have an opportunity to earn extra money, I tucked the note into my pocket.

SIXTEEN

Lily handed me her sketchbook, stepped back, and studied her feet.

I flipped through the pages, smiling. "Your progress is impressive!" All the sketches were self-portraits, morphing from a primitive first effort, with uneven eye placement and an outlined nose, to an accomplished rendering with full shadows and depth. "I especially like the range of dark, medium, and light tones. This last one has a great expression." She'd drawn her long curly hair in a wild, rapid fashion, as if it were windblown. "See how this denotes movement? Good work."

"Thanks. Most of them were done as I looked in the mirror, but for that last one, I printed a *selfie* and placed it upside down to copy—like you told me."

"Yeah, that way, instead of seeing a face, you see abstract shapes. They're beautiful. Bet your mom is proud."

"She probably would be. My mom loved art—she was a tour guide at the museum." She quickly turned her back and stood before my large angel, for which she'd been posing. "I wish she could see this," she said in a thin voice.

Smiling, I said, "She's welcome anytime. I'd love to meet—"

"She's *dead*!" Lily blurted. She drew in a deep breath and exhaled slowly. "I mean, she died five years ago. Damn breast cancer."

"You must miss her," I said quietly.

"I still get sad when the holidays come...or her birthday." Lily brushed her long mane away from her swan-like neck. "Mother's Day is a hard one."

"Do you feel like modeling today?" I asked.

"Yeah, hanging out here and drawing with you helps me." Her lips curled into a slight smile. "Besides, you have to finish this angel so I can be famous!"

"Let's have at it." I donned my paint-stained big shirt. "Oh, and you have to name this one."

"Margaret. Her name is Margaret. After my mom."

"Perfect!"

* * *

After our long modeling session, I treated Lily to high tea at The Victorian Tea Room downtown. It was a sunny, crisp day, so we sat outside overlooking the river. Our food was presented on three-tiered silver trays and fine china hand-painted with pink-moss roses. We snacked on tasty, tiny, crust-less sandwiches, buttery cookies, and scones bursting with berries on which we piled clotted cream. Lily ate like a linebacker and asked for seconds.

"Cucumber sandwiches! So good. *Who knew?*" Lily said, talking around the food.

"Good, right? My mother used to bring me here. I like the egg-salad ones," I said.

"And these little crème-puff-thingys are divine! I do believe I'll have another *spoat* of tea," Lily said in a thick British accent as she extended her little finger.

"Hey, that accent is pretty good. You could be an actor and an artist," I said.

I offered to drive Lily home, but she said the weather was so pleasant that she'd rather walk.

* * *

Merlin greeted me with his plaintive cries for treats. Tweaking his ears and rubbing the ultra-soft fur under his chin, I placed some healthy food in his dish. I played with him, throwing his fake mouse at him, which he retrieved every time.

"I think you have animal-identity disorder—you're a cat, not a dog." I reached for his brush and knelt on the floor with him, brushing his long gray fur as he flattened out on the floor like a rug, making his happy-cat noises. "Have to get to work, Fuzzy Buddy." He settled down, washing his paws with his sandpapery tongue.

After mixing paint on my palette and setting up, I took some time to read Sister Gertrude's diary—my new guilty pleasure.

February 20, 1939

Dear Diary,

Sister Ignatius assigned me to be her assistant today. We had a full and productive day. Sister made her daily rounds visiting each and every patient, asking if they needed anything or if she could do something for them.

Next, I helped her answer the mail. We had a mountain of unpaid bills, one concerned the new surgical wing for two thousand dollars! Which we did not have! Sister Ignatius calmly wrote the check, but did not sign it. She placed it in the outstretched hand of our St. Anthony statue and said, "St. Anthony, you have never let us down and I have every confidence that you will help us now. Thank you."

The next letter Sister opened contained a check for payment of a patient's bill in the amount of two thousand dollars, which did not surprise her.

We left to visit the back door of the kitchen, where a long line of hungry people stood. It was common knowledge in Verdant Valley that Sister Ignatius of St. Anthony's Hospital never turned away a hungry person.

She signaled to Sister Raphael for a conference. "Please make certain everyone gets a hot bowl of soup and a loaf of bread. I realize the line is longer than usual, but these are hard times. No one will go hungry on my watch."

Sister Raphael furrowed her brow and rubbed her forehead. "But, Sister, our supplies are already low. After I give away this food and feed the patients, there won't be any food for the convent."

Sister Ignatius smiled. "God will grant you what you need if you ask in good faith. If you have little faith—you will receive little. Be sure to save the potato skins, we shall have a lovely soup for supper this evening."

A reporter from The Valley Chronicle approached Sister. The tall young man removed his hat and said, "Good day, Sisters. How many in the bread line? I see quite a number of hoboes."

Sister recoiled, "My dear fellow, please do not say hoboes, 'tis offensive to me. They are Knights of the Road."

"Sorry. Mind if I snap a photograph? It'd be good publicity for St. Anthony's"

"I mind very much indeed! No photographs. These people have suffered enough. Let us not embarrass them."

Sister Ignatius is tireless in her industry. I do not know where she gets all of her energy!

March 10, 1939
Dear Diary,
Our Sister Ignatius is bedridden, recovering from surgery. She had been ill for some time, but never complained. Finally, Doctor Kaplan operated on her and discovered a large mass in her intestines, which has metastasized. He wept in the operating room. Sister Ignatius has been running the hospital from her sickbed, but the end is near. Whatever will we do without her? She is like a mother to me.

March 14, 1939
Dear Diary,

Dead Nuns Talking

Sister Ignatius experienced a glorious quietus, the kind re-
served for saints. The newspaper ran a banner headline: SISTER
IGNATIUS, VERDANT VALLEY'S ANGEL OF MERCY, HAS
DIED.

I clapped the diary shut and tossed it on the cot. I blew my
nose and doused my face with cold water.

SEVENTEEN

On Friday I sprang out of bed, excited about the installation of my commissioned painting. Sister Xavier had selected the hallway outside the cafeteria as the home for it. She said it'd serve as "spiritual nourishment" for the employees as they filed past it to get their "physical nourishment."

Up before dawn, I looked forward to visiting my river and viewing the sunrise reflected on the mirrored water. I was gifted with a brilliant mango-to-magenta spectacle. I had plenty of time to swim laps at the "Y." After my pool workout, I cruised over to McDonald's for my morning bolus of coffee.

I'd spent weeks working on this painting and was pleased with it. I hoped it'd be well received.

* * *

I breezed into Mamma's room and found her reading the morning paper, sobbing. "*Mamma Mia!* What's wrong?"

"Arté, take a look at this article. It says St. Anthony's is slated for possible closure—*first* on the list! Is that true? I told you I've heard rumors about that. Now here it is in black and white." She punched the paper and reached for her handkerchief from its dwelling place between her ample breasts. "*Oh, Dio!* Where would I go? This is my *home.*" She sucked in a ragged breath and coughed. "I'll be moved far away…I'll never see

103

you again." She buried her blotchy face in her gnarled hands. She coughed and wheezed. I quickly handed her the inhaler and she took several puffs.

I hugged my mother. "No, Mamma, I wouldn't let that happen."

She was inconsolable. I'd never seen her this way. A spasm gripped my chest and I wondered if it were a heart attack. I chewed a Bayer's Baby aspirin just in case.

"Mamma, are you ready to go to the cafeteria for the unveiling of my painting? I'm very excited," I said, trying to take away her worry.

"I don't feel like going anywhere."

"That's a shame—they'll be serving refreshments. I know how much you enjoy those tiny sandwiches...Sister X told me she'd ordered Italian cookies."

"I'll get my ...pocket . . . book." She sniffed. Attacking her nose with her linen hankie once more, she reached for a plastic bag with which to line her purse.

* * *

As I glided Mamma's wheelchair into the cafeteria, a large crowd greeted me. I didn't expect that many. There stood Joe Goodman. Okay, that was grounds for nervousness. Now I had to contend with a broken-hearted mother, a swarm of people, *and* Goodman's famous one-sided dimple.

The rich timbre of Sister Xavier's voice welcomed the audience warmly. "I'm delighted to have so many friends and employees here to view the portraits of the seven founding Sisters of St. Anthony's Hospital, which is celebrating its one hundredth year of caring for the disadvantaged."

The group applauded roundly.

"It's my pleasure," Sister said in her deep husky voice, "to introduce the artist who created this wonderful painting, Artemisia Credo. Artemisia, please come up and say a few words about your beautiful artwork."

Was she *freakin' kidding* me? She didn't mention anything about public speaking being part of the commission. Is there a back door?...I wagged my head left and right. Okay, get a grip...Breathe.

A prick of panic pierced my gut and nauseated me as I stumbled to the microphone.

Don't puke in front of Joe Goodman again! My acid reflux ignited and I thought flames might shoot out of my mouth. "Jeez...I'd rather have a public colonoscopy on Main Street than give a speech," I said.

The crowd erupted into riotous laughter.

I took a huge gulp of air. "Uh...did I just say that out loud?" More laughs.

Joe shook his head as he displayed that killer grin of his. That mono dimple! A smirk like that should be against the law.

My innards made a hollow-gurgling sound, like a clogged pipe draining.

"Well...um, thank you, Sister X ...I mean Sister Xavier for your kind words." I stared at her groin and quickly glanced away. Looking out at a sea of faces, I tried to collect my thoughts, which scattered like cockroaches when a light was turned on them. "Um...when Sister asked me to take on this commission, I wanted to know all about the seven nuns—their histories, you know, in order to paint authentic portraits. I wondered who these women were before they'd dedicated their lives to God. Anyway, I didn't want the painting to look like a stiff copy of a photograph." I focused on Mamma and saw her sneaking Italian cookies into her pocketbook.

I blew out a puff of air as I heard the whoosh of blood surging through my arteries, sounding like Niagara Falls. "So, um, I've been researching in the archive room and I've discovered many interesting facts about the nuns' hardships. Turns out, most of them came from Ireland." Sweating like a Sumo wrestler, my mouth felt like it was full of cotton balls and my upper lip stuck to my teeth. I pretended to talk directly to Mary, who stood in the back of the room swaying like an elephant, but that made me seasick.

Why was there never a fire drill when you needed one? I watched the minute hand on the clock inch its way full circle.

"For example, the seven Sisters would make sure the patients had the very finest food and they never turned away a hungry person from the kitchen door of St. Anthony's—to the point where they had nothing left to eat, except for a watery soup made from potato skins...Can you imagine?"

After a long pause, trying to think what else to say, I fidgeted with the St. Anthony medal around my neck. I grasped it and slid it along it's fine silver chain. It began to heat up, radiating a comforting warmth. The odor of old wool and lavender whirled around me.

Sister Ignatius whispered in my ear! I felt the hotness of her breath. She had garlic for lunch: *"Tell them how St. Anthony always answered me prayers to keep the hospital open."*

My body twitched as if I'd been electrocuted. I did a double-take and turned around to see if someone stood behind me. Nope. What was happening?

I took a big swig of water. "And...and...um, you wouldn't believe how many times St. Anthony's Hospital almost closed because there was never enough money to pay the bills, until Sister Ignatius—the first administrator—prayed to St. Anthony for help and then the money always—and I mean *always*—appeared in the exact amount needed!"

Where was I going with this?

Sister Ignatius whispered again, *"Reassure them."*

I jumped and turned around again. Nobody was there.

The drumbeat of my heart played *"Wipe Out."* My hand flew to my ticker, which was beating so fast it made my jacket quiver. "And we should have complete trust," I said glancing over my shoulder, "in St. Anthony too."

My voice found volume and I became lucid. "I guess what I'm trying to say is this: St. Anthony's was founded on an *unshakable faith*. *Mercy*. And *pure intention*—that's why it's one hundred years old and will continue to be here for many years to come. In addition to its earthy staff, St. Anthony's has a heavenly CEO. That's what I've tried to convey in this painting through the nuns' countenances. I've titled it, *Remember the Mission.* Um... thank you...and , uh, peace out."

Did a dead nun just talk to me? Yeah. Pretty sure. Man, this was crazy!

The audience clapped loudly and sincerely. The hospital staff had viewed my remarks as a pep talk and it eased their worries.

Mamma clapped wildly and yelled way too loudly—like she was at the opera or something, "BRAVO...BRAVO!"

Jeesh, how embarrassing.

Whew! That was over. Rivers of sweat trickled between my breasts.

Dr. Goodman smiled at me. He unclipped his pager from his belt and read a message. Leaving abruptly, he waved to me.

I rushed over to Mary. Dripping with venom, I said, "I went to the college to see about that *job*."

"Oh, Arté, you don't have to thank me."

I squinted and clutched her collar. "Mary McKee," I said, gritting my teeth, "if you ever send me on a job to model in a college life class...for *nude drawing*...I'll rip your arm off and beat you over the head with the bloody stump."

Mary's wounded expression looked like a child whose ice cream dropped out of her cone. Her eyes widened. "*Whah?* It paid fifty dollars an hour! If ya don't wanna work odd jobs, then take the frickin' solo exhibit and make money from your art!"

I stomped over to Mamma and wheeled her to the buffet as Mary scuttled out the back door like a raccoon running from a garbage can.

Mamma Mia and I stayed to nibble on the miniature

sandwiches and cookies that were artfully arranged on the silver trays. Mamma opened her black, faux-leather purse and dumped a bunch of Italian cookies into it.

"What's the matter, getting tired of Lorna Doones?" I asked.

"It's a shame to waste good cookies," Mamma said, "and I never met a cookie I didn't like." She swiped a banana from the fruit bowl. "Have banana, will travel," she said with a giggle. "I want to go back to my room, I'm tired now. By the way, honey, you did a good job speaking. I'm proud of you. But next time, don't look over your shoulder so much." Mamma munched on a cookie. With a huge smile, she said, "And your painting!" She made her clam-hand, kissed the tips of her fingers, then opened her hand widely, and exclaimed. *"Bellissimo!* You sure captured Sister Ignatius's likeness—I still remember what she looked like."

"Thanks, Mamma. I'll be back around dinner time. We can eat together and then I want to watch the news with you."

Mamma's favorite aide, Cass, took her back to the skilled-nursing floor.

* * *

I trekked to my studio to work on my second painting of the nuns—the one for my personal collection.

After painting several hours, I returned to St. Anthony's to dine with Mamma and watch the news to find out what's going on with the hospital.

Good evening. In our lead story, Governor Scanlon O'Shea, of New York State, has ordered a commission to study the viability of New York State's hospitals. The commission, which will meet in Albany, was formed to determine which hospitals will be closed due to budget cuts. Many skilled-nursing floors, which are home to thousands of American senior citizens, are losing money for the hospitals, of which they are part. The ever-increasing annual financial losses are magnified by recent reductions in New York State Medicaid reimbursement rates. The Medicaid funding has been cut to such a degree that certain hospitals, which already carry enormous debt, may find it impossible to survive. St. Anthony's Hospital in Verdant Valley, New York offers dual services that the competing hospital, The Valley Hospital, also provides. Governor O'Shea says that is redundant and expensive. St. Anthony's Hospital carries massive debt and is the first slated to be closed."

Mamma threw her pillow at the TV. We clutched each other for support.

"It'll be okay, Mamma Mia. Please don't cry."

"But what are we going to do? You know the Governor can do whatever he wants." She blew her nose. "Oh, *Dio!* "

In a state of panic, I tried to think of something. John Lennon's anthem popped into my head. "No! The *people* have the power. For starters, we're going to collect signatures on a petition. This is an election year—actually, it's weeks away—we'll send the governor a strong message."

Mamma reached for her asthma inhaler and took a few hits.

"Breathe easy, Mamma. Calm down. You collect here at St. Anthony's—be sure to ask every employee, visitor, and resident on the skilled-nursing floor. And I'll collect all over town—Mary'll help, she knows *everybody!* Where's that legal tablet I gave you?"

"Right there in my bureau. Bottom drawer, under my brassieres, next to the Lorna Doones."

I located the tablet, drafted a few scathing paragraphs, and handed it back to Mamma. "Okay, time to get your Italian *up!*"

Mamma flattened her hand, bit the edge of it, and waved it. "*Va bene!* I'll give that governor *the-what-for.* "

"I'm going back to my studio to work on a massive email campaign, which will be quite effective—remember, signatures will carry the most weight. I'll include the governor's phone number and email address so he'll be inundated with angry messages."

EIGHTEEN

On Sunday morning I received a phone call from Sister Xavier, whom I'd avoided like a swarm of hornets. "Artemisia. Your mother has gone A.W.O.L.! We can't find her anywhere. We've never lost a resident before!"

* * *

I rushed over and passed St. Joseph's Catholic Church on the corner across from St. Anthony's Hospital. I spied my little Italian mamma sitting in her wheelchair, holding a sign, which read: HELP ME! GOVERNOR O'SHEA IS GOING TO MAKE ME HOMELESS. Her eyes rolled heavenward like in Mantegna's painting of martyred St. Sebastian tied to a tree— the only things missing were the arrows piercing her body.

A huge crowd spilled out from the church and Mamma solicited for their signatures on our petition. She must have wheeled herself across the street. Talk about laying it on thick! She fleeced the crowd for sympathy as she puffed on her empty asthma inhaler. Everyone signed her petition, except for one man, on whose shoes she spat!

I parked my car and strode over to her.

"I was worried sick about you," I said, with my hands on my hips like a superhero. Wagging my finger at her, I said, "You're grounded!"

"What? You said to collect as many signatures as I could. Well, I didn't let the grass grow under my feet—I went all over Hell's half acre to get my signatures."

"Yeah, but I didn't say to give me a heart attack while doing so."

"So far, I've collected 2,000 signatures! That *panty-waist politician* is *not* throwing me out of my home!"

"That's fantastic news! Wow, together we have about 3,000 signatures and I'm sure Mary has a bunch too. Everyone in V.V. is outraged at the proposal of closing St. Anthony's. And the governor is moving so fast. He's over confident too—he's in for a huge surprise on election day. Man, never underestimate the power of the people."

"Arté," Mamma said, "I didn't eat yet and my blood sugar is getting low."

"C'mon, let's grab some breakfast."

I spotted Sister X in the cafeteria and before I could hide, she stopped me.

"You found your mother!" she cried, her hand over her heart. "Thank God. I was about to fill out an accident report."

"Good morning, Sister," I said, fixing my glance above her waist. "She's fine. Found her outside St. Joseph's collecting signatures after Mass. We've collected over 3,000 signatures in favor of St. Anthony's. That'll get the governor's attention!"

"It certainly will. Good work, ladies."

Sighing deeply, I said, "I wish I could do more." I shook my head.

"Do you mean that?" Sister X asked.

"Excuse me?"

"Artemisia, if you testified before the committee as a concerned daughter of a long-time resident of St. Anthony's skilled-nursing floor, I believe that would have a huge impact on the hearings. You'd assign a name and face to the problem of dislodging the residents. Perhaps you'd play to their sympathies."

"Oh, I, uh, I don't think...um, I have a lot of work. I'm behind on my projects...and there are deadlines."

Mamma wheezed and puffed on her asthma inhaler. She unfolded her hankie and honked her nose like a trumpet.

I shrugged. "If you think that would help...I guess I could try."

"Excellent! The meetings have been behind closed doors, but the next one is open to the public. I'll arrange to add you to the schedule to speak. You can ride along with me."

"Thank you, Sister, I appreciate that." *Great!* Just what I needed. More public speaking and a road trip with a transgendered nun! The Universe must think that was funny.

My stomach churned as I sniffed the smoky, porcine aroma of bacon, sizzling and crisping in the pan. I inhaled deeply. "Ahh, bacon!" I murmured.

"If you dab bacon grease behind your ears, I guarantee you'll nab a man!" Mamma said. She rolled her chair towards the doughnuts and we enjoyed a fine feast.

Afterward, Mamma was exhausted. We returned to her room. Settling her into bed, she opened the covers and beckoned to me. "Arté, you do so much for me and never take time for yourself. Here, honey, climb into bed with me and take a little nap."

"I'd like nothing better, but I have a lot of work to do at my studio."

"It's just as well," Mamma said, trolling for a laugh, "I'm due for my enema and the nurse might get the wrong *coolie.*"

* * *

Sister Xavier rolled up in front of my studio in her tan Dodge Dart and gave three staccato horn toots.

I tossed back two Advil tablets, grabbed my personal canvas of the seven dead nuns, and sprinted to her car. I opened the back door and stowed my painting. As I slid into the passenger seat, I was assaulted by an odd odor of a ghostly fish fry, pine air freshener and stale cigarette smoke. Was Sister X a secret smoker? Just add that to her list of surprises. I'd googled the distance to Albany and was in for an eight-hour, round-trip with Sister X-rated.

We rode in a painful silence for thirty minutes. I gave her a sideways glance, inspected her face, and found no trace of a beard—probably had electrolysis. Focusing on her Adam's apple, I suspected she had surgery to shave the prominent bony cartilage because it looked feminine. When we hit the thruway, I said, "Sister, you might want to slow down a bit—you're over the limit at eighty." Man, this nun had a heavy foot!

"It's fine. We're making good time."

I shrugged as I double-checked my seat belt.

A whiney police siren punctuated our quietude. Sister muttered, *"Damn!"* as she pulled over. She adjusted her mini-veil headpiece and reached for her nun-purse.

"Mornin' Sister," the state trooper said with a dimpled smile as he nodded and touched the wide brim of his hat. "Where're you off to in such a blazin' hurry?"

"Good morning, officer," she chirped. "We're going to Albany for a meeting with *Governor O'Shea.* What seems to be the problem?"

Did she just name-drop?

"Do you know how fast you were driving?"

"No, sir. I believe I was within the speed limit."

What the crap! She was a cigarette-smoking, lipstick-wearing, lying, trans-woman nun. She probably had a tattoo and a nipple piercing too. I got your number, *Twisted Sister.* I eyed her suspiciously. Maybe…she's not a real nun…I shook my head. Nah, who'd want to be a nun imposter? Maybe she felt safe living as a nun…or figured she could do more good if people didn't know her secret. Who am I to judge?

"I'll let you off this time, but slow it down."

"God bless you, sir," she said.

He tipped his felt-brimmed hat and swaggered back to his cruiser like John Wayne.

"Hee...hee...hee. Works every time," she said and merged into traffic.

NINETEEN

I didn't know TV cameras would be present at the Albany meeting. Wasn't it bad enough to give a speech in front of a bunch of professionals? Jeez, it was *Recitation Time* all over again in Sister Attila the Nun's classroom where her prime entertainment was to make me stand—emotionally naked—in front of the class and humiliate me to the point of tears. What the hell did I get myself into?

Sister Xavier and I waited in a huge conference room of the hotel where the public hearings were about to begin.

"There's Governor O'Shea!" she said. She squinted and hitched one side of her upper lip. "He thinks he's so powerful."

What the—didn't know he'd be at the meeting. Wait! Maybe that was a good thing. I'd direct my pointed questions to him. And if he responded with his political-speak non-answers, as he always did, I'd call him out… in front of everybody. Go ahead, Gov, make my day!

I placed my large painting of the seven founding nuns of St. Anthony's on the easel. This rectangular canvas was my favorite. I'd rendered close-up views of each nun's face, right on the picture plane—they looked as if they would burst through the painting. Their expressions arrested the viewer and the graphic black and white patterns were dramatic. I studied my notes and prayed for calmness, which eluded me so I asked St. Anthony to help me find it.

I was first on the schedule to speak. Sister Xavier introduced me to the audience, which was standing-room-only.

I inhaled a deep cleansing breath.

Slowly exhaling, I reached for my St. Anthony medal around my neck, grasped it tightly, and hiked it back and forth along the chain. It grew hot and an enormous dose of confidence infused my body.

"Thank you for the opportunity to speak. My eighty-nine-year-old mother, Loretta Credo, is a long-time resident on the fifth-floor skilled-nursing unit of St. Anthony's Hospital in Verdant Valley, New York." I halted and swept the audience with my gaze. "It is her *home.*" I took a sip of water, pausing intentionally to let that remark stand alone. "My mother considers the other residents and the nursing staff to be her extended family. I am her only relative. This question is to you, Governor O'Shea." I looked squarely at him, holding him prisoner with my gaze. He sat there in his handmade-Italian suit and red silk tie, looking like an ad for *GQ.* I wanted to become Samantha from *Bewitched,* twitch my nose, and turn him into a braying jackass. "What will happen to the residents who *live* on the skilled-nursing unit if *you* close down St. Anthony's Hospital?" I took a small step back from the microphone, folded my arms, and waited.

The governor scowled. His mouth looked like an upside down letter *U* and his face reddened as he whispered something to his assistant—probably asked *Who let her speak?* Sneering, he said, "We haven't discussed that yet. I suppose they'd be placed at various openings throughout the state," he said, as he ran his fingers through his five-hundred dollar haircut.

I stepped up to the microphone. *"Placed? Things* are placed. We are discussing people. *Beloved family members.* Governor O'Shea, you are suggesting shattering families, separating loved ones—who are at the end-stage of their lives—and creating hardships in terms of being close enough to visit elderly family members. I visit my mother every day."

I pierced the piffling politician with a look that transfixed him, like a butterfly pinned to a corkboard. "That, Governor O'Shea, is *not* okay with me."

I approached my painting and picked up the pointer stick. "I'm a professional artist and was commissioned to paint the portraits of the seven founding nuns of St. Anthony's, which hangs in the hospital. Before executing that painting, I did extensive research on the nuns and the origins of St. Anthony's. This painting I created for my *edification*...and *yours.*" I scanned the audience and noticed a few bored expressions. Some people checked their watches. "I promise I won't go over my allotted eighteen minutes, but I warn the sleepyheads, I have a squirt gun and I know how to use it." That comment was greeted with a small ripple of chuckles.

Tapping each nun's portrait with the pointer stick, I introduced them. "Sister Ignatius, the first administrator of St. Anthony's. Sister Augustine. Sister Tomasina. Sister Eucharia. Sister Bridget. Sister Raphael. Sister Gertrude.

"These are the names and faces of the nuns who cared for the poor; the names and faces of the nuns who gave their blankets to the patients while they slept in their winter coats in a house without a furnace; the names and faces of the nuns who gave all of their food to the poor—who lined up daily at the backdoor of St. Anthony's because it was common knowledge that Sister Ignatius never turned away a hungry person; the names and faces of the nuns who often dined on a watery soup made from potato skins because that's all there was left for them."

Now I had everyone's attention.

"These magnanimous women had entered a teaching order, but God had other plans for them. Doctor Eamon Rooney, the co-founder of St. Anthony's, had made a passionate plea to the bishop to enlist the help of these Sisters to initiate a hospital to care for the poor and disadvantaged.

"Even though there was another hospital in Verdant Valley, there was a great need for St. Anthony's because the other hospital was exclusive. That is to say, the other hospital turned away patients if they could not pay. In addition to turning away charity cases, the other hospital discriminated against people of the Jewish and Catholic faiths—remember that was one hundred years ago.

"Doctor Rooney also founded the school of nursing with the help of the seven nuns. He personally trained and taught the nursing students after working full days in surgery."

I pointed to the first administrator's portrait. "I ask you to study the face of Sister Ignatius, who was a brilliant language and mathematic teacher. At the age of thirty-two, she operated St. Anthony's Hospital." I lightly touched the image. "This sainted woman fought countless battles with the welfare commissioner to protect the basic human rights of the poverty-stricken of Verdant Valley. When the welfare commissioner denied a patient's case, she forgave the patient's debt. Sister Ignatius was a relentless champion of the poor.

"An example, which is one of hundreds from Sister Gertrude's diary, is about an extremely ill man who wandered into St. Anthony's and rested in the lobby. He told Sister Ignatius he was in great pain with end-stage rectal cancer. She was very kind to him and excused herself to call the welfare commissioner, who'd denied the case. Sister Ignatius admitted the poor man to St. Anthony's and according to Sister Gertrude, 'he was treated like Rockefeller himself!'

"Sister Ignatius was known for her charity and compassion. During the Depression, Sister Ignatius was a legend and she grew St. Anthony's with grace and grit."

As my eyes became misty, the TV camera panned in for a close-up. "When Sister Ignatius died in 1939, she was known to the citizens of Verdant Valley as *An Angel of Mercy.* When Doctor Eamon Rooney died in 1920, the banner headline in *The*

Valley Chronicle called him *The Doctor of the Poor.* What glorious epitaphs!"

The room grew silent. As Mamma was fond of saying, "It was so quiet, you could hear a flea fart."

I took a sip of water. "My research included extensive genealogy searches and I discovered information for you, Governor O'Shea." I held my gaze steady on him. "You are a direct descendant of Sister Ignatius—the former Molly O'Shea. Her father's brother was your great-grandfather. Your great aunt Molly dedicated her life to St. Anthony's. Your great aunt Molly performed countless works of mercy at the hospital *you* are about to close down."

An audible gasp arose.

Governor O'Shea's face deepened to puce. He looked like a heart attack waiting to happen as he extracted his handkerchief from his breast pocket and mopped his sweaty brow. His mouth turned down as he shot a murderous glance at me.

He irritated me like a seed trapped between my teeth. "I also have a brief message for you, Governor, from my mother, Loretta Credo." I reached into my pocket for a slip of paper and read: "Governor O'Shea, your decision to close St. Anthony's Hospital—my *home*—would separate me from my daughter and make me homeless. I have a news flash for you: I don't get mad; I get even. I've collected 3,000 signatures in favor of keeping St. Anthony's open. With your election a few weeks away—make no mistake—we, the people who signed the petition, will use the full measure of our voting power to vote your sorry — " I stopped abruptly. "*Self* out of office. But, hey, no pressure. Signed, Loretta Credo."

A few muffled laughs.

"So here's my point: St. Anthony's is one hundred years old and has survived World War I, the 1918 influenza pandemic, two major floods, which greatly damaged the hospital, World War II, the 1950's polio epidemic, countless financial crises, and political warfare. And now, Governor O'Shea, *you*, the great-grand nephew of Sister Ignatius—the co-founder and first administrator— want to close down St. Anthony's! That's wrong on so many levels. I mean, you don't need special brain cells to figure that out."

The audience was agitated. Loud whispers arose. Taking advantage of the momentum, I again addressed the governor personally, which infuriated him.

"If, after learning you are directly related to Sister Ignatius, who worked tirelessly to keep St. Anthony's running, and you still continue to *push so hard* to close it down, then shame. On. You."

There was a low murmur in the audience and several people nodded.

"In closing, I need to improve the knowledge of Governor O'Shea and this commission by informing them that St. Anthony's Hospital is much more than bricks and mortar. St. Anthony's Hospital is greater than Doctor Eamon Rooney and the seven noble nuns who had initiated this charity institution. It is greater than the 1,000 employees who stand to lose their jobs, thereby devastating the economy of Verdant Valley. It is greater than this commission and, most certainly, St. Anthony's Hospital is greater than *Governor O'Shea!*

"St. Anthony's Hospital is not an ordinary hospital…it is *extraordinary.* St. Anthony's Hospital, which is cloaked in a Higher Power, was conceived with *pure intention* in a spirit of *mercy* and *charity.*"

The TV cameraman was in my face. I stared at Governor O'Shea unblinkingly. "My final remark is to you, Governor. Having been made aware of St. Anthony's Hospital history and your relationship to Sister Ignatius, I say to you, Governor O'Shea now you *know* better and you can *do* better."

The camera quickly panned to a close-up of Governor O'Shea. He pulled his eyebrows together, creating an *eleven* sign above the bridge of his nose. His wide-opened eyes glared at me and his lips formed a straight line. Bet his blood pressure spiked fifty points.

The commissioner said, "Thank you, Miss Credo. That certainly was informative. Sister Xavier, do you have anything to add?"

Sister hitched her chin toward me. "Ditto what she said." The audience applauded. I quietly picked up my painting and exiting saw seven hooded figures in the back who looked like the dead nuns of St. Anthony's. But, of course, that was not possible.

Sister Xavier joined me in the hallway. "Artemisia, that was powerful!" She gave me a high-five.

"Jeez, Sister...I think I channeled Sister Ignatius!"

A group of reporters huddled around Governor O'Shea. I actually heard him say in a condescending tone, "You can't believe the drivel of a *spinster!* She's obviously co-dependent on her mother. She's probably one of those older women who lives alone with twenty cats. Actually, I've heard she has a drinking problem."

Spinster! Drinking problem! That cretin served me a fresh shit sandwich and I was supposed to eat it and say thank you? Okay, Gov, that's how you wanna play? *Gloves. Off!*

I marched up to him. "You *gormless, feckless politician,* you couldn't govern your way out of a paper bag, *you bloated bureaucrat!* By the way, you should see the *interesting* footage from the security camera in the archive room at St. Anthony's. It's *X-rated,* if you get my drift! I'm sure I could convince Sister Xavier to share the information with the press before your election. Talk about a *sizzling visual!*"

His jaw slacked open as the reporters swam around him like sharks during a feeding frenzy.

* * *

I stewed over my run-in with O'Shea on the ride home, but at least the dreaded public speaking was over.

"Artemisia, thank you for testifying. It's been rough on me fighting this battle alone. I appreciate your help." Sister X gave me a playful punch to my shoulder. "You're alright, *kid*. I'm treating you to dinner."

"First of all, thanks for calling me kid—you're not so bad yourself! And second, I'm glad I could do *something*. I will not let O'Shea kick my mother out of her home!"

"Governor O'Shea is not to be trusted," she said scowling, "he's a wolf in sheep's clothing."

"Oh," I nodded, "I've got his number.

TWENTY

I returned home from the Albany meeting beyond exhausted—more tired than an aged ballerina. It had been a long day of public speaking, sparring with a slime-ball governor, and palling around with a trans-nun. And my bra was killing me. Couldn't wait to de-bra. I unsnapped my instrument of torture and it sailed across the room. Merlin took cover under my bed. No wonder it'd felt like a boa constrictor around my ribcage. Sure, the *girls* were up where they once had been, but at what price? I'd been on a mission for years to find the perfect support bra—like the search for the Holy Grail. Finally, I'd gone to an expert. The preppy, smart-ass bra-fitter had trilled, "How old is this *thing*? Bras are not immortal! Eighty percent of women wear the wrong bra size. Your cup size was too small and band size too large." What the hell did she know about sixty-year-old *manuccis*? I rubbed the deep grooves etched into my shoulder blades as I heated my buckwheat neck pillow in the microwave. Retrieving the toasty U-shaped pillow, I slung it around my neck, feeling the warmth erase the muscle aches.

I switched on CNN. There was a close-up of me with my right eyebrow highly arched, spouting off at O'Shea. Anderson Cooper said, "There you have it folks, Governor O'Shea and his formidable opponent Artemisia Credo, facing off at the Albany meeting." He chuckled, "*Gormless, feckless politician*—my new, favorite saying!"

"*Basta!*" I shouted at the TV as I clicked the remote and threw it across the room. "How much crap can I handle in one day?"

I rushed through my bedtime routine and stumbled into bed. A powerful thirst awoke me around three AM. I padded to the kitchen where Merlin greeted me. He begged for a treat as he snaked between my feet, tickling my legs with his fuzzy overcoat.

I opened the refrigerator, reached in for the orange juice, and took a huge swig right out of the carton—a fringe benefit of living alone. I swished the tart liquid around in my mouth as I kicked the fridge door closed with my foot.

And there stood Sister Ignatius!

Spraying orange juice all over her—like a spit-take in a movie—I convulsed, coughing and sputtering. A squeeze of bile jetted into my system and my body vibrated as if I'd stuck my finger in a light socket. My blood felt like molten lava. Thought I was having a coronary. She scared the Holy Hell out of me.

Merlin's feet were a blur of motion, skidding on the linoleum. He sprinted out of the kitchen, knocking over his food dish as the dry kibbles bounced around the floor.

The logical side of my brain told me it wasn't possible for Sister Ignatius—dead since 1939—to be in my apartment. Yet, her fine Irish face with its alabaster skin, blue denim eyes, and overgrown eyebrows stared into my face. I wanted to reach out and touch her, but feared she'd slap my hand. I pinched the skin on my forearm tightly and twisted it to see if I'd wake up. Nope. Not dreaming.

She smelled of lavender and old wool. And when she moved, her long habit swished and her black rosary beads, which hung from her waistband, clicked.

Definitely not an apparition!

Merlin hissed and jumped into the wastebasket.

The orange juice dripped down her long garment.

"S...S...*Sister Ignatius?* H...how is this possible?"

She spoke in an Irish brogue as she extracted her linen handkerchief from her deep pocket and dabbed at the juice on her habit. "Och, Mother Machree! T'was that really necessary?"

"I don't understand."

"It's called sarcasm. I am not pleased that you sprayed orange juice all over me."

"No...I mean you're, um, like...*dead.*"

" Oh, *that.* Well, you summoned me to help you and St. Anthony's Hospital. All the hours of your research, your painting process, and the strong desire to help your mother made it possible...and, of course, me St. Anthony medal you are wearing." She continued cleaning off her wool serge garb. "Thoughts are pure energy. They have enormous power, don't you know."

Sister Ignatius sighed deeply, which made the hefty crucifix on her chest move up and down. "Alas! I fear St. Anthony's is still in grave danger of closing and you are not doing enough to save me hospital."

"*Me?*...Not doing *enough* to save St. Anthony's?" I thumped my chest. "I am *waaa-ay* out of my comfort zone here, *Sister!* I've collected signatures on a petition *and* publicly told off the governor *and* informed him that he's your great grandnephew—that should count for *something.*"

"Oh, that *ninny!* He has had everything served to him on a silver platter. And closing St. Anthony's Hospital has nothing to do with politics. He has a personal reason."

"But...but, Sister Ignatius, I tried. I'm so sorry the governor might close St. Anthony's. I just testified at the hearings in Albany...you know, I'm terrified of public speaking, yet, I really *tried.* And that petulant politician bad-mouthed me to the press! He tried to ruin my reputation. I don't want to do any of this—it's too much!"

The dead nun stood with arms akimbo and stabbed me with one of those classic no-nonsense, nun expressions. "Well, people in hell want ice water, but they don't get it. Wipe that helping-Jayus look off your face and try again."

"*Huh?*"

"When I had insurmountable problems, I placed my *complete* trust in God and St. Anthony. After that, I got my Irish up! I rolled up my sleeves and fought like a junk-yard dog with my teeth in my opponent's ankle—I never let up." She slapped her fist in the palm of her hand. "Artemisia *Credo*. Your name, Credo, is Latin for *I Believe*. God will give you as much as you trust and believe in Him, if you believe little, you will receive little."

"Are you telling me I don't believe enough? I feel like I'm doing my very best," I said, running my hands through my long hair. My frustration meter zoomed off the charts.

"You must save St. Anthony's. *Posthaste!* Artemisia, 'tis up to you now. This is your mission. Do more research on the governor. He always was full of gas...and remember the '60s."

The dead nun's voice echoed and became faint as she...as she, uh...transubstantiated into a smoke ring of aromatic incense and disappeared.

TWENTY-ONE

It was a crisp fall day, which put me in mind of back-to-school shopping and football games. I walked along my neighborhood, smiling as the dried, curled leaves crunched and crumbled under my feet. I loved that sound! I'd visited Mamma, and then —to top it off—Joe Goodman had called and asked if I wanted to go for ice cream.

Ice cream? Was that a rhetorical question?

* * *

Joe and I sat in the shaded park on a scrolled-arm bench under the gingko tree, watching small whirlwinds of colorful leaves dance around our feet. Two nervous squirrels spiraled down the thick trunk of a massive pine tree playing tag as a blue jay squabbled territorially and a train whistle blew softly off in the distance. I deeply inhaled the clean pine scent mixed with the loamy aroma of dried leaves, like dehydrated basil and oregano. The sun filtered through the thinning canopy, warming me as if I were wrapped in a cashmere shawl. The riot of color reminded me of a rich tapestry as I released a sigh of contentment.

We thoroughly enjoyed our peach ice-cream cones as a city bus rumbled to a stop in front of us, belching a charcoal puff of diesel smoke.

I could *not* believe my eyes. There—in full color on the side of the bus—was a life-sized photograph of *me* wearing Depend adult *diapers!*

Me. In. My. Bra. And. Diapers.

I was going to kill Mary McKee and no jury would convict me.

I prayed for a giant sinkhole to open up and swallow me. I just wanted to disappear into the maw of the earth. Maybe Joe wouldn't notice. Please, God, don't let Joe see me in the Depend diapers. I promise I'll tame my big, fat, Italian temper and I'll never budge in line at the grocery store again and—

Joe doubled over with a conniption of laughter.

He looked at me.

He glanced at the bus.

He pointed at the bus, but couldn't speak. Then he made wheezing noises. Was he choking on his ice-cream cone? Should I perform the Heimlich Maneuver?

Horrified, I watched as Joe slapped his knee over and over, as if that would help him breathe.

Mercifully, the traffic light morphed to green and the bus slowly chugged away, as my dignity flew out of my body and landed curbside like an old eviscerated plaid sofa on the side of the road waiting to be rescued.

I asked curtly, "Are you going to sit there and make fun at my expense?"

Joe stopped howling and said between gasps for oxygen, "It *depends.*"

* * *

Mortified, I retreated to my studio to hide out from Joe Goodman and the entire town of Verdant Valley, as I entertained the thought of spray-painting graffiti on the city bus. With my luck, I'd probably get caught in the act and end up with my picture and a banner headline in *The Valley Chronicle*: Diaper Lady Arrested For Vandalism.

My only option was to join the Witness Protection Program and start my life over.

My life had taken on the aura of an absurd reality show: *The Artist, Her Zany Jobs, and the Zombie Nuns*—except there were no TV cameras, only wacko jobs and dead nuns scaring the snot out of me.

I fell asleep on the cot in my studio and had another dream in which all of the St. Anthony nuns talked to me. When I woke up…I wasn't so sure it was a dream. It seemed like the dead nuns were in my studio. Crazy, right?

It was time for my hair appointment and I was in dire need of color and a trim. I enjoyed my hairdresser because she wasn't into gossiping, which I detested. We had interesting conversations about books, organic food, and history. We were history buffs, so I knew she'd be interested in my research of St. Anthony's Hospital.

"How's your commission and research going?" Janet asked as she ran a comb through my wet locks.

"It's fascinating to me. I have so much respect for the seven founding nuns of St. Anthony's. They sacrificed daily for the poor of V.V. Sister Ignatius, the first administrator, always forgave the patient's debt when they couldn't pay."

"Arté, as you know, I live right on the river. What's interesting about that is, years ago, my house was given to the same nuns you're talking about. I researched the deed and discovered that the cottage had been gifted to the convent in lieu of payment for a hospital bill."

"That's amazing," I said. And I wasn't so sure it was a coincidence.

"Also, I found a few black and white photographs of the nuns sitting at the water's edge reading the newspaper."

"How cool! Can I see the photos?"

"Sure. And the other day I was cleaning out the attic and found a family bible that had belonged to one of the nuns."

"*What!* I'd love to see that."

"Actually, I'll donate them to the hospital. It seems like that's where they belong."

"Thanks, Janet. We'll include it in the centennial celebration. I'll stop by your house tonight to pick them up."

* * *

Lily tapped on my studio window and breezed in. "Hiya, Angel Lady!"

"Hey, Lilypad, just in time to work on this new shipment of clay." I demonstrated some clay techniques for her.

Lily sat on the bay window seat, propped up with lots of pillows, and happily pushed and pulled a lump of clay. "Maybe I can make a Christmas present for my dad." Beams of sunlight dappled on her corkscrew curls. She had no idea how stunning she was with her red/mahogany hair, aqua eyes, and pale skin.

I reached for my sketchpad and rendered a few gesture drawings, when an idea came to me. "Say, Lily, how're your computer skills?"

"Pretty good. Why?"

"Because mine stink! I'd like to hire you as my studio assistant. The pay is not great, but I have a little money from my big commission and I could really use the help. You could blug and chirp for me."

Lily grinned. "Um, that's *blog* and *tweet.*"

"You see? When it comes to computers, I'm a mechanical moron. I don't know a computer chip from a potato chip or a mega byte from a mosquito bite. I'll write out the *blog* and you can operate and maintain it. Same for Facebook. And anything else out there in Internet Land." I began talking faster. "I want to open an online art gallery too. Need help with my mailing list for Open Studio and you can ring out customers when I have to run errands and visit my mother."

Lily's thumbs performed gymnastics on my phone pad. After a frenzy of clicks, she said, "Look. I've set up your Twitter account already!"

Frowning, she asked, "Who's this O'Shea dude?

"Governor of New York State. Why?"

"He better shut his *piehole!* He's bad-mouthing you on Twitter."

I snatched the phone from her hands. My mouth fell open as I read his rant. *'Don't believe a wanna-be artist who's co-dependent on her mommy. Has anyone ever heard of Artemisia Credo? Who names a kid Artemisia?'*

I stomped my foot. "What the—*co-dependent?* He'd be co-dependent on *oxygen* if Mamma Mia found out!"

Lily was indignant as she wrinkled her nose. "He can't talk about *my Artè* that way!" She squinted. "You want me to call him an idiot?"

"No, that would insult idiots. Tweet: '*You Witless Wonder, if only you had another neuron, you might have a synapse. Sorry your prefrontal lobotomy failed.*"

Lily laughed as she gave me a bear hug. Then she squealed like a piglet. "Oh, Artè, I have real job! It's going to be fun working for you. My dad has been on my case about finding work. *Now* he'll be proud of me. Gotta go tell him." She ran out the door and down the street.

TWENTY-TWO

I visited Mamma to tell her about the Albany meeting. As far as talking to a dead nun, I wasn't telling *anyone* about that.

Mamma was still in bed and hadn't bothered to get dressed, which was highly unusual. Her eyes and mouth looked droopy.

"Mamma Mia, don't you feel well? Why aren't you dressed? It's 11:30, almost time for your lunch tray."

"I'm not hungry. Too worried about St. Anthony's closing," she said bleakly. She held her handkerchief balled up in her fist, which trembled. "I heard some nurses talking outside my door while they waited for the elevator. They're looking for jobs already! Did you give the governor my message?"

"Oh, yeah," I said, sitting on the foot of her bed. "I presented it to him wrapped up with a big red bow!"

"Did you tell him the part about voting his sorry ass out of office?"

"About that *sorry ass* comment. Couldn't cuss in public."

"I should have said *sorry coolie*," Mamma said.

"Don't worry, Mamma, I got your message across. It got quite a response from the audience. They *loved* it!"

I poured a glass of ice-water and she drank most of it.

"I gave a brief history of St. Anthony's Hospital—you know, recounted how hard the nuns and Dr. Rooney had worked. I personified the hospital to convey that St. Anthony's is extraordinary and represents one hundred years of charity work in our community. Took my second painting of the nuns and used it in the presentation because I wanted the committee to *see* the nuns, make them real…and dramatic."

"*Bene*," Mamma said, "that's the ticket!"

"And then, *The Big Reveal!* I informed Governor O'Shea that Sister Ignatius—the former Molly O'Shea—was his great aunt. Man, that got everyone's attention. Wish you could've seen his face."

"*Ha!* That'll show him. What a dumb-bunny."

"Then—you'll love this part—I said that my mother, Loretta Credo, has been a long-time resident on St. Anthony's skilled-nursing unit, which is her *home*, and she had a message for the governor. When I told him about the 3,000 signatures and that we'd vote him out of office, he almost fell out of his chair. His face froze as if he'd overdosed on Botox."

Mamma Mia squealed with delight. "Hot-diggity-dog! Now we're cooking with *gas!* The poor fool, doesn't he know he should not mess with the Credo dames? He'll rue the day he heard of us."

"Have to go now. I'm meeting Mary for lunch in the cafeteria."

"Okay, honey. Don't forget my pocketbook with your Lorna Doones. *Ciao Bella.*"

We traded *baci.*

* * *

Mary and I sat in a booth in the cafeteria eating hot turkey sandwiches with gravy and fluffy mashed potatoes when Lily called. "That *scum-magnet, sleaze-bucket, douche-bag* O'Shea dude tweeted more rotten stuff about you! *He stinks on ice!*"

"What'd he say *this time?*"

"Sure you wanna hear it?"

"Give it to me straight."

"Quote: '*Artemisia Credo is a starving artist because her paintings suck. Nobody buys her garbage art. She's a loser with a drinking problem.*'"

Lily hyperventilated.

"Calm down, Lily. Tweet: '*Only an insecure, foolish, flaccid little man would tweet such lies. To view my artwork, visit www.artemisiacredo.com.*' There are two c's in flaccid."

"Aye, aye, Captain. Over and out."

Mary asked, "What was that about?"

"O'Shea is ranting about me on Twitter again."

Mary checked her phone. "Wow! He's unbelievable. Want me to go Boston on him? Maybe fit him with some cement shoes?" Then she laughed as she perused her phone. "Lily's tweet from your account just went viral. Let me see how many hits your website got. One hundred people just checked out your art on your site. And you got 200 *likes* on Facebook. Ha! Joke's on him! If he keeps it up, you'll be famous."

Three O.R. nurses dressed in sky-blue scrubs sat in front of us. They traded Dr. Joe Goodman stories and laughed hysterically. I sat up and took notice.

The nurse with the heavy eye makeup said, "Dr. Goodman's practical jokes crack me up! I request scrubbing with him just for entertainment. Today he operated on his good friend, who was morbidly obese —he removed his gall bladder. After he'd put in the last staple, he put out his hand and said, 'Sharpie.'" She laughed so hard she couldn't talk for a second. "I handed him the Sharpie and next to the Penrose drain he wrote: *Pull To Deflate.*" They giggled like schoolgirls. "I had to work in I.C.U. and Dr. Goodman called the desk, so I answered, 'I.C.U.' He said, 'That's funny, I can't see you.'"

The whippet-waist nurse said, "That reminds me of the time Dr. Goodman did a hemorrhoidectomy on his good buddy, who was a Navy fan. Of course, *everybody* knows Dr. Goodman is a staunch fan of Notre Dame—his alma mater. So, again, he requested the Sharpie. On his friend's butt cheeks he wrote: *Go Irish!*" They howled. "Then," she said, "his patient was constipated so he ordered '*M.O.M. in the A.M. for a B.M. in the P.M.*'"

Mary and I tried not to laugh. Then she let out a mega-burp, which sounded like a monster roaring, and said, "Excuse my *gas,*" as she thumped her diaphragm with her fist. She had a way of igniting laughing fits in me and I couldn't stop.

Now the nurses were trying to outdo each other. "Remember the time Dr. Goodman operated on Father Paul," the short nurse said, "and he wrote *Pray For Me* on Father's feet, which he didn't notice until he was in the shower?" She laughed so hard, she actually snorted. "Father Paul told the parishioners all about it in his Sunday sermon."

I whispered to Mary, "No wonder he enjoyed tricking Mamma Mia about her acute appendix. I hadn't realized he was a prankster."

We had to hurry with our lunches because Mary had to get back to work in the business office. As I walked her to the elevator, Mary said, "Hey, I have another job for you...um, hope you're still not mad at me...you know, on account of the adult diaper thingy."

"A *job!* Oh, let me guess. A stand-in for a firing squad...a print ad for denture cream...removing deer carcasses from the highway...a volunteer for bikini waxing...a vomit collector at the theme park...a TV commercial for relieving that embarrassing vaginal itch—*Try new and improved Crotch Crème.*"

"I get it! I get it, *already.* Not for nothin', I'm just trying to save you from starving."

* * *

I motored back to my studio to work for awhile and returned to St. Anthony's in the evening to have dinner with Mamma and watch the news with her. I treated her with a hamburger and fries from McDonald's. We finished just in time to watch the news.

"Mamma, now you can see a bit of the Albany meeting." I was surprised when they showed so much of it on the national news. Had I known it was to be televised, I'd have dressed up. My frayed bell-bottom jeans didn't look too bad. Mostly, I was shot from the waist up with a lot of close-ups. My turquoise earrings looked good with my pale skin tone. My hair could have looked better, but at least I sounded strong and confident. When I informed the governor of his relationship to Sister Ignatius, he showed no reaction—as if his face were carved in stone…like he was part of Mount Rushmore.

When I said, "You know better and you can do better," Governor O'Shea looked as if I'd thrown a pie in his face—oval mouth and wide eyes. When I informed him about the 3,000 signatures and voting him out of office, he was speechless.

I was surprised Mamma hadn't commented. I expected a zinger from her, but she didn't seem interested.

Mamma took the remote and watched the animal channel. She talked to the giraffe and lion. "They were in my room this morning and I fed them Lorna Doones."

I furrowed my brows. "The animals are on TV. They aren't real. Mamma, are you okay?" The usual spark in her eyes was missing and her visage was mask-like.

"I'm confused, but the odd thing is I *know* I'm confused." Then she sipped her water and her hand had a distinct tremor.

I called Doctor Higgins and he said my mother exhibited signs of Parkinson's disease and she's receiving treatment for that along with narcotics for pain management.

TWENTY-THREE

I headed out to Lucky Plucky Chicken to work one of Mary's *wonderful* jobs. Just shoot me now. Have you noticed that Mary was missing in action?

If I were a senator, my first order of business would be to introduce a bill to make The Chicken Dance illegal on grounds of …stupidity. Everyone looked stupid doing that silly dance and don't get me started on the music! Once that music got inside your head, it looped for hours. So you can imagine how thrilled I was when the manager of Lucky Plucky Chicken informed me that I *had* to perform The Chicken Dance every time a customer requested it. And, lucky me, I got to wear a twenty-pound, bright yellow chicken costume. Oh well, at least I was incognito.

I stood outside Lucky Plucky Chicken waving at cars like a fool, flapping my wings so hard I thought I might take flight. Someone tapped me on the shoulder.

"Oh, I'd *love* to see The Chicken Dance," Joe Goodman crooned.

Seriously? God, were you trying to punish me? Maybe if I did The Chicken Dance really fast he'd just go away.

Defeated, I hung my fowl head and signaled the owner to cue The Chicken Dance music and danced like a chicken on steroids with bright yellow feathers flying around me.

Joe Goodman laughed with gusto while doing that knee-slapping thing. "Thanks, Arté," he said, "that was *priceless!*"

"Dude," I said in a deep raspy voice, "you must have me confused with another chicken."

"Your Birkenstocks gave you away." He laughed all the way into Lucky Plucky Chicken.

Already hotter than a pizza oven in that ridiculous costume, he made my temperature soar as I contemplated my laughable life. What ring of Hell did I inhabit? I flipped him a double-bird salute.

Another tap on my shoulder. Sister Ignatius said, "I would like to see The Chicken Dance." Were you *freakin'* kidding me?

* * *

The next morning I swam laps at the "*Y.*" I got my best ideas and inspirations while propelling my body through the turquoise water. I loved the way my measured breathing produced sparkling champagne bubbles dancing to the surface and the gentle rocking motion of my strokes put me in a trance-like meditation. I thought—over and over—about Sister Ignatius talking to me the other night and it scared me every time. I tried to figure out the meaning of her cryptic message. Why didn't she clearly explain what I was supposed to do? Why would a dead nun give me nonsense clues? I was stumped… Interesting –yesterday the word *gas* was repeated several times. Sister Ignatius said Governor O'Shea was *full of gas*—an odd thing for a dead nun to say…Mamma said *cooking with gas*…Mary said *excuse my gas*…wait a minute, I just read an article in *The Valley Chronicle* about *natural gas* and the fracking protesters. Could all of this be related to St. Anthony's Hospital? And Sister Ignatius instructed me to do more research on Governor O'Shea…Man, could I buy a vowel?…My next step was to research the O'Shea family history and New York State's natural gas deposits and the hydro-fracking process.

* * *

I worried about Merlin. The shade of Sister Ignatius really spooked him. My poor Fuzzy Buddy had feline neurosis. He slunk around the apartment on his tiptoes like a cartoon cat, and his long fur stood straight up in the air. The other day I found him hiding in the wastebasket, shivering with fear and hissing at his shadow. He needed to see a cat psychiatrist.

After my pool workout, I visited Mamma and she looked feeble and disoriented. I observed her walking into the bathroom and her gait was stiff and she shuffled her feet. Her condition had downgraded rapidly. She had been bright and witty—the sharpest resident on her floor—but now she was dull and unexpressive. What if she wouldn't recognize me? The thought paralyzed me. I couldn't bear it if Mamma didn't know me. It must be the opiates causing the symptoms because it all started when she was on that pain patch. I called Dr. Higgins and requested that my mother be taken off all her medications except the insulin. He said we could give her "a holiday from her strong medicine" and use Tylenol around the clock to treat the pain.

Waiting in front of the elevators at St. Anthony's, I glanced down at the floor and noticed my reflection because the linoleum was highly polished, which put me in mind of Sister Gertrude because she was famous for mopping and waxing St. Anthony's floors. Jeez, couldn't get those dead nuns out of my head.

The elevator doors slid open and out walked Joe Goodman. *Really?* Could I catch a break here? Next time, I was talking the stairs. I hadn't talked to him since the Depend-Adult-Diaper fiasco and the more recent Lucky-Plucky-Chicken incident. My embarrassment had marinated into ripe anger. My hot Italian temper reared her on her haunches.

"Arté! It's good to see you. Actually, I was about to call you."

I pursed my lips. "Why? So you could make fun of me some more?" My right eyebrow shot up. "I'll have you know, Joe

Goodman," my finger wagged at him, "I have to work a lot of odd jobs to make an honest living—jobs I don't like—and I do *not* appreciate being your prime source of entertainment!"

I pulled my dignity tight around me like a pashmina shawl and marched away striding like a power walker trying to win a race. I found myself in the cafeteria eyeing a lone piece of chocolate cake with butter cream icing. Smacking my lips, I reached for it and clashed hands with someone. Glancing to my right, I saw Joe Goodman's dancing blue eyes peering at me as he held onto the plate. One side of my lip curled. "Just lost my appetite." Retracting my grip, I left in a hurry as if I just remembered I'd left my stove on.

I dashed to my studio to forget my troubles and bury myself in my work.

TWENTY-FOUR

Mary sailed into my studio. "Listen, Arté, ya gotta take that solo exhibit at Community Arts! It's a big-time opportunity—I'll help ya hang the show. You need to get over your shyness, it's crippling ya." She swayed back and forth waiting for my response.

"You don't understand. There's too much going on in my *pathetic life*." I glanced out the store-front window and saw Sister Ignatius stroll by, her sheer veil blowing in the wind. She waved. "You have *no* idea!" I ambled over to the door and locked it—as if that could keep her out! I felt like the plate-spinner on the old Ed Sullivan Show with that annoying music, way too many plates twirling, and all of them about to come crashing down fracturing into a million shards.

My cell chimed and I recognized Joe Goodman's number. I disconnected and tossed my phone into the maw of my purse, mumbling, "Never should have given him my number."

Mary recoiled, looking at me as if I were an ax murderer and she just discovered the bodies hidden in my studio. She extended her hands out, palms up. "Are ya nuts?"

"He had no right to make fun of me…to demean me…to humiliate me—"

"Don't let your hot Italian temper blow this. Doctor Goodman is a catch!"

"Goodman! *Ha!* What's *good* about embarrassing me? He should change his name to *Mean-man.*"

She shook her head and drew in a deep breath. "Jeet?" Mary asked.

"Pardon me."

"Did. You. Eat?" She hitched up her eyebrows. "Maybe you need a hearing aid."

"Not hungry... a drink sounds good—and I'm not even a drinker!" I sighed.

We chatted a few more minutes. Said I'd think about the exhibit. I uncovered my latest angel and said, "Meet Margaret, Angel of Peace."

Mary flipped out over it. "That's bee-u-ti-ful! So life-like."

We parted company and I worked on my angel.

After a few hours had passed, I received a call from Lily. She said she really needed to talk to me and asked if she could stop by my studio. I threw a sheet over my angel and snacked on some peanut butter and crackers.

* * *

Lily rapped on my window and I motioned her in.

"Have a seat, Lily." I stole a sideways glance at her, noting her paleness. She was uncharacteristically quiet. "Let's have some ginger tea and Lorna Doones," I said brightly.

Lily slurped her tea loudly. "That's good quality tea," she said and nibbled on a buttery cookie.

Finally, I asked, "Is everything okay?"

She hesitated, swallowed hard, and said, "Not exactly. I'm *kinda pregnant.*"

I strove to hide my shock. "I see. Um...have you told your dad?"

"Not yet. Don't know what to say. Been hiding it from him," she said, staring into her teacup, as if she'd find the answer to her problem floating in her tea.

"What about the baby's father?"

"He doesn't want anything to do with me...or my baby. He moved out of town."

"Sounds like he ran away." I put my cup down on the table and gave her a hug as she let out a ragged cry. The poor kid— what a time to be motherless.

I held her a moment as she shivered. "Have you thought about options?"

"I am *not* going to *kill* my baby...so don't even say the word *abortion*. And...and I won't *give my baby away* and have it grow up feeling rejected."

I handed her a tissue and she honked her nose loudly.

After a few quiet seconds, I said, "Well, then. You need to talk to your dad. Let him get used to the idea. Lily, you can talk to me anytime." I smiled at her.

"Thanks, Arté. Just had to tell *someone*. I'll...I'll be okay. I have to be strong for my baby."

"You look exhausted." I said, "here, stretch out on the cot and take a little snooze." I covered her with Mamma's hand-crocheted afghan and she fell asleep immediately with her arms cradling her belly.

I sat on the white wicker settee, which I'd scored curbside. I delighted in finding furniture on the side of the road—*road kill*—I called it. I'd load it into my cruiser, take it to my studio, sand and paint it. Oftentimes, I'd display it in the storefront-window and the fresh cottage-look furniture would sell at a neat profit. Merlin leapt onto the back of the settee, draping himself over the back like a furry doily. As the sun warmed my back, I read for a few hours until Lily woke up then I gave her a ride home and returned to my studio to paint.

TWENTY-FIVE

Joe called again so I turned off my phone. Who did he think he was? I would *not* give him the satisfaction of making fun of me again. *Jerk!*

I slung thick mounds of paint on my canvas and swirled it around with a palette knife, while wildly dancing to the Beatles' "Twist and Shout." John Lennon's lead vocals drove me crazy with his raspy voice scraping against the lyrics. Then the music segued to George Harrison's "While My Guitar Gently Weeps" and filled my studio with honey-dipped notes. I expertly played air guitar and rubber-necked to the rhythms of Clapton and Harrison.

A loud rapping on my studio window startled me. I did a double-take when seeing Joe Goodman.

Seriously?

I let him in and exhaled a big gush of air. *"What?"*

"I'm here to apologize. So don't run away." He waltzed in like he owned the place.

Surprised to see him, I remained quiet and listened.

"I am *sincerely* sorry," he said, hand-over-heart, "I never intended to hurt your feelings." The handsome surgeon paused, searching for his words. "I see now that I was insensitive...and I'd like to make it up to you with a nice dinner at The Valley Steak House."

I waited for a punch line as a heavy silence hung in the air. Well, that was awkward.

"This is the part where you say something," he said as he leaned against my work station and folded his arms.

"My bull-crap meter just went off the charts."

He studied me intently. After a short pause, he said, "I'm serious."

Hands on my hips, I said, "You know, Goodman, I've heard you're a professional practical joker. What're you planning? To *lure* me with *filet mignon* and make me wear a giant meat costume?...so you can laugh at me? Or... or write on me with a Sharpie?"

"*Sharpie?* What the *hell* are you talking about?" He lowered his brows and frowned. "No! I'd like to treat you to a nice dinner." He drew in a deep breath. "Look, Arté, I really like you... and your mother is a great lady, not to mention a laugh riot—"

"What? Wait!" I said, narrowing my eyes. "Did my mother put you up to this?"

"Nope." He peered at me. "This is *me* telling *you* that I'm *sorry* and I'd like to take you to dinner. You don't have to forgive me if you don't want to, but remember, that's a sign of weakness."

He changed positions to that sexy stance football players use—you know, hands on hips, weight on one foot, thinking of scoring a touchdown.

"Okay." The word slipped out of my mouth like a wayward hiccup.

Joe smiled and looked around my studio, studying my paintings. "Your work is excellent." He picked up a small study of an Angel of Peace with gold-leafed wings. "This is stunning. What do you plan on doing with all of these angel paintings?"

"I'd love to exhibit all of them together... *someday*." I sighed.

"Wow, these large angels are striking!" He was about to lift the cover from my latest one.

"No peeking!" I shouted. "That's a work in progress."

He dropped the cover as if it were a hot coal. "Sorry." Bet he thought I'd get mad again.

"My dream is to have a one-woman show, but...it's complicated." I won't tell him about my stage fright and give him more ammunition to make fun of me. "I believe my eight-foot angels would have a strong impact."

"How'd you market your work? Seems like you keep all of this secret."

"Well, I really don't have the time, much less the money, to effectively market my work. In a perfect world, I'd have an agent."

"I see." His gaze traveled from painting to painting. "What are your goals?"

"You know, Joe, all I want in life is to create my work. The work I *believe* in...that's important. You know, *authentic*... without worrying about money, rent, supplies, and all of that. I long for creative freedom. I'm sixty. Time is precious and, creatively speaking, I have unfinished business."

He nodded, as his lips curled upward.

I sighed deeply. "A lot of time is wasted scrambling to make ends meet. I teach here at the studio, hold Open Studio during the holidays, write grants, and work wacky jobs—*as you know!* And the whole time I'm doing all of that, I'm *aching* to paint my Angels of Peace." I smiled weakly.

"It must be difficult for you. I'm such an ass!"

"I'm not complaining. Nobody likes a crybaby."

He grinned at me with his head tilted to one side. "Why angels?"

"Angels are messengers of peace. The very name, *angel,* means messenger. And what singular message does mankind need to hear the most? What is it that *man* does not have? Peace!"

I tented my fingers together. "I strive to paint my angels as beautifully as possible in order to capture the attention of the viewer long enough to deliver my message of peace."

"I get it. You're an artist with ideals."

I cracked a half-smile. "And I lend new meaning to the term *starving artist.*"

"You also must be a devout Catholic."

I frowned. "Not anymore." I studied my feet and placed my hands in the back pockets of my jeans.

His eyebrows shot straight up. "But all these angels—"

"Just because I paint angels doesn't mean I'm a practicing Catholic. Used to be—never missed Mass! I'm outraged with the Church's egregious crimes against innocent children and the intentional cover up. The last time I attended Mass, during the homily—where the congregation sat there," I said, waving my arm through the air, " as if everything was *peachy keen*— I almost stood up and demanded that the priest address the elephant sitting in the aisle atop the *steaming* pile of dung!" I swallowed hard, shaking my head. "I can not go to Mass anymore— I didn't quit the Catholic Church, the Church quit me! They can add another crime to their roster, grand larceny of my religion. *Don't get me started!* " I had to do some deep-breathing exercises to calm down.

Taking a step back, he said, "Take it easy, Tiger." He ambled over to a self-portrait and stood before the full-length figure of a wild woman. I'd titled the work *Rebel in Menopause,* which I'd painted while in the throes of a hot-flash-marathon-from-hell. The large canvas depicted me in a black leather vest over a rolled-arm white T-shirt, a long, hand-made Peace amulet, and vintage bell-bottom jeans, from which peeked black motorcycle boots. I looked like a menopausal member of Hell's Angels. The expressive *alla prima* work portrayed a mad-as-hell woman with messy, thick, long hair and a right, highly arched eyebrow, which conveyed the message: Do Not Mess With This Chick.

"Whoa!" he said, holding his hand up like a stop sign.

"What's this one called? Hot Italian Temper?"

"Something like that."

Then he stood before a large canvas, swirling with figures bound in flames. He studied it and scratched his head. "Is that Newt Gingrich?"

"Yep."

"Is he in hell?"

"Uh-huh."

"Can you tell me about this painting?"

"Remember when Newt—who must be named after a small reptile—spearheaded the movement to close down the federal government? Like a spoiled brat? And even his own party was ticked off? His ego was so over inflated, I was amazed he didn't become airborne. And he voted to *kill the N.E.A.!* Without the support of the National Endowment of the Arts, most artists couldn't survive in the art world. So, I sketched his gas-bag mug on wanted posters, which read: Wanted For Attempted Murder Of The N.E.A., and hung them all over town. And I painted this," I pointed with my chin at the canvas, "parody of Michelangelo's Last Judgment. Substituted Gingrich for the central character in hell with the giant serpent wound around his body, ready to strike at a delicate part of anatomy." I rocked back on my heels. "A politician of his ilk should not piss off an artist."

"*Jesus-George!*" Joe said, smirking. "I'm afraid of you."

Looking at more of my paintings, he nodded. "Impressive." Then his pager went off, making that high-pitched noise like Mickey Mouse on helium. He sighed. "If there's a sound in hell, it's a doctor's pager sounding off." He read his message and said, "Have to go back to St. Anthony's, but I'm not on call tonight. Pick you up at 7."

"Peace out."

Joe grinned broadly. "I like how you always say that."

* * *

I had only four hours to get ready.

I dialed Mary. "Mare!" I said, breathlessly, "this time I have a *real* date with Joe Goodman. Tonightseveno'clockTheValley SteakHousewhatshouldIwear?"

"Wicked Pissa!" Mary shouted. "Wear that black-sleeveless dress with the leopard panel down the front—very slimming... and those sexy red-patent stilettoes, uh, and the red clutch with the wrist strap. And you have to promise to call me after your date—no matter what time it is."

"Will do. Gotta go and shave my cucumber-y legs."

* * *

I made a quick trip to check on Mamma Mia and she looked slightly better. The mask-like expression was gone and she was more alert. I showered her with *baci* and she responded with a smile!

"Are you in pain?" I asked.

"I'm feeling a bit better. Don't worry so much, Artemisia, you'll get more wrinkles!"

"More wrinkles!" I laughed.

"Yeah, you'll look like a Chinese Shar-Pei puppy. Your wrinkles will have wrinkles!" Her eyes glistened and she rolled up a belly laugh.

She was cracking jokes. *I had my mother back!* It was as if she had died and resurrected. She had a bad reaction to the opiates, but now she was Don Rickles.

TWENTY-SIX

Joe Goodman and I sat at a table-for-two at The Valley Steak House. The intimate table was dressed with white linens. A cut-crystal vase held a bouquet of miniature pink roses. Flames flickered from the candles in the silver candleholders as we listened to Vivaldi's *The Four Seasons.*

Joe looked handsome outfitted in khaki pants, navy blazer, white dress shirt, and burgundy tie with tiny figures of *Snoopy Joe Cool.*

The waitress was adorable with her hair piled on top of her head in an explosion of red curls. The beautiful young woman was embroidered with several tattoos all over her porcelain skin, even on her neck. Had it been painful to have had the needles piercing her neck? Mentally, I sketched her and thought she'd be an exquisite model for one of my Angels of Peace. Hmm, a tattooed angel. Could be interesting. I'd change the tatts to peace signs.

"Will you join me in a glass of wine?" Joe asked.

"Jeez, don't think I'd fit."

"You're just like your mother."

"Sorry. That's an old joke. I'll try to come up with some fresh material."

He grinned. "Think I'll have a glass of Pinot Noir."

"Water for me, with lemon, please," I said, shrugging. "Not much of a drinker."

The waitress left to fill our orders.

The menu made my mouth water. Couldn't remember the last time I had steak for dinner. After all, I'm a Ramen Noodle-poor artist.

"Oh, man!" Joe said, "I'm having the rib-eye with the crumbly blue-cheese topping." When our server took his order, he said, matter-of-factly, "I'll have the Big Mac and fries."

She laughed hysterically. "That's so funny! Especially in *this* restaurant."

I decided on the filet mignon, potatoes au gratin, and Green Beans Amandine. Both of us ordered the tomato-mozzarella fresh-basil salad.

The yeasty aroma from the bread called my name and I didn't hold back from diving into the breadbasket. The warm rolls were homemade, crusty on the outside and soft inside. I could've made a meal out of the bread.

"So, tell me about the Albany meeting," Joe said.

"I was so nervous—felt as if someone were knitting with my nerves. Had *a lot* to say and only eighteen minutes to say it." I spackled my bread with a thick layer of butter. "But, just before I spoke a veil of serenity…and confidence fell over me."

"Saw the coverage," Joe said, "you did a great job, Arté."

"Thank you." I took a sip of water. "Did you notice Governor O'Shea's reaction when I revealed his relationship to Sister Ignatius? Everyone in the room seemed shocked except him."

Joe said, "I thought he looked pissed off."

"Exactly."

"How'd you manage to get 3,000 signatures in favor of keeping St. Anthony's open, not to mention voting O'Shea out of office?" He tasted his wine.

"Mamma collected most of them. One Sunday she went rogue and wheeled herself out of the hospital without telling anyone. She rolled over to St. Joe's and collected signatures after Mass. Sister X nearly had a stroke when she couldn't find my mother. She called me and yelled in her deep, gravely voice, '*We lost your mother! We've never lost a resident before!*' I lowered my voice to a deep pitch and clutched my chest.

Joe laughed. "You should do a stand-up comedy routine about your mother."

I enjoyed my delicious salad with its fruity olive-oil dressing. After finishing it, I excused myself to go to the ladies' room. Actually, I just wanted to check in the mirror to see if I had basil stuck in my teeth.

I peered into the mirror and behind me saw Sister Ignatius, Sister Augustine, and Sister Gertrude. What was this? The holy trinity of dead nuns?

"Oh, for the love of God!" I cried, wringing my hands, "are you trying to kill me?"

Sister Gertrude said, "Now relax, Artemisia, we just want to tell you that you're doing a splendid job helping to save our St. Anthony's Hospital. By the way, we *love* your painting of us!"

I shut my eyes tightly then opened them. Yep. Still there.

What could be worse than being stalked by a pack of dead nuns? *Nothing*. Nothing at all.

Sister Gertrude said, "Now, we know you're on a lovely date with Doctor Goodman." She giggled. "You can thank us for that later. But tomorrow you really need to do that research."

Then—*poof*—the three of them were gone—vanished in a veil of smog, which smelled like incense smoke. I looked behind me. Searched each stall. I was alone in the bathroom.

I hurried back to our table and sat opposite Joe. "I'll take you up on your offer of wine."

A broad grin spread across his lips as he signaled to the server. "A glass of Pinot Noir for the lady."

The inked waitress retrieved the bottle, poured a glass, and turned to leave. I grabbed her arm. "Leave the bottle." I downed the glass in one gulp and refilled it.

Joe hitched his eyebrows. "Everything okay?"

"Just dandy. You're right, this wine is delicious."

I willed myself to forget about St. Anthony's and Mamma Mia. Most of all, I vowed not to let a gaggle of deceased nuns ruin my date with Joe Goodman. I drew in a deep breath and felt a pleasant warmth, like a mustard plaster stuck to my chest as I exhaled with a smile. Calmness washed over me.

Our server set down our dinners on white china. The potatoes au gratin were housed in a small oval ramekin topped with bubbling browned cheese. The green beans were uncut, arranged in a basket-weave design, and crusted with slivered almonds. The star of the show, a petite filet mignon, wore a bacon shawl drizzled with Béarnaise sauce. My dinner was almost too beautiful to eat.

Joe snatched the bottle of A1 Sauce, upended it, and pumped the bottom with his palm, covering his ribeye. It splattered on his Snoopy tie. *"Jesus George!"* His face contorted. "I *always* do that. How can I be a meticulous, neat surgeon and yet manage to slobber food on me at every meal?"

"You're *talented?"*

"That was a rhetorical question," he said as he dipped his napkin in water and rubbed the spot vigorously.

I laughed and reached for my wine.

Joe said, "So, a few of the docs are looking for jobs already."

"Would it be all right if we didn't talk about St. Anthony's? The whole situation is dragging me down."

He nodded, playing with the silverware. "Done." He polished the knife with his napkin. "So, Arté, tell me something about yourself that I don't know…start with your unusual name."

"My mother named me after an incredible Baroque painter, Artemisia Gentileschi. I think Mamma had hoped that her talent would rub off on me, but I only inherited the *'broke'* part."

153

He chuckled. "You have a huge talent."

Smiling, I said, "Thank you, Joe, I appreciate that," and gobbled another roll.

Worry lines creased his forehead. "I don't want to step on a land mine here, but I'm Catholic too…uh, isn't it weird not to attend Mass?"

"I miss the ritual of the Mass. But, the crimes and cover-up committed by the Catholic Church were not a few isolated cases. I researched it. It was widespread and went on for years. That's not what I'd signed up for. We're talking about *children! Innocent children.* I don't want to be part of any organized religion…when men make the rules," I brushed my bangs off my forehead, "humanity suffers. I mean, look at the Crusades . . jihads…*Holy Wars!* Wow, there's a classic oxymoron."

"Agreed!" He patted my hand. "Didn't mean to upset you. Moving on."

I chewed on the tip of my thumbnail. "Um, lemme see… most mornings I swim continuous laps at the 'Y'. Painting and swimming keep me sane—you know, like therapy."

"Got ya. For me, it's running. What music do you love?"

"Every Beatles' tune. All John Lennon and Paul McCartney songs. Um, Classical, of course. Paganini… Are you familiar with Paul McCartney's *Ecce Cor Meum*? So beautiful!"

"No, but I'll look for it."

"And C.C.R."

"Excuse me?"

"Creedence Clearwater Revival, you know, *Proud Mary, I Heard It Through The Grapevine.* Of course, I love Motown music. And Gregorian chant, which I listen to while painting my Angels of Peace."

"You have eclectic tastes. I like that. Besides music, what else do you love?"

"I *adore* my cat, Merlin—my fuzzy buddy. Rescued him years ago at the SPCA as they were about to put him to sleep.

He's a silver-gray Maine Coon who is, really, my best friend.
Also, I have an ongoing love affair with the river."
He hesitated. "What about your real love life?"
I blew out my cheeks. "I had one great love, early in my
life...Michael...died in Viet Nam." I fell silent for a full minute.
"We'd planned a big Italian wedding. We'd set the date—June
twentieth. Had my gown." I sipped my wine and blotted my lips
with the cloth napkin. "Michael had volunteered for a second
tour of duty—I begged him not to, but he said the combat pay
would buy a house for us." I gazed down at my lap. "Anyway...
uh, had a few minor loves, and dated a whole lot of losers and
a few creeps. My greatest...deepest regret in life is I never had
a child." I downed the rest of my wine. "Sorry, didn't intend to
get so serious. Your turn."

Joe brushed the bread crumbs off his Snoopy tie. "When
I'm not working or running, I read, mostly novels—love poetry...Frost, Browning, Neruda."

I smiled at Neruda. Now there was a manly-man who enjoyed love poems.

"Um...play classical guitar." He sipped wine. "Enjoy a
good crossword puzzle."

"You didn't mention your love life."

"I also found the love-of-my-life. Was married to a wonderful woman for thirty-three years." He frowned. "Margaret died
of breast cancer five years ago."

I reached out to touch his hand. "I'm truly sorry."

He nodded. "You know that pain. Margaret and I had wanted a big family. We were blessed with one daughter." Joe shook
his head slowly. "I worked through my grief by running like
a maniac and working non-stop...but my poor daughter was
completely lost."

He folded and unfolded his napkin. "She's too fragile to live
alone, so she lives with me. She's been hanging out with some...
low-life people." Joe scowled. "Dating this one guy—Margaret

would have been horrified. I just want to punch him in the face!" Inhaling deeply, he shrugged. "You can't ground a thirty-year-old." He briskly rubbed his face with both hands as if that could erase his troubles. "That's not all. Lily just told me … she's pregnant."

What? Lily was his daughter? *My Lily?* "Is Lily tall and thin? Long curly hair and mesmerizing blue eyes?"

"You know her?"

"Been spending a lot of time with her at my studio. I'm giving her art lessons in exchange for modeling for my large Angel of Peace. She never told me her last name."

I stroked my chin. Should I tell him what Lily said about keeping the baby? "Wow! A grandchild." I studied him. "Maybe your only grandchild."

He stared off into middle space.

"Lily's a delight. I really enjoy her. She's so funny and has raw artistic talent—she's improving rapidly. Did she show you her self-portraits?"

"No. I didn't know."

"If there's any way I can help, please let me know. I'm a pretty good listener."

"I can see that. Didn't mean to get serious either." Joe smiled thinly.

"Joe, you've been through a lot in life, as have I. We've been knocked down, but sprang up, swinging. Everything will work out. It's like Mamma always says, 'Everyone has *something*. Life equals pain plus joy.'"

We were silent for a few moments.

"Hey. They have amazing pie here. Homemade!" Joe said.

"*Pie!*" I could barely push the word out of my mouth. "I can't even *look* at pie since Mary McKee signed me up for that pie-eating-contest."

Joe and I closed down the restaurant. The cute waitress had sent to McDonald's and presented Joe with a Big Mac and fries along with the check. We had a good laugh over that. Just what we needed. "Thanks, Red," Joe said.

I took some of my beef home for Merlin and Joe left our waitress a big fat tip.

"It's a beautiful night," he said, "would you like to walk by the river?"

"I'd like that very much."

The Valley Steak House Restaurant was located in downtown Verdant Valley, next to the River Park. The park was lovely with three fountains, exquisite landscaping, and antique benches. The water fountains featured colored plumes of turquoise and pink water and every tree was adorned with tiny clear lights.

Outside we were greeted by a balmy Indian-Summer breeze. Sighing, I said, "We won't have too many warm fall nights like this. It's perfect." And I wasn't exactly referring to the weather.

We ambled down the pebbled path near the river. The soft glow from the full moon cast its golden rays on the velvety sage-green Mullein plants and the pink wildflowers danced in the gentle wind like tiny ballerinas in rose-hued tutus. The tangy air smelled of dried leaves and earth, like raw potatoes. The water lapped the edge of land as it'd done for thousands of years. We strolled under the same moon that'd illuminated the earth for eons, but the moonbeams in the star-dotted sky seemed to be shinning on us alone.

"Just *look* at that moon!" I said, pointing my chin heavenward and spreading my arms like an eagle to take in my moon nourishment.

Joe took his hand in mine and it was warm and soft. I held the hand that saved human lives and I felt safe.

We made our way up the little hill to the grassy knoll of the park. I slipped off my four-inch stilettoes and curled my toes into the cool moist grass. It was soft and spongy. We sat on a park bench in a comfortable silence admiring the lunar aura.

Finally Joe said, "It's getting late. Guess I should take you home."

"Okay."

We stood facing each other and the moon cast a spell on us or *something.*

I studied Joe's face, admiring his pillow-lips and thick hair. He searched my eyes. "I have to kiss you."

"You better hurry up."

And we just melted…into a leisurely…wine-sweet kiss.

TWENTY-SEVEN

Merlin had been waiting for me in my kitchen. He fixed his jade eyes on me and meowed forlornly, as if to say, *"Hey! Where have you been? You missed my treat-time."* I stroked his thick pelt and gave him a little piece of steak. He made clicking noises with his teeth then hummed like an electric fan.

"Oh, Fuzzy Buddy, what's happening to me? I'm so attracted to Joe! It's really bad timing with Mamma's situation at St. Anthony's. We have the fight of a lifetime on our hands and I can't fall in love now."

Fuzzy Buddy studied me and angled his fury head. Then he padded over to me and bumped against my legs as he wove in and out between my feet. I reached down to bury my fingers in his fur.

Joe and I had talked late into the night. I didn't call Mary—didn't want to break the moonstruck spell.

I shot out a text to Mary: *Lovely date. Joe's a nice guy. Had filet mignon. We'll talk soon.*

I wasn't telling Mary about Lily—that was confidential. And I wouldn't tell her about The Kiss (capitalized because it was *some kiss*). I tucked that away in my breast pocket for myself.

* * *

Enveloped in the fuzzy cocoon of Joe's kiss, I slept in for the first time in years. After getting dressed, I had a fierce craving for coffee.

I pulled up to the drive-thru at McDonald's and ordered an extra-large coffee. You know how you look forward to that first cup in the morning? I *really* needed that caffeine infusion.

I sniffed the nutty aroma and smiled, completely serene.

"Aw, fresh coffee! T'was one of me favorite earthly pleasures," Sister Ignatius said.

In my passenger seat sat the dead nun. I heard a scream and realized it'd come from me. My hands shook and I spilled my coffee. The other six dead nuns of St. Anthony's Hospital were crammed into the backseat like clowns in a comedy circus.

"I loved fresh coffee in the morning with Irish soda bread," Sister Augustine said.

Sister Gertrude chimed in, "I never could drink coffee—it gave me the *runs.*" She covered her mouth with her hand. "Um, perhaps that was too much information."

I pulled into a parking space and turned off the ignition. "You *have* to stop sneaking up on me. My heart can't take it!"

"We have only a few minutes," Sister Gertrude said.

"Yes," Sister Ignatius said, "now, Artemisia, be sure to look closely at me bible."

And then the wraiths disappeared—dissolving into confetti particles— leaving my nerves fried and my coffee cup empty.

I sat there for some time trying to ease my tachycardia and questioning my sanity.

Needing to see my mother, I ordered two more coffees, two hash browns, and drove to St. Anthony's.

* * *

I strode into Mamma's room and found her in bed again, still in her night-clothes.

"Mamma Mia. *Come stai?"*

"Meh," she replied, extending her hand, palm up.

"I have delicious coffee and a hash brown for you."

"I'm not hungry," she said, slicing her hand through the air.

Mamma's toenails needed trimming. "Let's take care of your toenails," I said. That might get her up and dressed for the day. As I finished clipping and massaging peppermint lotion on her feet, Sister X knocked on the door.

"May I come in?" she asked.

Sister's rounded shoulders and hollowed eyes were not her normal appearance. She looked pale.

"This is difficult," she began, "so I'll just say it…after one hundred years…St. Anthony's Hospital is closing. It's official. Just heard from Governor O'Shea's office. I wanted to be the one to tell you—didn't want you to hear it on the news."

Mamma winced and reached for her asthma inhaler.

I tried to manage my anger—didn't want to swear at a nun again. "Is there any chance St. Anthony's can stay open? What about a hospital merger?"

"Artemisia! Be realistic," she said in her deep gravely voice.

Jeez, she acted like I'd asked her to donate a kidney for a transplant. She didn't have to be so snotty.

"That's not possible in this case. St. Anthony's has carried a massive debt for years. No other hospital is willing to acquire that debt. Because our mission is to care for the downtrodden, St. Anthony's rarely receives payments, and reimbursements are at an all-time low. The governor has pushed hard for the closure and has taken swift action."

My voice rose. "What about the residents on the skilled-nursing floor?" Sweating, I wailed, "St Anthony's is their *home.*"

"I honestly don't know," she said quietly, "I'll keep you informed. I need to go and tell the other residents." She handed me a sheet of paper with optional nursing homes, most of which were fifty miles away.

Just like that? She was resigned to the fact? Sister X may be the administrator of St. Anthony's, but she was nothing like Sister Ignatius—she never gave up! That Super Sister was like a pit bull. Jeez, where was her complete trust in God?

My hands balled into fists. "*Sister*, I cannot accept that."

"*Artemisia*," she said, as if she were talking to a child, "it's a government *mandate*. Signed by Governor O'Shea. There's nothing we can do." She left to inform the rest of the residents on the floor.

Mamma rolled over in her bed, quietly weeping.

"Please don't cry," I said, "everything will be okay."

"You heard Sister. There's nothing we can do! Where will I end up? Oh, *Dio!*"

"Mamma Mia! You taught me to always be positive. You said, 'Life boils down to one essential decision: To be positive or to be negative. Always choose positive!' I've never seen you this negative."

"Oh, Arté, you don't understand."

"I understand perfectly…don't see the moving trucks yet. We are *not* taking this news sitting down!…Wait a minute… that's *exactly* how we're taking it. *Sitting down!*" I slapped my forehead as if squashing a mosquito and chuckled. "So that's what Sister Ignatius meant when she said, 'Remember the '60s' …Aw, the '60s—those were the days!"

Mamma stopped crying. "What are you talking about? Arté, you don't make sense. *You* better *sit* down."

I vibrated with excitement, flapping my hands. "Mamma Mia, we're going to have a Sit-In! An old-fashioned, '60's type of protest. Civil disobedience."

My mother studied me. "Calm down! I think you need a sedative."

"See, my generation made strong political statements by

holding a Sit-In. We gathered in massive groups—there was power in numbers—and protested, peacefully of course, and chanted our beliefs. We held protest signs too. We seated ourselves and refused to move. We used our voices and our bodies and every fiber of our being to tell our truth. A large crowd would gather to watch and then the police would be called to break up the disturbance."

I paused to sip my coffee. "We refused to leave and defiantly sat on the ground. *Immobile!* We locked our arms or chained ourselves to something. We were stuck like superglue." Peering out the window into middle-space, I smiled wistfully as I nibbled on a hash brown. "We were willing to be arrested for our cause because that resulted in the media—newspaper and TV— to report our Sit-In, thereby giving mass coverage to our protest. Just what we wanted! *Capisce?*"

Mamma looked me up and down. "That's what you learned in the college I worked so hard to pay for? To get arrested?"

"Yep, among other things. It was highly effective. I came of age in the most powerful decade of history. Social change and reform were carried out by peaceful protests. Why, I witnessed the civil rights movement, the women's rights protests, the labor workers fight, and the gay rights movement. And I learned to stand up for my beliefs!"

Her dark eyes glistened. "Hand me that hash brown." She nodded and chomped down, talking around the food in her mouth. "*Va bene!* I'd be willing to get arrested and go to jail to save my home at St. Anthony's. I'll tell the gang and we'll make protest signs in the Arts and Crafts room."

"Remember, Mamma, it's a *peaceful* protest. Please make that clear to your cronies."

Mamma set her jaw. "I'll lock the brakes on my wheelchair so even Coxey's army wouldn't be able to move me!" She munched on her hash brown and washed it down with coffee. "Better pack a bunch of Lorna Doones in my pocketbook…and

Dead Nuns Talking

I'll have my trusty cane handy in case some hooligan tries any *funny business* in the slammer—I'll go for the cojones with my quad cane." A slow smile crept across her ruby lips. "I can't wait for the Sit-In. O'Shea will *curse* the day he heard the name Loretta Credo!"

TWENTY-EIGHT

Joe had called to invite me to dinner. We had fish tacos at The Cactus Flower Café and then went for a drive. We ended up at Valley View Hilltop. *Parking!* At my age! We made out like teenagers. I was crazy in love with Joe and wanted to have sex with him, but what if Sister Ignatius decided to show up? That'd make her veil roll up like a window shade. A dead nun talking to me during sex would definitely kill the mood. And what if Joe asked what was wrong? Couldn't tell him a dead nun was present. Watching us. I kissed him with one eye open, on the look-out for a hooded specter. As if I didn't have enough stress in my life. *Oh, good heavens!* What if all seven dead nuns showed up? A sorority of shrouded sisters gawking at sex! They'd have to cover their eyes with their veils. I mean, they wouldn't watch us, would they? I...I couldn't even deal.

"Why so nervous, Arté?"

"Um, dunno."

"You seem distracted." He studied my face. "I want to talk about taking our relationship to the next level."

I gulped. "You mean...*sex?*" The word squeaked out like a rusty door that needed oil.

A throaty chuckle came from him. "Well, that too." He

stroked the side of my face. "What is it? The guilt from your Catholic education?"

"Uh, you could say the nuns are, I mean, *were* a problem." I twirled a lock of my hair. I couldn't meet his gaze.

"Arté, I'm very serious. I'm in love with you."

I got a little misty as I reached for his hand. "I love you more than I ever thought I could love a guy…but, what're you saying? Move in together?" If I told him I'd been stalked by a flock of dead nuns, he'd run for the hills—faster than a Kardashian taking a selfie.

"I want *more* than that. It's been a lonely five years since Margaret died. Lily and I are getting closer and we're preparing for the baby. You've been great with Lily." He cupped my face with his hands and kissed my puffy lips. Tender at first and then hard and long. My fingers clutched his thick hair as my stomach did flip-flops. Jeez, I was hornier than a rhino.

* * *

Joe dropped me off at my apartment. He wanted to come in, but I said I wasn't quite ready for the next step and he understood.

Lily taught me how to manage my Twitter account and she'd used Instagram to jettison images of my Angels of Peace into the internet universe. I was amazed by the power of social media. I'd been answering O'Shea's tweets because he upset Lily. A governor tweeting manic rants late at night as a form of bullying was my definition of a coward. I checked my account and read O'Shea's latest salvo. *"Artemisia Credo is a pathetic old maid and her art sucks! Did she even go to college?"*

My thumbs attacked my phone's keypad. *"FYI, I graduated Summa Cum Laude from Verdant Valley College with a double major in studio art and art history. Thanks for asking. Where did you earn your degree—Cretin College?"*

* * *

Mary and I snacked on French fries and tossed salads in St. Anthony's cafeteria, hoping the salads would cancel out the fries.

"So, howzit going with you and Dr. *Good*-Man?"

I put my fork down and blotted my lips with my napkin. "Uh, he's getting serious."

"Whadda mean?" Mary's red-penciled eyebrows raised up.

"Well, says he wants more than me moving in with him." I smiled weakly.

"Like marriage?" Mary asked.

"He didn't use that word, but what else could it mean?" I salted my fries.

"*Hot sweaty monkey-sex!*"

"Okay, changing the subject now." I dipped a long fry into a well of ketchup as my cell rang. "Saved by the bell—Credo Art Studio."

"I'm looking for Artemisia Credo. This is Margo Morningstar from Morningstar Gallery in New York."

"This is she. What can I do for you?"

"I looked up your work on your website because of Governor O'Shea's terrible tweets. I'd expected to see the work of an amateur. Instead, I was mesmerized by your stunning Angels of Peace. You are an accomplished artist! How can you let him get away with lying about your work?"

"I don't have the money to hire a lawyer to fight back. And, for the record, I am not an alcoholic—I'm practically a teetotaler."

"How about you fight back with a solo exhibit at my gallery? I have an immediate opening due to an artist's illness. Artemisia, I'd love to show your work. If you will agree, you'd show the world that Governor O'Shea lied about you and your work."

Mary's mouth fell open. She had her ear glued to my phone and nodded her head vigorously like a bobble-headed doll.

Dead Nuns Talking

After I disconnected my call, Mary held up a long flabby fry and wagged it at me. "Listen, Doll Face, if you say no to a solo exhibit in *frickin'* New York city, I'll flog you with this soggy French fry."

* * *

At the gloaming hour, I sat on the springy grass at the river's bend with my head resting on my bent knees. I ballooned my lungs with a deep intake of river air. Exhaled dreamily. Sniffed the loamy scent of the riverbank and listened to the bird's concerto, as I watched the smudged colors of the fading sunlight. My thoughts flowed like the river. Maybe I should take another chance on marriage. I couldn't compare a marriage to Joe to my miserable marriage to Dickk—that wouldn't be fair to Joe. As Mamma was so fond of saying, "Joe was a fine man!" Perhaps I wasn't too old—Mary said, "Sixty is the new fifty." Joe and I were in excellent health, might have another twenty or twenty-five good years left in us...*The man read poetry to me!* And we'd have a complete family with Lily and a baby. I'd love that. Marriage to Joe would be a new adventure. Joseph Campbell had written, "The big question is whether you are going to be able to say a hearty yes to your adventure."

I just wasn't sure about the dead nuns...were they always going to be popping up like a Jack in the Box?

* * *

I said yes to the New York one-woman exhibit. All these years, I'd guarded against ambition ruling my art and wanted to keep my work pure. I knew of artists who had licensed their work—mass marketed it on QVC and pimped their paintings with images on nightlights, coffee mugs, lamps, ceramic figures, afghans, and toilet seat covers! I'd rather be a starving artist. But, a New York solo-exhibit would be different. It'd be legitimate—the real deal.

Joe took me to New York. George and Mary offered to drive the truck with my over-sized Angels of Peace. George was born and raised in the city and knew his way around. The gallery had massive floor-to-ceiling windows and grey/taupe walls, which served as a neutral background for the art. A hand-scraped, wide-planked, dark wooden floor gleamed. The gallery owner, Margo, who wore her black hair slicked into a severe bun, pearls, red lipstick, and sported the New York City uniform of an all-black outfit, was innovative and included me in a lot of the details, which was a great experience. Her four-inch black patent leather heels clicked a Morse code as she marched across the wooden floor. Patches of bright red flashed on the underside of her stilettos. She looked like a super model in her fitted turtleneck and knee-length pencil skirt.

"Artemisia," she said in a low, warm voice, "so nice to feature your work in my gallery—and on such short notice." She shook my hand. "Don't be nervous. I'm here to help in any way I can. I like to collaborate with my artists—we're in this together!"

I had a specific vision as to the placement of the large angels. The four eight-foot Angels of Peace, which looked majestic, were positioned in the four corners of the gallery symbolizing the cardinal directions of the world. They seemed to relay the message of peace to the North, South, East, and West. My intent was to convey that angels were everywhere, imparting their singular wisdom. The miniature angel paintings with the shimmering gold-leafed wings contrasted starkly with the gigantic angels. They stood out like jewels. There was something about a miniature painting that made the viewer lean in and examine it. Margo lit the artwork as if it were a movie set. My body of work, displayed together with cinematic lighting, glowed. I was nervous and excited at the same time—my stomach constantly did that giggling thing.

Margo click-clacked over to me, her Pilates-toned body

straight and slender. "I've set up a book-signing station for your book, *Weeping Angels,* which, by the way, is *stunning* and I want to be the first to buy one. I'll signal you just before your Gallery Talk and we'll end with the book-signing. In the meanwhile, try to meet and greet as many spectators as possible. They love meeting the artist—makes them feel invested in the work."

I took a final glance around the gallery and could hardly believe I'd created such a cohesive exhibit. I wished Mamma could be here. Hopefully I wouldn't mess up the Gallery Talk.

It was lunchtime and the opening wasn't until 7 PM. George was eager to show us around his city. He knew a great Italian place for lunch not far away. As we walked, I practiced deep-breathing exercises to calm me down, but was way too edgy to eat.

Joe asked, "Hey, are you okay?"

I let out a nervous laugh. "Is it that obvious?"

Joe clasped my hand and squeezed it. "You're going to be just fine." He raised it to his lips and brushed a kiss across the back of my hand.

"Aw, that was wicked sweet," Mary said.

* * *

When we returned to the gallery for the opening, I was taken aback upon entering. We were greeted with soft strands of Gregorian Chant, rising and dipping, mingled with a sweet scent from the floral bouquets. Burled-wood pedestals of varying heights were topped with cerulean hand-blown vases filled with an assortment of fresh white flowers and lacy green ferns. The soft lighting was otherworldly. When my glance swept the room, taking in the angelic countenances, I thought of Dante's *Paradiso* .

Taking my cue from Margo, I wore a black shell and, since Joe once told me he was a *leg man*, a black, knee-length, straight skirt with a short black leather jacket with studding detail on the collar—for a rock'n'roll vibe. To brighten up the black, I wore my favorite chunky turquoise necklace and earrings. Tucked underneath my tank top was Sister Ignatius's St. Anthony medal.

I opted to wear leopard-printed high-heels, which Mary made me buy. "Ya can't wear those granny Birkenstocks for your Gallery Talk!"

Man, my dogs were barkin'. Okay, the killer heels were a mistake…and that industrial-strength support bra, but I was in the big leagues now. The pain took my mind off my nervousness. As Mamma was fond of saying, "Sometimes you have to suffer to be beautiful."

I talked with dozens of gallery goers, nibbled on cheese, crackers, and canapés. Even sipped a little wine. George and Joe huddled in a corner talking Notre Dame football while Mary chatted it up big time with the crowd.

Tiny red dots appeared below the miniature paintings, as if the wall were sprouting measles. *Sales!*

"Thank you, ladies and gentlemen," Margo said in her husky actress-voice, "for attending the opening of this *heavenly* exhibit, *Wingbeat.*" Her manicured hand stretched out, waving at the artwork like Vanna White. "*This* is the *bravura* work that Governor O'Shea has been calling '*garbage*' on Twitter at three o'clock in the morning." She used air quotation signs. "I ask you, What is wrong with that man? It's my pleasure to introduce you to a master-artist from upstate New York, Artemisia Credo."

I grasped my St. Anthony medal and slid it along the silver chain. I waited for the applause to quiet down as I ambled to the podium. My stomach flipped-flopped as I cleared my throat. Scanning the room, I spotted Sister Ignatius at the buffet, sipping wine and tossing a tiny crabcake into her mouth. She smiled and waved as the other dead nuns mingled with the New Yorkers.

"Good evening. It's such a pleasure to be in the greatest

city in the world! It's been lovely meeting with many of you. Margo, thank you for your kindness and warm welcome, I appreciate it." I drew in a deep breath and slowly exhaled. "So, why angels?" I clasped my hands together, then released them. "According to my research, every religion believes in angels. The name, *angel*, means messenger. And what is the message that mankind needs so desperately to hear? *Peace!*" I peered into the audience and saw smiling faces and nods. "Joseph Campbell—the late scholar and mythologist— reminded us to 'find what best fosters the flowering of our humanity in this contemporary life and dedicate ourselves to that.' For me, it was creating Angels of Peace."

I recounted my experience on the Ponte Sant'Angelo and said that some kind of angelic alchemy had taken hold of me and I knew my artistic mission was to paint Angels of Peace.

"The type of peace I'm referring to is that *quiet* peace within us—*individual peace,* which radiates outward to family and friends, to community, and in turn, to nation, and to world. This quiet peace doesn't come naturally or automatically, we must strive for it. Peace takes conscious effort. One way we can achieve individual peace is by performing random acts of kindness and to practice giving in a non-calculated way.

"When my mother and I traveled to Italy, we spent two days touring the Vatican Museums." I grinned, then let out a chuckle. "Actually, my mother almost started a fist fight in the Sistine Chapel." Some giggles. I recounted the *Get-Your-Hands-Off-My-Ass* story, which earned a big laugh. "Upon leaving the Vatican, I encountered a homeless elderly woman, sitting on the cobbled pavement, resting against a large box, which must have been her shelter. On a warm day, she wore layers of clothing, a long wool coat, and a shawl over her head. I'd just viewed hundreds of paintings of the Blessed Mother and it was clear to me that the elegant woman was the Madonna of the Street—*Madonna della Via.* People filed past her as if she were invisible. The sainted woman hung her head low as she held out her dirty Styrofoam beggar's cup. Her curved torso folded into itself like a question mark, as if her body asked, *Why me?* I ambled over to her and tucked a couple of dollars into her hand, which I held for a few seconds. She slowly raised her head and peered at me. I smiled warmly and stroked the side of her face and offered her the sign of peace. She was grateful that she'd been acknowledged…had been validated…had been shown that she mattered. Her chestnut eyes misted as she beamed at me. Her face illuminated as if a spotlight shone upon it. We made a spiritual connection. My small gesture filled me with an intense feeling of well-being and physical warmth. Because when you conduct acts of kindness, peace will follow. Spreading peace *gives* you peace."

I took a sip of water, paused, and inhaled deeply. "Artists are empathic. As I paint, my thoughts are of that graceful beggar and many homeless folks I've encountered, who are mired in their social position for *our edification.* I paint pondering peace. That's how I create my Angels of Peace, with *pure intention…*well, pure intention and a little paint. This positive thinking is translated into the painting because thoughts are units of pure energy. There is enormous power in a single thought, so make sure it's positive! My mother taught me that. Sometimes, I'm in a trance while painting where I lose track of time and place. Painting for hours seems like a few minutes. And when I sit down and study the work, I'm surprised."

I talked briefly about the application of the twenty-three-karat gold leaf. I said there's an image in my book of *Madonna della Via*, with a Vatican angel overseeing the mendicant, which caused a stir of murmurs.

"In closing, I'll leave you with a quote from my book, *Weeping Angels.* Then we'll have time for a few questions and on to the book signing.

"Make yourself familiar with the angels and behold them

frequently in spirit. For without being seen, they are present with you. Saint Francis DeSales ."

Smiling, I scanned the audience and waved my two-finger hand signal. "Peace out."

* * *

The next day Joe whisked me away to the Metropolitan Museum. What a guy! On our feet for hours, we welcomed a chance to sit down for a lovely lunch in The Petrie Court Café with the stunning backdrop of Central Park for our viewing pleasure. After lunch, Joe said he had a surprise for me. He guided me to the gallery with Artemisia Gentileschi's painting, *"Esther before Ahasuerus."* It depicted the Jewish heroine swooning before the king. We sat on a wooden bench, studying the oil painting.

Joe said, "You know why she's fainting?"

I shrugged.

"Because he proposed!" he said as he reached into his tweed sport coat and pulled out a Robin's-egg blue velvet Tiffany's box. He didn't do the cheesy kneeling thing, just said, "Arté, I love you and want to marry you."

A classy proposal at the Met in front of my favorite artist's work. How romantic!

And without hesitation, I said, "Yes!"

He slipped the ring on my finger.

"So, you don't think we're too old for marriage?" I asked.

Joe kissed me, smiled, and whispered in my ear, "We have miles to go before we sleep."

TWENTY-NINE

L ily had called me and asked if I could take her to a prenatal appointment. As we waited for the doctor, I noticed information on the bulletin board for free birthing classes. Then Lily invited me into the examining room to watch the ultrasound. The P.A. prepared her by squeezing warm KY Jelly all over Lily's rounded bump and slid the wand around her slippery, swollen belly.

We watched the darkened monitor, which looked like a moonscape with a skeleton folded up like origami floating in the center. Lily clutched my arm as my hand covered my mouth in awe when we saw a miniature hand waving at us. *Waving! Like the Queen of England!*

"Do you want to know the gender?" the P.A. asked.

"Oh, yes! I think it's a girl," Lily said.

"Well, you're right." Then she pointed out that the baby had a lot of hair. "Everything looks good. Are you taking your prenatal vitamins?"

"Of course," Lily said, "every day."

I said to Lily, "I'd love to take you to the birthing classes. Hey, I could be your birth coach—if you'd like."

"You wouldn't mind doing that?" Lily asked.

"Are you kidding? This is so exciting. And I love babies. Just *love* them!"

* * *

So many thoughts swirled in my mind. I needed to carve out some time for heavy-duty research. I returned to my studio and fired up my Mac to learn about the hydro-fracking process of natural gas in New York State.

Wow! Hydro-fracking was a method whereby highly pressurized chemicals and water were pumped deep underground to break up Marcellus shale, which released the natural gas. The gas was then held in storage wells. Hmm, what kind of chemicals? How much water? Where would they get the water?

The pro-fracking camp could insist on the safety of fracking all day long, but it was the gas-holding wells, pipes, and seals that were problematic. From what I'd gleaned, the water supply was contaminated due to leaky pipes and seals in the storage well where methane leaked into the drinking water. Also it was responsible for explosions. Of course, this serious problem was directly related to fracking. Apparently the gas company has been well aware of the leakage situation. And get this— a long-range study had determined that fracking caused earthquakes!

I definitely fell into the anti-fracking category.

I had to question the so-called *safety reports* that Governor O'Shea constantly cited. I read them and the information was outdated, therefore, incorrect. The earthquake information wasn't even included.

The pro-fracking population argued that it was good for the local economy, while the anti-fracking gang said: *At what cost?* Contaminated drinking water? Earthquakes? High-traffic patterns of heavy equipment and eighteen-wheelers rolling through town all day long? Sky-rocketing rent for the gas-company employees, which would result in unaffordable rents for local residents? Our Pennsylvania neighbors did not have a good experience with the hydrofracking. There had been reports of crime rates spiking twenty to forty percent!

But, why was the Gov pushing so hard to allow the fracking in New York State weeks before his election? According to my research, most New Yorkers were against it. It didn't seem a political decision.

Curious about the actual amount of Marcellus shale in our area, I continued researching. It took awhile, but I discovered a website with maps of natural-gas deposits. *Holy crapballs!* My eyeballs almost sprang out of their sockets like Felix the cat. St. Anthony's campus was built on top of the largest, richest Marcellus shale deposit in all of New York State!

I printed several copies of the map.

Then called Joe Goodman.

"Joe! It's Arté. Can you meet me at my studio right now? It's urgent."

I put in a call to Mary and continued to research.

Fifteen minutes later Joe arrived at my studio. "What's up? You don't look so good."

"Have you talked to Sister X?"

"No, I was in surgery."

"She met with me and my mother and informed us St. Anthony's is closing—a government mandate from O'Shea's office."

He jerked his head as he hiked up his eyebrows. "When the hell was she going to tell the docs?"

I shrugged. "Guess she told the skilled-nursing residents first."

"What's going to happen to them?"

"Apparently, nobody knows that answer." I made air-quotation marks. "Said she'd *keep me informed.*"

I took a deep cleansing breath, trying to compose myself. "Sister X handed me a list of nursing-home options." I punched the paper with my fist. "These facilities are fifty or more miles away. I couldn't afford to visit Mamma every day like I do at St. Anthony's."

Joe raked his hands through his thick hair. "A government mandate is pretty final."

"I'm mad as hell," I spat, "and Mamma and I are fighting back."

He cast a sideways glance at me. "That sounds ominous. What're you two planning?"

I folded my arms. "A Sit-In." I nodded. "With a good old-fashioned dose of civil disobedience. Mamma and I are willing to go to jail to make our political statement. We could use your help with organizing the protest. I need you to solicit the doctors."

He bobbed his head. "I'm in."

I heaved a sigh and blew out a puff of air that lifted my bangs off my forehead. "I'm trying to figure out why the Gov acted so swiftly to close St. Anthony's *and* approve the fracking. It's related somehow."

"Yeah," Joe said, "what's the rush? I'd always heard rumors of St. Anthony's closing circulating around the hospital. Usually we'd have a huge fund-raiser and that'd save good old St. Tony's."

"O'Shea's actions seem like political suicide." I paced back and forth, biting my thumbnail. I couldn't reveal a bunch of dead nuns were feeding me hints like nuts to a squirrel. "Take a look at this," I said, handing him the map.

Joe let out a low whistle. "Now, this is a game changer. St. Anthony's land is worth a *friggin' fortune*. Nice work, Arté." He let out a frustrated sigh. "You know, New York State has the distinction of the most governmental officials to serve jail time."

I said, "We should print tee shirts, *New York State, Home of Political Jailbirds.* I could sell them from my studio."

Mary burst through the door like a gust of wind. "Arté, what's shakin'? Hiya, Doctor Goodman."

He nodded. "Call me Joe."

Mary studied us. "You two look like someone died."

I filled Mary in on everything. "Wicked Pissa! Half of

Verdant Valley will be without jobs—including me and George. Our local economy will go down the crapper. We're screwed."

"We can thank O'Shea for that," I said.

"I'm not voting for that moron," Mary said.

I snarled, "That political gasbag has the IQ of a can of *scungilli*."

Joe commented, "Arté, that's insulting to *scungilli*…what the hell is *scungilli*?"

"What if…the Gov," I said, stroking my chin, "doesn't want to get re-elected?"

"What are you talking about?" Mary asked, swaying back and forth like sea anemones, "the Chowddahead is running for office."

"Yeah. One would assume he'd be adamant about winning. But his actions belie that. Mamma always taught me : *Never Assume*. What if the Gov is doing all his dirty work now, while he has the power of his office?"

"That's an interesting take on O'Shea," Joe said.

"I better go and tell George about the closure," Mary said, "he'll be wicked pissed."

I hugged Mary. "Call you later. Tell everyone who participates in the protest that it must be peaceful. Non-violent."

After she left, I glanced at the paper with the nursing-home information. Damn! I would not do the ugly cry. Snot dripped out of my nose as my face contorted.

Joe handed me a Kleenex as he folded me into his arms. "We're going to beat this, Arté."

THIRTY

I had a restless night, expecting another visit from the drove of departed nuns. I never thought I'd say this, but wished they'd show up and tell me *exactly* what to do.

I needed to clear my addled head so I went to the "Y."

While lapping in the turquoise water, free-associating thoughts circled in my mind, as if my thoughts were swimming too. I tried to make sense of all my information.

Why would the Gov approve the fracking and shut down St. Anthony's so close to the election? Didn't make sense. Unless my hunch was correct and they were related…but how?…And why?

As I swam back and forth pushing off the ends of the pool, my flutter kicks became stronger. I propelled my body through the silky water faster than usual. Why the hell didn't Sister Ignatius tell me what was going on with the Gov and what to do about it? I wasn't a damn mind reader.

I stopped at the end of the pool to adjust my goggles. As I gave a strong push off the end, Sister Ignatius said, "I *did* tell you what to do. I said to look closely at me bible. And watch your language!"

I sucked in a mouth full of liquid, coughed, and aspirated the water. Had to grasp the ledge of the pool so I wouldn't go under. I choked, gagging and retching. Chlorine burned my lungs as I sucked in ragged breaths. She knew what I was *thinking!* Glancing around at the other swimmers, I realized they couldn't see a dead nun—soaking wet in a long habit and veil—talking to me.

"I'll say it again. Look closely at me bible," Sister Ignatius instructed, as she flipped over on her back like a killer whale, back-stroked to the opposite end of the pool...and disappeared into water droplets.

I hopped out of the pool—wheezing and fighting for air. Then I showered, dressed, and headed back to my studio to locate the bible. Didn't even stop for coffee.

* * *

Where had I placed the bible? Rooting around my bookcase, I found it among my art books. Inside of the front cover, in beautiful Palmer-method script, I read : *To our beloved daughter, Molly O'Shea, commemorating her entrance into the convent. May God bless you. With much love, Mother and Father.*

I welled up with awe. Sister Ignatius's bible! I held a relic of a saint. I handled the same book from which Sister Ignatius had prayed. The special tome included a section that was also a missal for the Latin Mass. She must've used it every day. Why would Sister Ignatius have left this important book behind?... at the river cottage? Surely it would have been given to a family member or housed at St. Anthony's in the display cabinet in the lobby along with the other artifacts. I thought of manifest destiny and wondered if *all* of this had been preordained? Was I meant to come along after Sister Ignatius in order to find this holy book for the purpose of saving St. Anthony's? Was that why zombie nuns were scaring the bejeezus out of me? Had Mamma Mia been fated to have trained with Sister Ignatius and to have worked there...and end up living at St. Anthony's? And what about Joe and me? Had our meeting been predestined?

My head hurt.

The gilded-edged paper of the bible smelled like faded incense. As I slowly turned each tissue-thin page, I found holy cards from funerals tucked inside the thick book. Dr. Eamon Rooney's funeral card tumbled out with an image of St. Anthony on the front and a rendering of a Celtic cross and a prayer for Dr. Rooney's soul on the back.

Along with the prayer card was a pressed faded-red rose—probably from his burial bouquet. Misty-eyed, I recited the intercession for Dr. Rooney.

I chanted some of the lyrical Latin Mass, recalling my childhood and yearning for my stolen religion. Having learned the Latin Mass in Catholic grade school, I remembered the meaning of every word. The poetic cadence of the ancient language mesmerized me just like Gregorian chant, which I still listened to while painting my Angels of Peace.

In the center of the bible, marking the Offertory of the Mass, was a folded onion-skin paper. I carefully opened it. The heading read *Land Lease*. Dated January 1, 1908, it was written with a fountain pen, with a few drips of black ink staining the document.

I, Seamus O'Shea, brother of Patrick O'Shea and uncle of Molly O'Shea, do hereby gift to Molly O'Shea my land in Verdant Valley, New York on which St. Anthony's Hospital is built. This said gift is in the form of a Land Lease for 101 years. In the event St. Anthony's Hospital is not successful, my land will revert back to the O'Shea family. However, in the event St. Anthony's Hospital is successful, after 101 years, said land will be given, free and clear, to St. Anthony's Hospital and the Sisterhood which operates it.

May God bless you in your charitable work.

Seamus O'Shea and Robert Bird, Barrister-At-Law

So, what did this mean? Surely, this was what Sister Ignatius wanted me to find. But what should I do next? What was a Land Lease? I turned to my computer to find out.

I learned that a Land Lease was a real estate agreement in which the land was owned by one party and the actual building on that land was owned by another party who rented the land. In other words, the building owner did not own the land on which their building existed. Was the O'Shea Land Lease for 101 years because they wanted to keep the land in the family? I'd share this information with Joe. Hmm, since this was a legal document, we would need an attorney. I know Joe'd help us.

So, this was in Sister Ignatius's bible. The document looked like it was original…Was there another copy of this letter? Would this have been recorded in the Hall of Records?

* * *

Even though I had an enormous amount of work to do in organizing our upcoming Sit-In, I trekked to the City Hall of Records downtown.

I searched for a few hours, but couldn't find anything. Finally, I asked the bleached-blond young clerk sitting behind the desk to help me. She sported a tight pencil-skirt and a taut, low, V-neck sweater. Whoa! *Those* had to be implants—if she wasn't careful, she'd poke someone's eye out. Looked like Madonna's breast-cones. She sat crossed legged, swinging her foot and filing her nails with an emery board.

I smiled. "Excuse me. I've been looking for a Land Lease, dated 1908, for St. Anthony's Hospital. Could you help me?"

"Oh, yes. That particular document," she said, chomping on a wad of gum, "is on loan to Governor O'Shea. He borrowed it for a family history book he was working on."

I jerked my head. *Borrowed?* Documents weren't allowed to be taken from the Hall of Records. Fishing for information, I said, "Boy, he's a terrific governor." Then trying not to gag on my words, I continued. "He sure has my vote!"

"Me too!" she said overly excited, like she'd been invited to the prom, as she stood and ironed the wrinkles out of her skirt with her hand. "Normally, I'd never let a document out of the building, but...after all, he *is* the *governor* of New York State." She extended both hands, palms up. "What could go wrong?" Teetering on her stilettoes, she leaned in, conspiratorially, and whispered, "And he's so handsome! Could be Alec Baldwin's twin."

"Ya don't say!" Wow! He was *that good*. And she believed he'd return the document! What a sucker. She must have the IQ of a Cheez-It. Probably would lose her job.

So, the Gov believed he had the only copy of the Land Lease and no one could piece together his scheme to take St. Anthony's rich land. Well now, he hadn't counted on a posse of dead nuns, had he?

THIRTY-ONE

I called Joe. "I need your help, again."

Joe Goodman entered my studio, sauntered over, and planted an Al and Tipper Gore-kiss on me. Thought he might suck my lips off. After he left me in a melted heap, he tipped an imaginary cowboy hat and said in a perfect John Wayne voice, "Pardon me, Ma'am, I had a powerful hankerin' to do that."

My fingers stroked my swollen lips, which tingled with pleasure from the seismic smooch. I kissed him back as if I were a starving dog and he had gravy smeared all over his mouth. I pulled myself away, brushed my hair back, and straightened my blouse.

"What's up, Arté?"

"I forgot ..." I said, completely flummoxed. "Okay. We'll have to ignore the sexual tension. We have a lot of work to do." I grinned. "We can make out later." *Make out!* What was I, in high school?

Grinning, he said, "If I told you that you have a beautiful body, would you hold it against me?"

"Later, Cowboy!" I put an arm's length between us. "Seriously, here's what I've discovered." I filled him in.

Joe read the letter from Seamus O'Shea. "Is this the only copy?"

"That's my guess."

"Is he next in line to inherit the land?" he asked.

"Don't know, but I aim to find out."

Joe studied the document again and his eyes widened. "What if that *bastard* has St. Anthony's demolished?"

I shuddered. "If that happened, he'd probably wait until all's clear and no one would connect the dots. Then he'd collect the mineral rights and become a multi-billionaire. Or... have a third party do his dirty work."

"You believe he's that crooked?"

"*Ah...yee-ah!* He's a *politician.*" I spat the word out as if it were poison that left a bad taste. "I'm also guessing he doesn't know about the letter I found in Sister Ignatius's bible." I paced back and forth. "This is really complicated. With this new information and the upcoming Sit-In, we'd better lawyer-up."

"Don't worry about it. That'll be my contribution—don't forget I have a high stake in this too. Don't want to lose my job." He furrowed his brow. "You know, if you're right about him, he would be committing a crime—it's illegal to use your political office for personal gain."

I nodded. "Correct. And look at the harm he'd do to V.V.— 1,000 jobs lost!" I balled both of my fists. "I will *not* let him kick my mother out of her home! And another thing—who'd heal the poor? No other hospital is like ours. St. Anthony's is ruled by the hand of God."

Joe smiled. "That's a beautiful way to describe St Tony's"

I glanced at my watch. "Gotta go. Promised Mamma Mia I'd help with the protest signs." I waited a beat. "Oh, who am I kidding? Have to make sure Mamma doesn't incite a riot with her cronies."

Chuckling, Joe said, "It's never dull around the Credo dames."

* * *

Kathleen Huddle

"Hee-hee whoo! Hee-hee whoo!" Lily and I practiced the Lamaze breathing technique in the birthing class. She was stretched out on my yoga mat with pillows supporting her bent knees. I had one hand on her abdomen, counting the breaths. I enjoyed spending time with Lily, who tried to act brave, but was frightened of the unknown. At least now she'd be prepared.

I found the classes fascinating, especially the breastfeeding section, which is an art! I always figured nursing a newborn came naturally and automatically. *Who knew?*

Spellbound, we viewed the birth videos.

Lily spouted, *"Eew-yoo!"* every few minutes. When the placenta delivered, she turned to me and asked, "Is that her liver?" Then she saw the umbilical cord, she asked, "What *is* that? An alien?" The C-section video was next and Lily turned lime-green, gagged, and covered her eyes with her hands. "*Yuck!* I'm going to toss my cookies!"

We learned about HypnoBirthing, the Bradley Method to help avoid pain, and the ever-popular epidural—the pregnant woman's best friend. Lily said she was determined to give birth naturally. I had my doubts.

We toured the labor and delivery room and the nursery. Lily practiced bathing the squishy life-sized baby doll and was proficient in diapering. She proposed a contest to see who could diaper faster. I practiced too because I planned on helping Lily care for the baby.

THIRTY-TWO

I bumped into Mary on the elevator at St. Anthony's. "Mare. I was about to call you. I need George's help on some Internet research. Ask him to find out if Governor Scanlon O'Shea is next in line to inherit the O'Shea estate. Have to know before the Sit-In."

"When's the Sit-In?"

"Saturday."

"Saddadee?"

I smiled at her charming Boston accent. "We're meeting in the cafeteria…*Saddadee* at 9. I need to go over some important aspects of the Sit-In. It must be non-violent, organized, and orderly."

"Gotcha. I'll have George get on the research and let ya know ASAP."

I handed Mary a stack of posters. "Could you hang these all over the hospital? One on each floor by the elevators, in all the break-rooms, bathrooms, and cafeteria. They explain everything about the protest."

"Will do."

"Thanks. Now listen. Mamma and I are going to serve jail time to make our point crystal clear."

Mary's over-penciled eyebrows shot straight up. "Get out!…the Sit-In will send a strong enough message. Sure you wanna do that?"

The elevator stopped at Mamma's floor and we exited. *"Oooh yeah!* This is personal. Mamma and I are on a mission. We're mad as hell. I've uncovered damaging information on the Gov." I glanced left, then right, and whispered, "He's a crook, but I can't talk here."

"Whoa! Ya better be careful. I don't trust that Chowddahead."

We walked down the hall and stood in front of the door to the arts and crafts room on the skilled-nursing floor. "I'll be fine. I don't expect anyone else to go to jail. Don't know how long the sentence will be so I need to call in a big favor."

"Anything for you. You know that."

"Take my key—it fits the studio and my apartment. Please take good care of Merlin. I have plenty of cat food in the kitchen and lots of kitty litter." I tucked a long strand of hair behind my ear. "Now, he hacks up some mega hairballs—don't be alarmed. The first time I saw my Fuzzy Buddy retching a hairball, thought he was dying...I'm afraid you'll have to scoop his poop. Hope you don't mind."

"Nah," she said waving her hand, "what's a little poop between friends?"

I smiled. "Thanks. I'm in a time crunch here. Have to pick up Mamma's meds for our jail time...remember, it's vital that George finds out that info on O'Shea. Oh, and don't tell me over the phone—better come to the studio to let me know."

"Jeez, Arté, this is beginning ta sound like a mystery movie. Where ya goin' now?"

"Have to check on Mamma—she's holding a rally with her geriatric gang. They're probably planning to tar and feather O'Shea."

* * *

I slipped into the back of the arts and crafts room and watched Mamma in action. The room was packed with elderly residents of St. Anthony's in various stages of mobility. Some were leaning on their walkers, some propped up by their canes, and a few in wheelchairs.

Strapped into her wheelchair, Lola inched her way into the room carrying her shopping bag and wearing multi strands of faux pearls around her wrinkled neck. "Out of my way! I'm late for Bloomingdale's big sale." Tess, Mamma's wingwoman, slid her walker with its neon green- tennis balls attached to the bottom over next to her. She backed up to a chair and plopped down with a huff.

Mr. Gomer, who had a crush on Mamma, sat next to her—a little too close, if you asked me.

Mamma slowly pried herself out of her wheelchair and hobbled to the front of the room with the aid of her four-pronged cane. She cried out, "Hail, hail, the gang's all here." Everyone cheered. "We all need to come together to *fight*," she said, as she pounded her flattened hand with her fist, "to save our home here at St. Anthony's. If we don't, we'll be scattered—*like garbage*—all over the state in nursing facilities."

Loud cries of indignation filled the room.

Mamma continued, "Now, I wanna know if you're gonna set sail on this ship with me...or wave from the shore?"

Gomer hopped up, saluted, and said, "Aye, aye, Captain!"

Mamma nodded. "If O'Shea thinks we're *too old* to fight back, he can think again. We've already collected over 3,000 signatures to keep St. Anthony's open. *Ha!* That's just the beginning. We may be at the end stages of our lives, but we have plenty of fight left in us."

Shouts of *"you betcha"* and *"damn straight"* rang out.

"So," Mamma said, "let's start by thinking of strong slogans for our protest signs."

Tess's eyes glistened. *"We may be gray, but we have plenty to say!"*

"Good one, Tessie." Mamma did a fist pump. *"Hell no, we won't go!"*

The geriatric group applauded.

Gomer placed his thumb and index finger in his toothless mouth and let out a loud whistle accompanied by a shower of spit. Then he shouted, *"We may be old, but we're still bold!"*

"Right on, Brother," Tess hollered in her gravely voice.

I took notes, recording their war cries, which sprang from their mouths like jewels.

Mrs. Mucci cupped her hands around her mouth and shouted in her horse voice, *"Hey, Governor, you think I'm an old goat? Well, I still know how to vote!"*

"Molto bene! Theresa." Mamma nodded. She narrowed her dark mahogany eyes and flashed her *Il Malocchio* sign. *"If you take away my home, you'll need Mercurochrome!"*

Gomer grabbed a nearby bedpan and beat it like a drum. His buddy, Jack O'Keefe, whose snow-white hair stood up in a cowlick, snatched an emesis basin and banged it with his cane. Polinski, the third Musketeer, rubbed his bald head for good luck and let out a roar. Tess took a rubber glove from the drawer and snapped it back like a sling-shot and laughed as it sailed across the room.

The crowd chanted, *"Hell no, we won't go!"*

Things quickly got out of control, like a teacher-less study hall. I sprang from my seat. "Ladies and gentlemen, I must remind you. This is to be a *peaceful* protest. *Non-violent!"*

I started up the coffee-maker and heated water for tea, then assisted the group in making their protest signs. I must admit, their slogans were excellent—sharp-witted and straight to the point.

* * *

Later that evening, Joe and Mary met me at my studio. We ordered pizza and snacks.

Mary handed me a print-out on the information about Governor O'Shea's inheritance. Just as I'd expected, he would inherit all the land St. Anthony's was built upon. And the mineral rights too.

Mary glanced at me, then Joe, and back to me. "What's up?"

"I did an extensive search on all the Marcellus shale deposits in New York State. Guess where the richest gas deposits in the entire state are? Right under St. Anthony's Hospital!"

Mary wrinkled her nose as she shrugged. "I don't get it."

"Nobody was supposed to get it! Look what O'Shea has been doing," I said, counting my fingers, "he *approved* the hydro-fracking, he's *about to close St. Anthony's,* he *stole* the document from the Hall of Records, and," I waved the latest information, "this *proves* he's a crook! You don't have to paint me a picture!"

"That *bha-staad!*" Mary said.

Joe leaned against the counter, tapping his fingers on the countertop.

"There's more," I commented.

"*More!* Hasn't that Craphead done enough?" Mary asked.

"I discovered a hand-written document from 1908 that could save St. Anthony's and put the Gov behind bars."

"How the hell did you find that?" Mary asked.

"As Mamma would say, *'By the grace of God.'"* If you thought I would divulge my dead nun source, you'd be mistaken.

"Does O'Shea know any of this?" Mary rocked back and forth like a metronome.

"Not yet. I have to figure a way to publicly expose him. You know how the political crooks operate—they're powerful machines that crush anyone in their way.

Joe commented, "Arté, the term *political crook* is redundant."

"Well, he's already tried to demonize me."

"But it backfired. You better be careful." Mary's eyes widened. "He might try to *off* you!"

The pizza-delivery guy knocked and Mary jumped. She

pulled a black comb out of her pocket and taking a defensive stance, held it like a gun. With arms extended straight and both hands on the comb, she said, "Don't' cha worry, Arté, I got'cha covered."

"Mary. That's a comb."

"The *perp* doesn't know that. I don't want ya to end up a *vic*."

"Uh…perhaps you've been watching too many episodes of *Blue Bloods.*"

Joe chuckled. "Open the door. I'm starving."

Our meeting broke up a few hours later when Joe got called to the operating room.

* * *

The ring of the phone startled me at 2:18 AM. Shaking from the loud ringing, I groped for the receiver.

Lily's raw voice said, *"Houston, we have a problem!* It's D-day—my water broke."

"Are you sure?"

"Yep. I'm standing in a puddle."

"Where's your father?"

"He's operating. There was a terrible car accident. He's doing surgery on a mother and her child. I hope they'll be okay."

"Any contractions?"

*"*No, the mother wasn't pregnant."

"Lily. Focus! Remember what we learned in the birthing classes? Do you feel a sharp tightening across your belly?"

"Uh-huh."

"Listen carefully. Unlock your front door and sit down. I'll be there in ten minutes."

* * *

I grabbed my labor bag packed with lollipops, a tennis

ball, small pillow, lavender lotion, and lip balm as I dashed out the door. Merlin looked confused. "I'll fill you in later, Fuzzy Buddy."

* * *

Lily was admitted and the nurse sent word to Joe in the operating room. "Tell him not to worry," I said, "I've got this covered."

I changed into the soft cotton scrubs and took my position by Lily's bedside, as she twisted and turned in pain. I reviewed the Lamaze breathing with Lily.

A few hours later, Joe bounded through the door and went straight to Lily, stroking her thick mane of curls.

Lily said, "Don't worry, Dad. I'm a tough chick."

I turned to reach into the labor bag for a root beer lollipop for Lily and bounced off Sister Ignatius. One minute the space was empty and the next, a dead nun standing there like a linebacker. Why was she here? I lost my balance and Joe steadied me.

"Guess I'm not the only nervous one." He studied my face. "You okay? You're shaking," he said as he squeezed my hand.

Wishing that dead nun wouldn't sneak up on me, I took in a deep breath and said, "Everything is going to be fine. Lily's doing an amazing job."

Lily was calm and almost Zen-like. She was dilated five centimeters and handled the contractions.

As Lily's cervix continued to dilate, she rocked and twisted in bed. No dramatics at all—just writhing and grimacing. Joe paced back and forth and I thought he'd wear a hole in the vinyl floor. I coached Lily through the rough patches. I was mindful of referring to the pain as *contractions* as I rolled the tennis ball over the small of her back to soothe the tight muscles.

The nurse examined Lily and said she was progressing nicely. She suggested a warm bath to help with the pain because

Lily had refused all medications. We'd learned about the bath in our birthing classes and Lily said she'd try it. Joe stepped outside to get some fresh air. I ran the water and helped her into the oversized tub.

"Ahh!" Lily said, as she eased into the warm water, *"Calgon, take me away!"* Then her face contorted and she rubbed the sides of her swollen belly. A tiny foot tented against her abdomen.

"You're doing the most amazing job!" I said. "You're stoic."

Huffing and puffing, she said, "I'm so thirsty."

I handed her a blue plastic cup filled with ice chips.

She crunched on the ice and swallowed hard. "I'm going to blow chunks!"

I snatched the wastebasket and she filled it.

"Ugh! Shouldn't have eaten that Chinese food," Lily said.

Retching from the miasma of the vomit, I helped her out of the tub and dried her off. I rubbed lavender lotion all over her, thinking it would help relax her. Rubbed some on my wrists too. Lily shook uncontrollably. I slipped her gown on, wrapped her in the towel, and called for the nurse—who was busy with two other deliveries—to help me get Lily back into bed. When she saw her shaking, the nurse pulled a cotton blanket out of the warming closet and shrouded Lily, who smiled and thanked her.

Again, Lily refused pain medication and the epidural. "I am delivering my baby without drugs. They're bad for my baby."

"But, an epidural would be okay. Pretty soon, there'll be a point of no return and they won't be able to give an epidural—remember, we learned that in class?" I said, rubbing her arm.

"No...drugs!" Lily vomited again.

I sent for Joe, who ran into the room.

Lily was severely dehydrated and they administered an IV with anti-vomiting medicine.

An hour later, Lily roiled in pain. No theatrical screaming, just quiet, elegant moaning.

The baby's head crowned. The fetal heart monitor made strange noises. Joe panicked.

Sister Ignatius stood by Lily's head and made the sign-of-the-cross.

I froze.

The doctor, calmly and silently, reached in and unwrapped the umbilical cord from the baby's neck. The baby's face was dark blue. Joe and I clutched each other.

The doctor instructed Lily to push hard. The nurse and I held Lily's trembling legs.

"I can't...push any...harder," Lily whispered.

The nurse helped by compressing Lily's abdomen.

Reminding Lily of the breathing techniques, I panted with her. "Okay, deep, deep breath. Ready for the big, hard push." I pushed right along with Lily—it was a wonder I didn't deliver something. The doctor rotated the baby's head and shoulders, coaxing it out.

"One more push. *Bear down!*" the doctor yelled.

To my wonderment, from her dark, cozy cave, a baby girl slid right out into the world! They suctioned the baby's mouth and her dusky complexion turned rosy pink. They placed two clamps on the umbilical cord and handed the surgical scissors to Joe. "The honor is yours, Grandpa." When the baby cried, I offered a prayer of thanksgiving. The newborn was wide-eyed and alert. Lily, true to her belief, had delivered her baby drug-free. Joe said that was why the infant was so keen and bright. The nurse cleaned some cheesy stuff off the baby, wrapped her in a warm blanket, and placed her on Lily's chest. Joe leaned in close to inspect his new granddaughter while the surgeon stitched Lily.

Lily, laughing through her tears, said, "Dad, meet Jo-Jo."

Dabbing each other's tears, Joe and I smiled. The exceptional gift of witnessing Jo-Jo's birth was the highest honor of my life.

We were so enamored with our new baby, we didn't notice the surgeon sponging up copious amounts of blood. Lily's monitor made a frightening noise. Joe snapped out of his reverie.

Lily's eyelids fluttered. Her lips were a strange pale lavender and she looked waxy-white. Joe's color wasn't too pink either.

Lily was rushed to the operating room to stop the hemorrhaging.

Joe said, "I'm going with Lily." Because he was on staff, Joe was allowed into the operating theatre.

* * *

We almost lost Lily. I camped out in the surgical waiting room. Stretched out on the brown pleather sofa, I tried not to worry about her. Even though we hadn't known each other long, I felt motherly towards her and I sensed her need for a mother—probably why we connected quickly and deeply.

Hours later, Joe ambled through the door and slumped on the sofa. "Lily finally stabilized. A birth and a near death all in one night!" He hung his head and wept. I held him, rubbing his arm with the fresh bandage, a vestige of his blood donation to his only child.

THIRTY-THREE

I prepared for our jail time and had Mamma's medicine and asthma inhaler in a large zip-lock plastic bag. We dressed in warm layers, as I knew the jail cells would be drafty. I wore a poncho to use as an extra blanket for my mother. I left my cell phone home and carried a TracFone—didn't want my real phone confiscated with all my photos and personal data. I had bottled water, lip balm, Sister Ignatius's St. Anthony medal, and Mamma always traveled with her rosary. We were all set.

Our group of insurgents met in St. Anthony's cafeteria. Joe had been kind enough to spring for doughnuts and coffee for everyone. I was quite relieved when Joe showed up with his lawyer.

I addressed the crowd and began with a prayer to St. Anthony: *"St Anthony, patron saint of this hospital and finder of lost things, grant us wisdom and guide us in finding a peaceful and successful solution to save St. Anthony's Hospital."*

Then I said, "Good morning. First, let me remind everyone this is to be a *peaceful* and *orderly* demonstration. Thank you in advance for your cooperation. As a group, we'll exit the hospital by the back door, march slowly around the hospital, and end up in the Divine Street parking lot." Scanning the room, I saw nods of understanding. "My mother, Loretta Credo— "
Gomer cheered as if he were at a football game and his chums,

O'Keefe and Polinski, egged him on. If my eyes had been out-fitted with lasers, Gomer would have a huge hole in his middle. "As I was saying, my mother and I will represent the entire group. So, when asked to move along by a police officer, please do so quickly and quietly." I glared at Gomer.

Mamma thumped her cane on the floor and yelled, *"Capisce?"*

There were some rumblings from the elderly mavericks.

"We expect the media to arrive—the newspaper and TV re-porters. Mamma and I have prepared our statements and will speak for the group, which will result in the coverage we desire. Rest assured, we will make certain the media understands it is *not* okay to kick skilled-nursing residents out of their *homes*."

That last remark set off shouting and whistles from the golden-agers. It was a spark in a bone-dry forest. I became more worried about our outcome. "Please. Settle down," I cried, flat-tening my hands and pumping the air. "My mother and I are prepared to serve jail time, but we *do not* want anyone else to do so. Is that *crystal clear*? We must be on our very best behavior. We need to present ourselves as good, law-abiding citizens—worthy of respect. Questions?"

Gomer's arthritic hand shot straight up. "What if a copper hits me over my head with a billy-club? Then can I clobber him?"

I shot a glance at Joe, who inspected his feet as he scratched the back of his neck.

"No!...no, Mr. Gomer, you may *not*." Oh great! Just what I needed—a loose cannon. "An officer of the law would not hit an elderly gentleman—*unprovoked.* Each of us is account-able for our actions. The police are not our enemies. Remember, there will be cameras recording everything. Do we understand each other, Mr. Gomer?"

"Yes, Ma'am." He nudged O'Keefe and Polinski.

Tess waved. "Don't expect me to be ladylike when I express

myself. That sumabitch is trying to kick me out of my home. Who the hell does he think he is? A *dic*tator?…Well, he's got the first part right."

I drew in a sharp breath. "We have to outsmart the governor at his own game. To be effective, we must be respectful. Good luck and peace out."

Outside, I assigned our positions. Leading the march were the present-day nuns who worked at St. Anthony's. Sister Xavier, tall and broad-shouldered, carried a sign which read, *Crusaders For St. Anthony's Hospital.* Another nun's poster proclaimed *Fighting A Holy War For St. Anthony's.* In a show of solidarity for the founding nuns, they wore the old-fashioned, long, black and white habits as they carried my second painting of the seven original sisters, which made for a strong graphic.

Mamma and I trekked with the nuns as I pushed Mamma's wheelchair along with pride. My mother's four-pronged cane rested on her lap as she held her *Hell No, We Won't Go!* sign. The side pockets of Mamma's chair bulged with small packets of Loorna Doones. I tucked in her afghan around her legs to ward off the brisk air.

Behind us, the aging residents of the skilled-nursing floor paraded with passion. Tess was strong enough to roll her walker along. Her protest sign: *Governor O'Shea Will Have Hell To Pay!* was taped to the front of her walker.

Lola, strapped securely to her wheelchair, inched her way, taking baby steps with her feet, adding to the poignancy of the protest. She probably thought she was finally going shopping at Bloomingdale's.

There marched Gomer, O'Keefe, and Polinski, like the three stooges. Gomer pumped his sign—*We Will Fight For What's Right!*—up and down. His buddy, Jack O'Keefe, with his ruddy complexion and snow-white hair, blew his red nose. His son had provided him with whiskey. He passed a brown bag to Gomer and Polinski and the rough riders cackled as they took long hits from it. The cortège of curmudgeons readied for battle. They didn't look frail or broken. To the contrary, they looked as if they could slay a dragon.

Proceeding behind the elderly were the doctors and nurses, outfitted in their blue scrub suits. They were followed by an infantry of St. Anthony employees. Mary, George and Johnny Mae locked arms as they marched. Johnny Mae wore her braids piled high on her head secured in a bright yellow turban which matched her caftan. As she strode, a voodoo necklace with a likeness of Governor O'Shea pierced with pins swayed on her chest. I'd arranged to have John Lennon's *"Power to the People"* broadcasted through the loud speakers and our cavalcade loudly chanted along.

I glanced up at the roof of St. Anthony's. The seven founding nuns, stationed like gargoyles, protected and oversaw our protest. The pack of nuns were spring-loaded, ready to pounce like cougars.

A large crowd—three hundred or more—had gathered. My pulse quickened when I spotted the TV cameras. I geared up for my least-favorite activity—public speaking, but this protest wasn't about my insecurities. I shifted my thinking to: This is an opportunity to publicly expose a crook. How enjoyable will that be? Let me count the ways!

The TV news reporter interviewed me. The glamorous young woman had perfectly arched eyebrows, veneered teeth, and wore a bold onyx and silver statement necklace. I guessed the boobs were fake too. In her phony voice she asked, "What's your name and why are you protesting?"

"My name is Artemisia Credo and my mother, Loretta Credo, is a long-time resident on the skilled-nursing floor here at St. Anthony's. It is her *home*. Governor Scanlon O'Shea has ordered St. Anthony's Hospital to be closed. Not only will that put 1,000 people out of work and ruin the economy of Verdant

Valley, it will evict the elderly residents, many of whom have lived here for years, out of their homes."

I peered directly into the camera as the whiz of the camera lens moved in for an extreme close up. I hitched my right eyebrow upward. "It is *not* okay with me for Governor O'Shea to *kick* my eighty-nine-year-old mother out of her home. And I question if the governor's decision is for the greater good of Verdant Valley."

Eyebrows raised, she said, "Explain."

"I have reason to wonder if Governor O'Shea is closing St. Anthony's Hospital for his personal gain."

"How so?"

"Let me be clear as cellophane. I am not accusing the governor of anything—I'll leave that to the investigative reporters and pundits. But, Governor O'Shea needs to explain the conflict of interest in closing St. Anthony's *and* approving the hydro-fracking in our state, *since* he owns the land—*and mineral rights*—that St. Anthony's Hospital is built upon. According to my research, St. Anthony's Hospital sits upon the richest Marcellus-shale deposit in all of New York State."

The reporter jerked her head. "You're making damaging claims. Can you prove them?"

"I am asking for an explanation from Governor O'Shea. I have in my possession a document proving the governor is poised to take possession of all the rich land upon which St. Anthony's is built."

I glanced at the growing crowd and then at the reporter. "May I ask you a question?"

She widened her eyes. "Of course."

"Isn't it illegal to use public office for personal financial gain?"

"Why, yes. It is."

I let the reporter's affirmative answer hang heavy in the air, like a fifty-pound weight.

Across the street my mother sat parked in her wheelchair next to the podium.

The protest had become organic.

The crowd swelled and the noise magnified, as if we were at a raucous political convention.

Gomer, O'Keefe, and Polinski passed the brown-paper bag back and forth.

Excusing myself and thanking the reporter for her time, I prayed she'd air the entire interview because I'd parsed my words to publicly expose O'Shea.

I sprinted across the street to Mamma and Gomer in time to hear him say, "Don't worry, Loretta, I'll protect you. I have a sock full of quarters in my pocket and I'll clobber any copper who tries to move your wheelchair."

Mamma Mia eyed his pocket. "I wondered what that bulge was. Thought you took Viagra."

"*Whoa!*" I said, "pump the brakes on that."

I signaled to Mary's husband to turn off the music because it was time for our speeches. "Mamma, I'll go first and save you for last. We'll end on a strong note."

"*Va bene,*" Mamma said.

"Are you ready?" I said as I squeezed her hand.

She nodded. "*Andiamo!*"

Sister X wanted to say a few words and snatched the microphone. She clutched it and slung her salvo. "Governor O'Shea, if you think a stolen kiss in the archive room gives you the right to close down St. Anthony's Hospital, you are sadly mistaken. *I am a nun!*"

Man, I didn't see that coming. A rumbling murmur arose from the crowd.

I stepped up to the podium. " Thank you, Sister Xavier. All of you who work at St. Anthony's know how extraordinary this hospital is." The crowd roared like a mythic beast. "I believe St. Anthony's skilled-nursing unit is the finest in the state."

Mamma's geriatric gang cheered as Gomer whistled loudly through his gums. "The residents who live on the skilled-nursing floor love their home and consider each other as family members."

"Damn straight!" Tess hollered.

"St. Anthony's Hospital has been a beacon of hope in our community for one hundred years. It was founded by Doctor Eamon Rooney and seven sisters of charity who worked tirelessly to care for the poor, which is the mission statement of the hospital."

The throng grew quiet and hung onto every word.

"Many times over, St. Anthony's was on the verge of closing, but *miraculously*, it always prevailed. St. Anthony's Hospital is *scrappy*—like Sister Ignatius, the first administrator and the other nuns who first operated the hospital."

Atop the hospital's roof, the seven hooded specters pumped their fists.

"St. Anthony's has survived the first world war, the flu pandemic, two major floods, the second world war, the polio epidemic, and endless financial crises…St. Anthony's has stood strong for a century. The sheer determination of the nuns coupled with massive fund-raising has kept St. Anthony's running. Everyone present and everyone watching on TV must question Governor O'Shea as to why he has ordered the closure of St. Anthony's Hospital."

The crowd became restless. People were moving around and talking.

"We are here today to say: It is *not* okay to close St. Anthony's Hospital! And it is *not* right to kick these senior citizens out of their homes!"

The mob went a little crazy as it roared like the ocean.

Gomer screamed, "Hell no, we won't go!"

Jeez, I thought he might burst an artery.

"Here's what I know for sure: We, who are gathered here

today, are *mandated* to protect St. Anthony's Hospital. To Governor O'Shea, know this: We place you on notice—we will use the full measure of our voting power to vote you out of office."

The TV camera turned to cover the crowd and then back to me. "Governor O'Shea, do the right thing."

My mother led the chant, "Down with O'Shea, He'll have hell to pay!"

I held up my hands to quiet the demonstrators. "Now my eighty-nine-year-old mother, Loretta Credo, will speak."

Mamma Mia slowly extracted herself out of her wheelchair. She grasped her quad-cane and dramatically thumped up to the microphone, milking the scene like a dairy farmer yanking on udders. "I may be gray, but I have plenty to say."

Gomer yelled, "Give 'em hell, Loretta."

"If Governor O'Shea thinks we're a bunch of dumb bunnies living on the skilled-nursing floor at St. Anthony's, he needs to think again. We've got your number, Governor, and we know how to vote!" My mother addressed the right, middle, and left of the audience like a skilled politician. "My mind is sharp as a machete! Still can recall my Latin, which I learned in high school. *Acta non verba*—actions not words. That's what we're doing right this minute…and we took action when we collected over 3,000 signatures in favor of saving St. Anthony's."

Tess hollered, "Power to the people!"

"Let me tell you something," Mamma said, as she squinted while wagging her index finger, "I do not tolerate bullies. When I was a young schoolgirl, a big bully picked on the entire class and no one dared to stand up to him. One day he snatched my new beret right off my head. My mother had worked so hard to make it for me. He threw it down a steep embankment into the creek and I watched it flow away to the river. And something in me *snapped!*" She clicked her fingers together into the microphone.

The TV camera moved in tight on my mother's expressive face. That cameraman knew drama when he saw it.

"I took off running after the big bully, tackled him, and beat him to a pulp—his face looked like raw hamburger. We rolled down the embankment. I pounded him at the top of the hill. I pounded him as we rolled down the hill. I pounded him at the bottom of the hill. I beat the *stuffing* out of him as my classmates cheered me on. I felt like Julius Caesar! He never expected anyone to challenge him and I took him by surprise. After that banner day, the big bully showed me respect...or was it fear?" Her eyes glistened.

"I have paid a lifetime of taxes and now Governor O'Shea wants to *displace me?* Not without a fight!" She wagged her gnarled index finger at the camera. "The government is supposed to be *for* the people and *by* the people. O'Shea, you work for *me,*" she said, thumping her chest.

"We, the people, are saying in one *loud* voice : Do *not* close our St. Anthony's Hospital and do *not* kick us out of our homes!" My mother tapped the podium with every word. "I fought a big bully once at the beginning of my lifetime. Now I'm eighty-nine-years-old—towards the end of my life—and I'm fighting a big bully named Governor Scanlon O'Shea." Mamma peered through narrowed eyes squarely into the camera lens. "And here's what: I have one great fight left in me ...and let me tell you, it's a *lulu*...I mean a *real doozy!"*

The rebels clapped and yelled as I helped Mamma into her wheelchair. "Great job, Mamma Mia," I said as I kissed her soft cheek.

Mary's husband, George, turned up John Lennon's "Power to the People," as the scene became electrified. The golden-agers pumped their signs up and down. Gomer, O'Keefe, and Polinski had two fingers of whiskey left, which they didn't bother to hide in the brown paper-bag.

A police siren screamed as a patrol car sped down Divine

Street. The black and white sedan screeched to a halt and two big-bellied officers rolled out of the car. "Who's in charge of these here shenanigans?"

I stepped forward. "I am, officer. Artemisia Credo and this is my mother, Loretta Credo."

"What's all this fuss about?" the policeman asked.

My mother spoke up. "Governor O'Shea is trying to close down St. Anthony's and kick me and all the residents who live on the skilled-nursing floor out of our homes! That's *what!*"

"Well, you can't protest on the hospital's property."

"That's *rich!*" I said. "My mother *lives* here. This *is* her property. That's the point of this protest."

The officer removed his hat and scratched his bald head. "Lemme see your permit."

"We don't have one," I said.

"Ma'am, a permit is required for a crowd this size, especially with amplified sound. Also, there could be multiple injuries."

"We didn't count on a crowd this size—it sort of mushroomed," I said.

"Ma'am, you and your mother have to move on now. No permit. No protest."

Mamma Mia's black-olive eyes shot sparks at me as she loudly clicked on the brakes of her wheelchair. "Artemisia. Don't move a muscle."

I nodded at her as I sat on the ground and locked my arm through hers. "I'm afraid we can't do that, officer. We're choosing civil disobedience instead."

Gomer shrieked, "*Geronimo!*"

"Holy mackerel, Murph, it's gonna be one of those days," the portly policeman said to his partner.

Gomer whipped out his sock full of quarters. With his comb-over flapping in the wind, he cried, "I'll save you, Loretta!"

I couldn't believe it when he socked it to the officer, knocking his hat off.

"Hands behind your back, ya old fart! You're under arrest," the officer said as he spun the elderly felon around and handcuffed him.

"Jeez, Mamma, what kind of a *lunatic* is Gomer?" I asked.

"He's trying to impress me."

That set off Tess, who said, "I'm not moving either!"

Mrs. Mucci screamed, "I'm with you, Tessie!"

The police officer said to Mamma, "I'm asking you one more time to move along."

"Touch a hair on this old gray head if you must," she said, "but I'm going to jail to save my home!"

Joe sat down next to me. "I'm not letting you go to jail alone, Arté." He grabbed my hand.

Lola, clutching her pocketbook to her chest like a personal flotation device, yelled, "Which way to Bloomingdale's?"

The present-day nuns dressed in the old-fashioned habits dropped to the ground and refused to move. They looked like a bunch of penguins that'd been bowled over.

I glanced up at the rooftop for the seven dead nuns to help. They weren't there.

"Stand your ground!" Sister Ignatius yelled in my ear, which produced a full-body shudder in me. She had some set of lungs. "And stop the demolition!" I felt as if someone had placed electric paddles on my spinal cord. She scared the juice out of me every time. If I ever made it through this, I'd need a heart transplant.

THIRTY-FOUR

I should have packed Advil.

The Sit-In was to have resulted in just Mamma and me arrested. What a fiasco! It took hours to settle all of us in our cells, one for men and one for women. The stench in ours was overpowering—top notes of disinfectant with pungent undertones of stale urine. The dreary gray cinder-block cells were rough and cold.

The Verdant Valley jail wasn't set up to house senior-citizen inmates. The officer debated whether or not to book them, but the elderly dissidents insisted on being arrested. It was their excellent adventure, kind of like Ferris Bueller. They refused to move from the jail. The police were skeptical about picking them up and physically moving them for fear of breaking their bones. The officer had to call the skilled-nursing floor and ask the nurse to send over the meds for Gomer, O'Keefe, Polinski, Tess, and Mrs. Mucci...and anti-embolism stockings, denture cups, Metamucil, adult diapers, pureed food, and bed pans.

I overheard Chief Ramirez talking to Joe—they'd been buddies since high school. "The governor called and he was mad as hell. Said to throw the book at Arté—Uh, I cleaned that up a bit. He said to teach her a lesson."

Joe clenched his jaw. "That bastard's a crook. When we're finished, you'll be *arresting him!*"

The young woman TV reporter showed up as if on a mission to win a journalism award. "Shoot the nuns," she ordered the cameraman, "I'll headline with *Sisters in the Slammer!*" The present-day nuns dressed in the old-fashioned habits created a striking black and white pattern. It was surprising to see nuns clutching the bars—sort of like seeing a tattooed nun. The reporter barked orders to the cameraman to shoot scenes of the wheelchairs and walkers lined up in the hall and the fuming senior citizens peering through the iron bars. I understood she was looking for a visual punch for her story. Part of me actually felt sorry for O'Shea. He hadn't counted on a swarm of dead nuns—like angry hornets—descending upon him. Not to mention the spunky elderly residents of St. Anthony's. Did he think he was dealing with a bunch of demented old fogies? He didn't stand a chance. How sad for him.

The reporter asked if I had anything to say.

"Ask Governor O'Shea why he snatched the original document of the O'Shea Land Lease from the Verdant Valley Hall of Records," I said.

"I'll get right on that," she commented. Then she interviewed Mamma's gang. "Mrs. Credo, what do you have to say to Governor O"Shea?"

Mamma's eyes blazed as she flashed her famous *Il Malocchio* sign. "A plague on both his houses."

Gomer flashed another hand signal, which was one half of a peace sign.

Tess yelled in her gritty voice, "Hey, O'Shea, take your election and *shove it!*"

Mary McKee rushed into the building like Seinfeld's Kramer. She panted heavily and had to stop to catch her breath.

"Arté!" she said breathlessly, "I have somethin' *wicked awesome* to tell ya. St. Anthony's business office has been *freakin' flooded* with phone calls and emails pledging money to save the hospital! It's because of the news coverage—local and national pledges! We have several thousand bucks already…and more coming in! I'm working extra shifts to take in all the donations. I'm not moving my Boston ass outta St. Anthony's—they'll have ta use dynamite on me!" She swayed back and forth like a palm tree in a hurricane.

The reporter had struck journalism gold. "Keep filming. Are you getting this?"

The police were exhausted and ordered all visitors to leave. Joe's lawyer was allowed to stay. The officers wanted to process out the old folks in the worst way, but the cantankerous crowd refused and the lawyer backed them up. They had to send out for food to feed their geriatric prisoners. Each had special diets and restrictions: no sugar; no salt; no cholesterol; pureed food, and lots of prunes. After everyone was fed, the officers tried to settle their jailbirds down.

I whispered to Joe who was in the opposite cell, "*Psst*…Joe, want some Lorna Doones?"

"Toss 'em over," he said in a low voice.

"Listen," I said, tucking a long tendril behind my ear, "I'm staying here for my full sentence—the longer I stay in jail, the stronger the message I'll send. But you should have your lawyer get you out tomorrow. Your place is with Lily and Jo-Jo now."

"Lily has recovered and I hired a private-duty OB nurse to care for them."

"Thank God Lily is better! But, you have to talk the bedpan-gang into going back to the skilled-nursing floor. And you should be on the outside to run interference. I need you to do some re-search with local construction companies to see if the Gov had contacted any of them regarding demolition of St. Anthony's."

Joe grinned and flashed his one-sided dimple. "You're an amazing woman. Most would've given up. How do you always know what to research?" He scratched his bushy head. "You psychic or something?"

"Nah," I said laughing weakly, "just a holy hunch."

THIRTY-FIVE

I helped Mamma Mia onto her cot and covered her with my poncho. Perched on a wobbly wooden chair bedside her, I administered Mamma's Tylenol and she expertly injected her insulin. She coughed and took a few hits on her inhaler.

Mamma's eyes shone and her face glowed. "Artemisia, this was the best day of my life—next to the day you were born. I've never felt more alive! For the first time in a very long while, I feel like I have *purpose*...I feel *useful.*" She drew in a deep inhale of musty jail air. "Boy, that Sit-In was a *hum-dinger!* No wonder you had fun in college." She wore a big grin. "We're going to win our fight. I can *feel* it."

My dead-nun stalker appeared behind Mamma Mia.

I jumped.

"Arté, why are you so jumpy? You look like you have a bee in your brassiere." My mother chuckled.

"Mamma, you were magnificent today. During your speech, you held the audience in the palm of your hand. I'm so proud of you."

"I spoke from my heart," she said, thumping her chest. "I meant every word." She reached into her pocket and handed me a small package of Lorna Doones. "*Mangia!*"

I obediently took a cookie and nibbled.

Mamma reached out to stroke my cheek and planted Italian

kisses all over my face. She grasped both my hands with her large, warm ones. "Arté. I have something to tell you. Been waiting for the right time," she said in a low raspy voice. She fell silent for a full minute. "The doctors...have found a tumor...in my pancreas."

"What are you talking about? No, Mamma, that's not possible. I just attended your monthly medical review and the doctor didn't say anything like that."

"I told him not to tell you, honey. Insisted on confidentiality—cited the HIPAA laws. Said I'd tell you in my own way, on my own terms."

I shook my head. "Not the pancreas...it's probably a cyst. Is it in the head or tail?" Mary and I had researched pancreatic cancer when her mother had been diagnosed.

"Doesn't make a difference. My bloodwork for tumor marker was off the charts."

I studied my feet. Mamma lifted my chin with her gnarled finger. "Don't take it so hard. Arté, listen to me. We all are born terminal. *Capisce?* We can't live forever. I, uh, need to know you'll be okay."

Head down, I mumbled, "Does Joe know?"

"Yes," Mamma said.

"I see," I said, balling up my fists.

"Don't be upset with him. Told him I'd sue his ass off if he violated the HIPAA law."

"Is this why you've been trying to fix me up on dates?" I said, slowly shaking my head.

"I don't want you to be alone, you know, after I'm gone. But the thing is, I won't be *gone.* I'll always be with you...just in a different way."

I peered into Sister Ignatius's blue eyes. She fingered her rosary beads. Sister Gertrude stood beside Mamma, dabbing her eyes with her veil.

"How do you feel?"

"Right this minute, I'm okay."

In the darkened cell, I sensed the color draining from my face. My stomach twisted. I tried to speak, but my throat tightened like a drawstring pulled tautly. I heard myself whimper like a small child. *"Mamma Mia."*

"Please don't. Don't cry, Arté," my mother said as she rocked me like a baby.

THIRTY-SIX

Mamma's protest speech had gone viral on YouTube.
The Valley Chronicle ran a huge photo of Mamma Mia on
the front page as she flashed her bull-horn sign of *Il Malocchio*.
The headline screamed : *Hell No, We Won't Go!* There were
photographs of some of the protesters holding their signs and
sitting on the ground, one of Mr. Gomer in handcuffs, and one
of the nuns behind bars—*Sisters in the Slammer!* The exciting
visuals made me want to reach for my canvas and brush.

The VC reported: *"Among the thirty arrested were the nuns
who work at St. Anthony's—sporting the old-fashioned long
habits—and several elderly residents of the skilled-nursing
floor, doctors and nurses. At first, the police cited that the elderly were trespassing on the hospital's property. At that point,
Artemisia Credo, organizer of the protest, was quoted as saying,
"That's rich. These elderly people live at St. Anthony's. How
can you arrest someone for trespassing on their own property?
Governor O'Shea is trying to kick them out of their homes."*

*The police officer arrested the rebels because they did not
have a permit and they refused to move.*

*Eighty-nine-year-old Loretta Credo, the co-organizer of the
protest, refused to move saying, "Arrest if you must, this old
gray head, but spare my home of St. Anthony's Hospital."*

Verdant Valley hadn't seen this much excitement since the

Suffragettes had marched down Main Street, were jailed, and went on a hunger strike.

Hosting the Geritol Gang proved to be too much for the V.V. police, not only was it too expensive, they had to act as nursemaids to the aged inmates. After one day, the residents were released back to St. Anthony's—even Gomer who'd assaulted a police officer. Mamma said she wasn't leaving me there alone, but Joe finally talked her into returning to St. Tony's.

My sentence was a $3,000 fine or three days in jail. I took one for the team. Yeah, like I had three grand to splurge. After my three days expired, they practically kicked my butt out of there. My aching back was killing me and I'd dreamed of swimming laps in the warm water, so that was the first thing I did when set free. The second thing was to drink two cups of McDonald's coffee. Believe me, jailhouse coffee was nothing to write home about.

Then I had a long visit with Mamma. She was doing okay, but didn't have much of an appetite. I brought her our favorite treat, warm fried dough. Most people like powder sugar on it, but we sprinkle salt. She took one bite and set it aside. Wearing a big grin, she talked at length about her recent adventure. I held her hand and didn't ever want to let go.

My lone elevator ride to the lobby stopped on the third floor. Joe hopped on and was glad to see me. It was supernatural how many times Joe and I met on the elevator at St. Anthony's. He leaned in to kiss me and I violently shoved him away with both hands. Almost knocked him over.

Wide eyed, he asked, "What the *hell* was that for?"

"You didn't tell me about Mamma!" I yelled. "My mother is *dying* …and you didn't tell me!" I cried like a baby with colic. Snot and tears dripped down my contorted face.

"Get a grip! I wasn't at liberty to tell you. Not because she threatened to sue, but because it was her *right*." A crease appeared in his forehead and his lip curled. "You know, there's help for people like you with anger-management issues." He couldn't get off the elevator fast enough.

I went to my studio to check on Merlin. I collapsed in my easy chair and sobbed to the point my ribs ached. Merlin ran to me and leapt to the back of the chair, draping himself around my neck like an angora scarf.

"Fuzzy Buddy! Mamma Mia is sick. What're we going do?"

Perched atop my shoulder, he kneaded his fury paw into my arm, patting me reassuringly.

I wiped my dripping nose on my sleeve. "That's not all!" I wailed. " I yelled at Joe, pushed him away…pushed him right out of my life. Me and my big mouth!"

Sister Ignatius sat on the window seat with the sun streaming through her sheer veil.

"Artemisia, you know it wasn't Doctor Goodman's fault. He was following your mother's wishes. You need to apologize."

I took in a ragged breath, nodded, and mumbled, "Yes, Sister." I glanced toward the window seat and watched her dissolve into pixels mixed with dust motes in the bright sunlight. I sighed again and called Joe's office.

He was understanding. For several weeks, I'd been tamping down the stress, like gun powder into a musket, until I finally exploded. Said I'd been under an enormous strain and the news about my mother was the tipping point. When Joe made a joke about my hot Italian temper, I knew he forgave me.

"I'm returning those steak knives I bought you," he said.

"As a peace offering—because you know I'm all about peace—you, Lily and Jo-Jo are invited to dinner here, 7 PM— it's chicken parm night! And because I feel extra guilty for being mean, I'm making homemade pasta and meatballs too."

"You had me at chicken parm."

"I really want you to see my Angel of Peace Lily posed for. She named her Margaret."

"I'd love that. See ya later."

"Peace out."

Then I headed upstairs to take a long, steamy, Epsom-salted bath. Afterward, I prepared my special dinner. I tightly rolled the meatballs between the flattened palms of my hands, and slowly browned them in olive oil with garlic cloves. I clipped fresh basil from the little green pot on my windowsill and simmered my tomato sauce with the meatballs all afternoon—just like Mamma had taught me. The aroma in my little apartment was a mixture of garlic, onion, and green pepper sautéed in olive oil with top notes of tomato sauce. I tore off the end of a crusty loaf of bread, mopped it in the sauce and slid it into my mouth—*molto bene!*

* * *

Joe, Lily and the baby arrived promptly at 7. Joe asked, "Is it safe to lean in for a kiss?"

I giggled as I pulled him close. He kissed my cheek then my lips as I inhaled his woodsy scent.

"Jeez, get a room," Lily said, smiling.

Joe handed me a bottle of Pinot Noir. "Remember?" he said.

"Uh-huh." I said, grinning widely. "Lovely."

Jo-Jo was asleep in her car seat. I stroked her rose-petal cheek and kissed her, drawing in that intoxicating baby lotion smell. Lily placed the car seat on the floor as she sniffed deeply and smiled. "Mmm, tomato sauce. Smells just like an Italian restaurant!"

I returned her grin. "Hope you guys brought a hearty appetite with you."

"Oh, yeah," Joe said. "By the way, here's that research you asked for." He pulled a folded piece of paper from his breast pocket and handed it to me.

It was a print-out from Rusinko Construction Company with an estimate made out to Scanlon O'Shea for the demolition of St. Anthony's Hospital campus.

"*Bingo!*" I cried.

"I already handed copies over to our lawyer, the authorities, and the newspaper," he said. "O'Shea's under investigation for corruption charges." Joe did a perfect Richard Nixon impersonation. He raised his shoulders, flashed a double peace sign, and wagged his head, shaking his jowls. "I am *not* a crook. I have no intention of resigning. I will be vindicated. I am not a crook." Joe always made me laugh, even when I was upset. "What's going to happen with the election?" I asked.

"Not sure about that one. Maybe the lieutenant governor will take over. Needless to say, O'Shea's days as governor are numbered. My lawyer said there's a moratorium on the hydro-fracking until they straighten this mess out."

"And St. Anthony's?"

"An enormous amount of money has been raised and more pledges coming in from all over the country. St. Tony's is in good shape and should stay out of the red for years. All because of the media coverage of the Sit-In!"

"You know, Joe, that really surprised me. All I tried to do was save my mother from being kicked out of her home. What I know for sure is: It was Divine intervention…just like always with St. Anthony's Hospital."

Joe said, "The saga of St. Anthony's Hospital plays out like a movie."

"Before we go upstairs, we'll have the grand unveiling," I said.

We headed to the eight-foot-Angel of Peace, which stood underneath the drape.

"Lily," I said, "the honor is yours."

She pulled the sheet off to reveal her likeness. The angel held a lily, a reference to Lily's name and a symbol of peace.

"*Day-um!* Doppelganger much?" Lily said.

Joe said, "It looks amazing…how'd you— "

A thunderous smashing sound rang through my studio.

A brick sailed through the store-front window, shattering it. Missile-like shards of glass jetted everywhere. Merlin sprinted past me and dove in a wicker basket under the counter.

Lily screamed, and reached for Jo-Jo.

Joe threw his body over the car seat, protecting his new granddaughter. "Lily, are you hurt?"

"*My baby!*" Lily shrieked. "*Is my baby hurt?*"

Joe said, "Jo-Jo is fine. Everything is okay."

But everything was not okay. An odd odor of gasoline and diesel oil fumes permeated the studio.

THIRTY-SEVEN

Joe called his buddy, the police chief, Andy Ramirez. After the patrol car arrived, they searched around the building and found more gasoline-soaked rags hidden in the hedges under the window. My studio became a crime scene for attempted arson. Mary had been right— O'Shea did try *to off me.*

Joe said it wasn't safe for me to stay in my apartment and wanted me to go home with him and Lily and the baby. But I had to call my landlord and have the window boarded up. Boy, was he upset! He said, "Do you know how much a store-front window like this costs? I'm hemorrhaging money!" I sent Joe and Lily home with the chicken parm dinner and extra meatballs.

I dropped off Merlin in his carry-box at Mary's. Merlin hated his carry-box because he associated it with a trip to the vet—I usually had to chase him around with treats to get him in it. He scuttled right in that time.

Then I spent the night with Mamma Mia. Didn't tell her what had happened. Told her we were having a pajama party and the nurse set up a cot for me. I tempted my mother with my Italian dinner, but she wasn't hungry. I brought Mamma's favorite movie, *I Remember Mamma,* starring Irene Dunne and we cuddled together watching it.

* * *

The next morning, Chief Ramirez called me to the station to fill out a report.

"We caught the crook. We went over the surveillance tapes your landlord provided. We had a lovely close-up of his mug on the tape."

"That's a relief. Now I can move back into my apartment and reopen my studio." I furrowed my brow. "But, I believe he was hired by Governor O'Shea—I just *know it*. But can't prove it." I tapped the pen on the desk. "I revealed in my TV interview that I had a damaging document against Governor O'Shea, *in my possession*. He probably figured a fire would destroy it."

Ramirez's eyebrows shot up.

"This guy you arrested, what's his name?" I asked.

"The perp's name is Sam the Man Slovinski—he's not exactly a stranger here. When we hauled him in and interrogated him, he babbled like a crazy guy...something about a ghost...a nun scaring the hell out of him. Kept mumbling *dead nun... dead nun.*"

I looked left and right and behind me for Sister Ignatius. Bet she kept that goon from torching my studio.

"Can you question him again about O'Shea? What if the Gov hires another thug?"

"We will certainly do that and, in the meantime, we'll give you special protection. If we offer Slovinski a deal, he'll sing like a canary."

I stood and shook his hand. "Thank you, I appreciate that."

I had to go Mary's house to retrieve Merlin.

* * *

I filled Mary in on my latest adventure.

Unblinking, Mary swayed back and forth like a field of wheat in the wind. "You okay? Told ya that lousy *craphead* would try ta make ya *kaput*. Whadda *puke-face!*"

"What a *fessacchione!* " I pushed out a deep breath. "I'm

holding up okay," I said, as I picked up Merlin and stroked his silver-gray pelt. He stared at me wide-eyed and blinked slowly.

Mary said, "I'm so sorry about your mother. How is she?"

"Not much of an appetite, but okay for now."

My cell buzzed and it was Lily. "Arté, I'm calling to see if you're okay?"

"I'm just fine. You and Jo Jo?"

"Me and *Mini Me* are good."

I disconnected and continued telling Mary about my saga. "A brick smashed my studio window and the police found gasoline soaked rags in the hedge."

"*Holy shitballs!*" Mary cried, "that *craphead, butt-face* tried to burn down your studio."

THIRTY-EIGHT

My cell chimed and it was Anderson Cooper! From *CNN's AC 360°*. He was working on a special, *Senior Citizens Who Made a Difference*, and wanted to interview Mamma and me. Said he'd interview Mamma Mia at St. Anthony's and then he'd meet me at my studio. More public speaking for me! I used to be that person who wouldn't say *poop* if I had a mouth full of it—now I was sort of getting use to the TV camera, thanks to a dead nun.

When I told Mamma that Anderson Cooper was going to interview her for TV, she fluffed her hair and said, "I'm ready for my close-up, Mr. DeMille."

Mamma had her hair styled at the skilled-nursing beauty shop and looked beautiful, like an older version of her favorite movie star, Loretta Young. Her salt and pepper short hair had a smooth curl. I plucked her high-arched brows and added a bit of dark brown pencil to define them. Preparing for the TV camera, we opted for a little mascara, red rouge, and glossy ruby lipstick. She looked regal in her Joan Rivers-faux pearls.

She had a fresh pot of coffee and a plate of Lorna Doones waiting for Anderson Cooper. I sat quietly in the corner to watch Mamma Mia in her glory.

"Thanks, Loretta, for the cookies. They're my favorite," Anderson said.

"*Mangia!* There're plenty more where they came from."

The bright lights flicked on and the camera rolled.

"Loretta, you and your daughter, *singlehandedly*, saved St. Anthony's Hospital from closure. That's an outstanding accomplishment."

"And we gave a crooked politician *the-what-for!* The big *ciuccio!* Did O'Shea think I was going to roll over and play dead? *C'mon!* You know, Anderson, people should not underestimate the elderly, especially an old crone like me. I do not suffer fools… or bullies…or intellectual eunuchs."

"When I saw you give that bully speech on *YouTube*, I was mesmerized, impressed, and amused. You're the real deal," Anderson said.

"I have eighty-nine years of life's scholarship behind me. I've learned a thing or two in my day. Society needs to learn this lesson: When you see a person with gray hair and wrinkles, don't discount them. Rather, think of gray hair and wrinkles as badges of courage and years of valuable experience." As she spoke, her large hands sailed through the air like a conductor of a symphony. "Also, I had thirty years of nursing experience. I've witnessed a great deal of sorrow and joy. Can size a person up in five seconds flat! I say what's on my mind and do not care one *jot* what anyone thinks—especially a *flaccid little politician. Faccia di culo!*" Mamma folded her hand like a clam and waved it. *"Capisce?"*

"Say what?"

"Literally it means, *face of a butt."*

"Well said." Anderson had a laughing spasm. "So, I guess you weren't fazed by your jail time?"

"When the police officer *threatened* me with arrest, I laughed. I'm eighty-nine—what the hell was I worried about? *A life sentence?"*

Anderson had a bona fide laughing fit, like the one I had in Sister Attila the Nun's classroom. He had to stop filming for a few moments and took a sip of water to compose himself.

"I believe *because* of my age, I made a strong statement. *Forte!*" Mamma made a fist and pounded it in her flattened palm.

"What was it like to be in jail?"

"It was the best day of my life—next to the day I gave birth to my Artemisia! A few of my *amici* joined me…Tessie and Theresa, Gomer—he has a crush on me." Mamma cupped her hand and whispered, "He tried to crawl in my bed one night and I went for the groin with my quad cane."

"What!" I said.

Anderson doubled over. "Keep rolling."

"That's why Gomer talks in a high-pitched voice now. Lola was at the Sit-In—she thought she was at Bloomingdale's. And O'Keefe and Polinski, Gomer's buddies—Larry, Curly, and Mo, if you get my drift."

"You're killing me," Anderson said, holding his belly.

"The police sent us back to St. Anthony's after one day because of our special medical needs. Ruined all our fun. Talk about an *escapade!*"

* * *

Anderson Cooper opened my interview with a beautiful shot of my eight-foot Angel of Peace holding the *PAX* sign. It was fortunate that my large angels were back in my studio after my NYC exhibit. The camera slowly panned down my angel to the globe on which she stood. When I'd composed my sketch, I made sure my angel stood right over the USA, shedding extra grace and protection over my country. I considered it my masterwork. Then the camera traveled around my studio as Anderson did a voice-over.

"We are in the studio of Artemisia Credo, painter of Angels of Peace, originator of a movement called Hunger for Peace and social activist." The cameraman moved in for extreme close ups of my angel paintings with the gold-leaf wings, which shimmered as the bright TV lights bounced off them.

"But Artemisia is in the news for another reason: Artemisia and her eighty-nine-year old mother, Loretta Credo, saved St. Anthony's Hospital—Loretta's beloved home—from closure."

"Thank you, Artemisia, for inviting us into your studio."

"Hello, Anderson. It's a pleasure to visit with you."

He chuckled, "My new favorite saying is your phrase, *"You gormless, feckless politician."*

"I sell tee shirts with that expression here in my studio."

"I'll take two dozen," Anderson said. "Not only did you save St. Anthony's Hospital, you toppled a sitting governor. He's serving time in prison!"

"Well, Governor O'Shea managed to do that to himself. All I did was shine a spotlight on his wrongdoing."

"Artemisia, I just interviewed your mother. She's a piece of work," Anderson said as he laughed.

Nodding, I said, "I get that a lot."

"Your store-front window was smashed," Anderson noted. "That's an act of violence and here you are an advocate for peace."

"It was more serious than a broken window. Gasoline-soaked rags were found under the window. We *miraculously* escaped harm. The police are handling it."

"You seem unusually calm about it."

"I have *infallable* protection," I said. Merlin skulked by, low-to-the-ground as if hunting. "Merlin usually sits in that window seat. Fortunately, he wasn't in the bay window at the time."

The camera zoomed in on Merlin as my handsome feline scurried away like the Cowardly Lion.

THIRTY-NINE

Mary stopped by to see how I was doing. "Arté, I tried to warn ya about that slime-ball, sleaze-bucket governor— that piece of *crap*—tryin' to *off* ya. Knew he was a crook. The *dipshit!*"

"I must have had an angel watching over me. You were right, Mare. O'Shea sent a bungling henchman to do his dirty work. Chief Ramirez told me when they interrogated the goon, he babbled like a crazy person. Said dead nuns spooked him." I laughed. "Isn't that a riot? *Dead nuns!* Two of the scariest words in the English language."

Mary said, "Yeah. If I ever saw a dead nun, I'd crap my pants. Had enough with the live nuns in grade school."

I giggled. "Ever notice how *nun* is spelled the same frontward and backward? A little creepy, don't you think?"

"Yah," Mary chuckled. "I wish I could have seen that interrogation. See, I know how it works. They put the *perp* in the *sweatbox* and *crack* him like an egg!" She made a hand movement as if she were breaking a twig in two. "That's how Danny the detective on *Blue Bloods* does it—*love* that show, it should win an Emmy."

"There had been so much excitement and havoc lately. Now that I've had time to process everything—St. Anthony's near closure, battling a demented governor, the Sit-In, *public*

228

speaking, attempted arson— " I drew in a deep inhale and puffed it out. "I have post traumatic shock." Because when you factor in the seven deceased religious women garbed in long black and white habits stalking me, that was reason enough for shock. "Also the stress of Mamma's illness," I added sadly.

"I saw you and your mother on Anderson Cooper. You looked pretty…and your angels just glowed, I mean, they truly looked heavenly. Your mamma was hilarious—how's she doing?" Mary asked.

"Hardly has an appetite." I mumbled, "Don't know what I'll do without her." I drew in a sharp breath. "I pray for her constantly. Have to keep my faith—did you know my last name means *I believe?* A very wise person told me that."

* * *

I spent the day with Mamma. I helped her get dressed into her black ponte-knit pants and flowered faux-silk Susan Graver blouse. Then I set her hair and styled it.

"Mamma Mia, you look beautiful!" I beamed at her as I snapped some photos of her. She wanted to sit for awhile.

After I eased her into her wheelchair, she peered at me for moment. "Artemisia, I am so happy about your engagement to Joe—it's what I prayed for."

"We get along great! I just hope I'm not too old for marriage." I furrowed my brow and shook my head.

"Why the worried look? He's a fine man." She added, shaking her clam-hand, " And that *hair!"*

"Well, I'm kinda set in my ways, you know?" I folded my arms across my body.

"*Horsefeathers!* What the hell are you talking about? He loves you—I can tell." My mother studied me intently. "I observe you around him and you can't deny you're in love with him. Lily sounds like she's crazy about you too. And that baby is wonderful—such a beautiful infant!"

"Yeah, Lily's a lovely young woman. She's an incongruous mix of immaturity and wisdom. Sometimes she's like a teenager, or younger, but then she'll say something profound. Said she wouldn't give her baby away and have that child always thinking it wasn't good enough. And, she delivered her baby without any drugs! Talk about stoic." I sat with my hands clasped in my lap. "I admire her. And she's very funny." A big smile spread across my lips. "I love helping her with Jo-Jo."

Mamma's face softened as she pressed the back of her hand to my cheek. "You always loved babies. You'll be a happy family with a baby! It's what you always wanted." Mamma smiled widely. "And now I can die happy knowing you won't be alone."

I grabbed her hand and kissed it. "C'mon, Mamma, I'll take you for a ride around the hospital. We can check out the gift shop and, if you feel like it, snack on some ice cream in the cafeteria."

I was happy when Mamma ate a little ice cream, but then she tired quickly and I returned her to her room.

FORTY

As our hands dovetailed, my soon-to-be husband beamed a mega-watt smile at me. "Come along and grow old with me. The best is yet to be."

We had a simple ceremony in St. Anthony's Hospital's chapel. Mamma Mia was well enough to attend. She was my matron of honor and told me later that she'd been *in cahoots* with Joe. Instead of a best man, Joe had a best woman, Lily. Mary, George, Johnny Mae, and Sister X sat in the front pew as Mary held Jo-Jo, who made soft baby coos of approval. After we were pronounced husband and wife, Joe planted one on me like that sailor who kissed the nurse on V-J Day in Times Square. *Wowza!*

Mamma cheered. *"Bravo! Bellissima!"*

Mary said, *"Wicked Pissa Awesome!"*

Before our reception in the cafeteria, I excused myself to touch up my eye makeup. As I reapplied my mascara, Sister Ignatius stood behind me watching. Jeez, I nearly poked my eye out!

"Artemisia, congratulations! You and Doctor Goodman make a handsome couple. I am happy you found each other."

I scrunched my eyebrows. "I have a hunch you and the other Sisters had a lot to do with Joe and me getting together. My wedding has your fingerprints all over it." I chewed on the inside of my cheek. "Uh…um, now that St. Anthony's has been saved, um, will you still *need* me?" I studied my fingernails. " I mean, uh…are you still going to *visit* me? Oh, I'll just come out and say it! Will I have to burn sage and waft the smoke with an eagle's feather to enjoy my honeymoon?"

Sister Ignatius chuckled. "I haven't much time. I want you to know that you did a splendid job saving our St. Anthony's Hospital. Well done!"

"May I ask you a question, Sister? Why didn't you tell me, *clearly,* in the very beginning, *exactly* what to do and how to do it? It would have been so much easier. I mean, you almost killed me! Every time you appeared, I nearly jumped out of my skin!"

"Yes. You are correct that would have been easy. But you would not have learned a valuable lesson: To believe in your-self. And, I hasten to add, you would not have become such an eloquent public speaker!" Her hand went to her mouth as she grinned. "T'was quite humorous to see you jump like that. You looked like a surprised frog."

A broad smile spread across my coral glossed lips. "Most of my life, I've been terrified of nuns—no offense. But, please believe me when I tell you, I admire you and it's been an honor to have been *stalked*…I mean, to have known you."

"I am afraid Sister Attila had done a great disservice to you. Part of my mission was to correct that. I had to right a wrong."

"Thank you, Sister Ignatius, I appreciate it… even though I nearly had a cardiac arrest." I scratched the back of my neck. "Is Sister Attila there with you? In heaven?"

"You must understand, Artemisia, that not all young wom-en entered the convent because they had a vocation. Some had problems and were sent by their families. Sister Attila did the best she could…under her circumstances."

"Uh, and what about Sister Xavier? Is she a real nun?"

"Poor Sister Xavier was born as a woman trapped in a man's body. Think of the heartache within that situation! Sister

Xavier had a deep vocation to be a nun since she was a child. Yes, she's a real nun and a good person. She chose the safety of the convent to do her works of mercy. She has an important ministry to the disenfranchised and worked hard to try to save St. Anthony's. Every person on this planet is a child of God. Jaysus said, '*All* of you come to me.'"

"I see… Mamma always taught me not to judge people because we didn't know what went on behind closed doors."

Sister Ignatius adjusted her veil and ironed her tunic with her hand. "One more thing. I know how upset and worried you are about your dear mother. She has lived a life of good deeds and was a compassionate nurse. Loretta has been edified. When the time comes, I will be there to greet her."

With head down, I expressed my gratitude again.

"Now, about your Catholic religion," Sister said.

I peered at her and held up both hands like stop signs. "I still believe in God, the Holy Trinity, the angels, and saints. But, Sister Ignatius—*respectfully*—I cannot, in good conscience, be part of the Catholic Church. Instead, I follow the example of Jesus and try to spread peace."

She smiled kindly. "Well now, Artemisia, ye cannot go wrong following the example of Jaysus. God bless and all the best." She drew the sign-of-the-cross in the air and evaporated like steam on the bathroom mirror, leaving the sweet scent of incense.

"Holy smokes," I mumbled. I would take my experience with Sister Ignatius and the other dead nuns to my grave because no one would ever believe it.

* * *

Mamma, my world-class mother, held on to her earthly bonds for as long as she could. Mamma Mia was a warrior. Her slow dance with Death was too painful for me to write about. The emotional truth was, because of her suffering, I actually celebrated her merciful release from the tendrils of her malignant disease. I envisioned Mamma's vibrant spirit rumbling a great belly laugh as it catapulted out of her ravished body, performing gymnastics of Olympic status, flipping, somersaulting, twisting, and cartwheeling away toward peace.

Like the ancient Egyptians who sent earthly items along with their dead for their journey to the afterlife, I tucked Sister Ignatius's St. Anthony medal into my mother's casket along with a small oil painting of an Angel of Peace with gold-leaf wings and Mamma's prayer-polished rosary beads.

I took great comfort in knowing Sister Ignatius had greeted Mamma Mia and escorted her to the other side. This I knew for certain: There were two shimmering souls in heaven—powerful allies—watching over my new family.

I wore Mamma's blue satin nightgown to bed and it felt like a hug from my mother. It still smelled like her—Lily-of-the-Valley dusting powder and olive oil. Nary a day went by that I didn't think of my mother. When the longing for my mamma overwhelmed me, I nibbled on Lorna Doones, my new comfort food. That shortbread cookie was emblematic of my mother—sweet, crispy, comforting, tasty, rich, delicious, salty, and crusty. As you know by now, Mamma Mia was one tough cookie.

FORTY-ONE

O'Shea continued to serve time in prison for misuse of his governmental office and attempted arson—hope he likes his orange jumpsuit.

I was so sad when my fuzzy buddy, Merlin, died of old age. He was a fabulous feline! As it turned out, I didn't rescue Merlin; he rescued me. I'll never be able to replace him.

Sister Ignatius no longer visited me. I guess her work with me was finished.

Four years had passed since my wedding and I was so happy to have said *yes* to my *adventure*—Joseph Campbell would have been proud of me. Even though I came late to the party, this marriage gig was pretty damn good.

My step-daughter, Lily, had gained a new confidence in herself and was a good mother. The way she played with her daughter made me wonder if she wasn't having more fun than Jo-Jo. Lily worked part-time at my studio and was a wizard on the computer. She'd grown my business to a comfortable point and sold some of her ceramic mugs and jewelry out of the studio.

Jo-Jo, a raven-haired, turquoise-eyed beauty, was four-years-old and attended pre-K. For her birthday, she'd requested *"a diamond ring and a jar of jelly beans."* She'd begged for a kitten, but I told her Pap-Pap was way too allergic and, without skipping a beat, she said, "No problemo, we'll just get a *bald* kitty!" She settled for a goldfish—named her Fluffy.

Our curly-headed little diva belted out Christmas carols in July and made "carpet angels" on her fuzzy pink rug in her room. She was worried about the ducks being cold in the winter and wanted me to make them "duck hoodies." As I tucked Jo-Jo into bed the other night, she grew solemn. Kneeling, she made a backward sign-of-the-cross and prayed, "Blessed is the Fruit of the *Loom,* Jesus." She peered at me, "Bella Nonna, why are you laughing?"

"Because you make me so happy."

"Well, get a grip!" she said. Then furrowing her brow, she asked, "Do angels wear underpants?"

"Hmm. That's a really good question. I don't know."

Joe retired right after Jo-Jo was born. I thought he'd miss surgery because he was talented at it, but he'd said, "No, I don't miss getting called out of my warm bed—especially now that you're in it."

As it turned out, Joe snored. Big time! He sounded like the Tasmanian Devil with a chain saw. On steroids! He didn't believe me, so I tape recorded him. Then, awake for hours because of the racket, I observed him as he stopped breathing! Once. Twice. The third time—when I feared I'd become a widow—I sprang into action. Straddling his chest, I raised my arms high in the air, ready to pound his chest and restart his heart. His eyes popped open!

"What the *hell* are you doing?"

"I'll have you know, you stopped breathing. Three times! I was about to save your life."

"Jesus-George! If that's how you *save* my life, I'd hate to see how you would *kill* me."

I told him we were in this family together and we had to stay healthy for Lily and Jo-Jo. I made him go to the sleep clinic and he had sleep apnea.

Our marriage had been an adjustment. Communication was the key. Every time I searched in the kitchen for the ripe bananas with their sugary brown spots to make banana buttermilk cake, they were gone. "Oh, I threw out those *rotten* bananas," Joe said, as if I were a sloppy housekeeper too lazy to toss spoiled bananas. So when I said, "Sometimes Joe drove me bananas," it was a literal statement. Post-It notes saved my marriage. I stuck them on …mostly everything. "*Joe, step away from the bananas. Now!*"

For my wedding gift, that sweet man purchased Mamma's house, which *miraculously* came on the market. He had the kitchen remodeled, added on our master bedroom with a spa bathroom and—cue the heavenly choir—a walk-in closet! Also, a private suite for Lily and Jo-Jo. Best of all, Mamma's original flower garden was still as she'd left it so many years ago.

Joe and I sat on the wrap-around front porch, side-by-side, holding hands. Nibbling on a Lorna Doone, I smiled at the squeals of delight as Lily and Jo-Jo ran through the garden among the rare antique moss-roses, and Snow Queen hydrangeas, which Mamma Mia had so lovingly tended.

I never thought I'd remarry. I'd given up on my dream for a loving husband and children years ago. I was reminded of John Lennon's song: "*Life is what happens when you're busy making other plans.*" And now I had Joe, Lily, and Jo-Jo. I hadn't qualified my prayers. Even though my life was not exactly as I'd imagined, it was precisely and completely what I'd prayed for.

Peace out.

About the Author

Kathleen Huddle is a visual artist. She and her husband of 46 years have four daughters and two grandchildren. They live in Upstate New York. You can find her work on the Internet at kathleenhuddle.com and huddleangels.com.

CPSIA information can be obtained
at www.ICGtesting.com
Printed in the USA
FFOW01n1715160417
34603FF